FIVE FAVOURITE CASES

The Continuing Chronicles of Sherlock Holmes

C. Thorne

ISBN: 9798333758170
Imprint: Independently published

Cover and interior design by: L. Thorne
Library of Congress Control Number: 2018675309
Printed in the United States of America

This is for my family, past, present, future, with love to you all.

CONTENTS

INTRODUCTION

The Continuing Chronicles of Sherlock Holmes: Five Favourite Cases, is a sampler from the series that includes five mysteries selected from the three-dozen stories in the canon, with all-new illustrations.

This is a way for fans old and new to read some of the most popular stories from author C. Thorne's *The Continuing Chronicles of Sherlock Holmes.*

Included in this collection are:

The Case of Cromwell's Cranium

The Case of Moriarty's Betrayer

The Adventure of the Séance Society

The Case of the Snowdonia Werewolf

The Mystery of Wyvern Hall

Journey back to a time in which dangers lurked ever-present in the foggy, gas-lit streets of London, and where for Sherlock Holmes of 221B Baker Street, the game was always afoot....

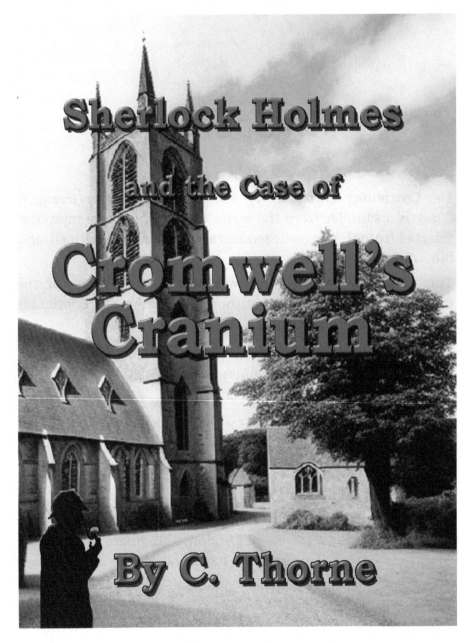

Sherlock Holmes

and the Case of

Cromwell's Cranium

By C. Thorne

THE CASE OF CROMWELL'S CRANIUM

I t had been a busy summer for my friend Sherlock Holmes, with one case after another vying for his attention, but oddly, as I found was often the scenario, a break came to his hectic schedule as the first cool days of autumn visited us, and Holmes was even able to slip off to the Italian lake country for a fortnight, while Mrs. Watson and I went in the opposite direction, to visit my Scottish relations.

Pleasant as the north could be, it was with no small joy that I greeted my friend the morning after his arrival home to Baker Street, his present lodgings, and a place still beloved to me some years after I'd departed from it for the second time upon my re-marriage.

"My dear Watson!" my friend called brightly upon spotting me at his door, brought up by the ever-kind Mrs. Hudson, the building's landlady.

"Holmes!" I called back. "It's good to see you, my friend! And how did you find Italy?"

"Hideous, Watson," Holmes said with a wrinkled brow. "Too quiet, too sunny, too dull, and the region around Lake Como was absent of any interesting acts of crime with which to nourish my starving brain cells."

"Oh, you make it sound Purgatorial, indeed," I jested.

"The most vexing problem I found in my time there lay in helping a little girl locate her missing cat, Aldo. But you arrive just in time, Watson, for in another few moments I expect a caller who may prove to be a client come to deliver me of my recent ennui amid law-abiding Mediterraneans!"

Holmes' prediction proved a valid one, as thirty seconds gone and there was a ring at the outer bell, and a moment past that saw Mrs. Hudson delivering to the door a fellow of stocky proportions, dressed in academic attire.

Knowing Holmes' methods, I tried, based on the pursuit of intellectual deductions, to discern something about this newcomer, yet beyond such obvious details as his age and gender, I found I perceived little, save that I did notice his fingernails appeared to have been recently bitten, perhaps, I gathered, hinting at some nervous complaint lately entered into his life.

Holmes, however, barked. "Ah! Mr. D.B. Curtis, author of this morning's telegram, I presume?"

"Your servant, sir," Mr. Curtis replied, making a little bow with his head.

"Mr. Curtis, may I present my friend and longtime

colleague, Dr. Watson, whose name doubtless will be as familiar to you as my own."

"Certainly, sir, for I feel as though I already know Dr. Watson well, from his own records of your cases which he is so kind as to publish, granting myself and so many others insights into your most fascinating undertakings. I especially admire that trick the good doctor describes you doing, Mr. Holmes, where you tell much about a man via minute clues upon his person. You know the one to which I refer, I am sure...?"

Unable to resist after so obvious an unstated plea for a demonstration, hungry to exercise powers apparently unused on his spirit-draining holiday, Holmes studied his putative client for a moment, left hand curled about his chin in serpentine fashion, then dazzled him when he revealed:

"My dear Mr. Curtis, from the almost indiscernible thickening of the skin on your left thumb, the digit most men use to turn the pages of a book, I would hazard to say you are employed in a capacity that sees you habitually handling many volumes on a daily basis. Furthermore, judging by the pleasant odour of aged paper that comes of long exposure to it, and which I detect on your suit coat, rising as it does above the equally agreeable scent of the Foster's Bay Rum Aftershave which you liberally applied this morning, and taking into account the blatant fact of the academic's clothing you wear, I would put your place of employment as being in a library, at an institution of learning which is not, I think, a university, but rather a boarding school where older boys productively study in preparation for entrance therein."

Curtis cried out: "That it is, sir, that it certainly is!"

"A telling pattern of wear on the outer heels of your shoes tells me you are in the habit of walking on rough cobbles more common in alleyways than on streets, where surfaces are, as a rule, more smooth. This tells me you often pass between a series of buildings in town, though the relative lack of wear contrasted against the age of the shoes, about two years, tells me part of that trek is across grass rather than pavement. As a rapid walking pace deteriorates shoe leather more quickly than a slower one, I would judge your fastest travels take place in mornings, when you are working against a deadline of time, rather than in afternoons, when you might proceed more casually, having no clock to judge you. Thus I'd say you are in the habit of using an unorthodox route as something of a shortcut to work, allowing yourself an extra five minutes at your tea and newspaper each morning; time being precious in any life."

"That I do!" Curtis agreed excitedly. "I cut a zig-zag through town and across the pasture to reach the school."

"One of the buildings you pass on your walk, in fact due west of your home by no more than fifty feet, is a restaurant that serves Hungarian goulash of some neighborhood infamy, owing, I believe, to its extreme spiciness, too severe for the more moderate British palate."

"However do you know that, Holmes?" I inquired, this seeming the oddest detail of all to me.

Leaving no mystery, Holmes added: "Elementary! Upon coming home a man will hang his hat in the foyer of his house, where a thoughtful wife will frequently leave a window open to provide a fresh breeze throughout the dwelling, and as I likewise detect an olfactory trace-residue of goulash suddenly in the atmosphere of Baker Street, this tells me that the hat which Mr. Curtis holds in his hand, Watson, has long hung in a place of exposure to an influx of the aroma of that dish being prepared nearby."

Curtis chuckled and looked happily toward me. "Amazing!" he chirped, "yet so simple! I did once try my neighbour's goulash, Dr. Watson, and as a result of my culinary curiosity was left gulping ice water for nearly five minutes!"

I granted the jolly librarian a smile as he chuckled in memory.

But Holmes was not done. "At your work," he continued, "you sit upon a stool rather than a chair or bench, I gather, because it eases certain strains upon your lower back. As you are not stooped-over now, I gather this is an old injury rather than a recent one?"

"I fell from a carriage as a boy," admitted Curtis, "and spent a summer recovering."

"Ah, you are marvelous as ever!" I told Holmes, though of course I'd seen him carry out this feat many times.

But still my friend had not reached his *denouement*.

"You are in the habit," he said, "of taking your lunches under the spreading boughs of a tree of some venerable age... a chestnut tree, I gather. You are wed to a wife with graying red hair who comes from the northwest...Lancashire, let us say, no....yes, yes, it is Lancashire, and it has been a happy domestic arrangement, despite some initial misgivings on behalf of both families, hers prejudiced against a southerner, while your relations feeling, if you'll forgive me, that she was perhaps of a background less suited as a match to your own middle-class origins."

Curtis nodded with delight and said, "And yet we proved them all wrong, those Doubting Thomases and nay-sayers!"

"Alas," said Holmes, truly in the thick of his observations now, "you and she are childless, though have, I gather, a loving attachment to a pair of white-haired dogs which I believe to be French poodles, each in the custom of sleeping each night at the foot of your bed."

Curtis stood agape and then gushed praise, saying, "Mr. Holmes, Mr. Holmes, you are amazing!"

"And would you care to know how I deduced the last parts of what I have just told you, sir?" Holmes inquired, pausing to draw on the pipe he'd ignored as he disserted. "I assure you it was all based on the most rudimentary of observations."

"So it always proves to be," I added.

To my surprise Curtis tendered a request I knew to be rare in a client when he said, "Please, Mr. Holmes, I beg you don't break the spell by telling me how you accomplished that last magnificent feat of describing my spouse, our shared past, and our current home life, for I gather from the Doctor's records of your work as well as your words that the explanations are often so simple as to shatter the illusion of your omniscience! I love my present sense of wonder more than I would the stark reality that accompanies enlightenment."

In truth I knew Holmes rather enjoyed revealing the methods behind his tricks, but here he emitted a sharp laugh and said, "A sentiment which has kept stage conjurers in business for millennia, but, then, as you desire, so shall you have it!"

Pleased with himself, he gestured to a chair by the comfortable fire, then after seeing his client seated, took a one himself, as did I. Thus with us all in place, Mr. Curtis was invited to reveal the nature of the problem which had brought him to Baker Street.

Here the previously jolly academic's demeanor changed, as I suspected it might, as few came to consult with Sherlock Holmes lest some matter heavily troubled him.

"You are doubtless aware, gentlemen," Curtis began, "of the identity of our nation's one-time Lord Protector, Oliver Cromwell, some nearly two and a half centuries ago, and the sordid history of his, er, well, to put it bluntly, his posthumously-detached skull?"

Holmes shifted, his interest in the morbid brought keenly alive, yet it was I, as a doctor, who answered.

"Indeed," I said, "it seems that due to King Charles II's ire the body of the former dictator was disinterred during the Restoration, a summer after his natural death, and his head displayed for a time on a spike mounted above Westminster Hall. There is, I believe a discrepancy in the accounts given as to the fate of the appendage for some years, til about the 18th century, when it reappeared in the hands of a private collector, only to vanish again from the record, I gather? A grim and distastefully macabre story at any length!"

Mr. Curtis, who had been nodding at my words froze at the last of what I'd said, and I sensed a sudden renewed awkwardness in his posture.

"Here, Watson, I fear you may have unintentionally

discomfited my client," said Holmes with a small smile of amusement. "Pray, Mr. Curtis, my friend meant no offense, and would be grateful to you, as would I, were you to take up the narration and fully enlighten us as to the nature of your call today. It pertains, I gather, to Cromwell's cranium, about which you may perhaps know something more than most of the rest of us?"

"It's only that, uh, well, er, you see...." He swallowed hard and said, "In confidence now..."

"Of course, sir," Holmes told him.

"Well, er, it is no mere story as you put it, Doctor, since long unknown to the public, we at St. Brendan's Academy for Boys, the school at which I act as librarian as well being among the masters there,... Well, I possess membership in a certain fraternal club which...."

He hesitated only another second and then the revelation burst out of him. "Well, we, sirs, at the school, had been in possession of the head of Cromwell for over a hundred years!"

"Your school has had the head of Oliver Cromwell?" I burst out. Why, then they had held the key to perhaps the greatest parlor-mystery in all of recent history!

The news was like a lightning flash in the room, sudden and quite shocking, though Holmes remained unruffled, and in contrast to me said only, "I see. And may I take it then that your call concerns this...*artifact*, and some recent disruption to the norm at the academy where you labour? I did not miss the past tense you assigned to the matter of its possession. The school *had* it."

"It's gone," Curtis confirmed shortly, his previous good mood dimming as worry showed on his portly face. "And worse, still, gone upon my own watch."

"And how was the disappearance discovered?" asked Holmes.

"By myself, yesterday evening," Curtis admitted. "I am a man of some nervous energy, you see, and the shock nearly prostrated me."

"Tell me the details of where the skull was kept, and whom else could access this relic of that turbulent period in our country's past."

I thought: *Relic? Artifact?* This was human remains! But I said nothing, merely took notes as the information came forth.

With what one might term delighted relish, Mr. Curtis informed us that Cromwell's semi-mummified cranium had been secretly gifted to the academy by a benefactor in July of the year 1780, an alumnus of the school who remembered his *alma mater* in his will with gifts of money, and also several other peculiar endowments.

Peculiar indeed, I thought to myself.

The head was immediately placed in a velvet-lined mahogany box, and was kept as one of the school's great secrets, less a mascot than a sort of object of pride that an otherwise undistinguished institution in the countryside of Suffolk might enjoy this questionable connection with so significant a personage from our nation's history. Any who knew of the possession were subjected to an oath of secrecy, to be broken only in the most dire of circumstances pertaining to what Curtis termed 'the cranium's well-being.'

"A condition which presently qualifies," I said aloud.

"Oh, I assure you," pressed Curtis, "there was nothing lurid in the possession of the cranium, gentlemen, it rested all but twelve nights of the year in a box kept in turn in the office of one of the masters of the school, I being Master of Books, you know, and then would be taken out for the private club banquet held on the final Friday of each month. We'd place the box in a spot of honour at the headmaster's table as the dinner began, and the night would begin with a toast: *'To the Lord Protector, our most honoured guest!'* At which time the Master in whose keeping the head rested would lift the artifact out of the box for a moment so that it might witness the toast offered in its honour. It was then returned inside, and at the dinner's conclusion was faithfully passed on to the next Master, who would in his stead keep it for the following four weeks in a show of mutual confidence in him."

The thought of dining with a desiccated human head did not sound appetizing to my earthy Scots' nature, but I knew well the odd traditions present in some schools---my own having us chase an oiled hare through the halls on Saint Andrew's Eve---but I still kept my silence as Holmes nodded, encouraging Curtis to go on.

"You see, this last month, September, had been my turn to host the Lord Protector in my own office, where he has sat in a place reserved for him inside my locked cabinet, the office feeling quite comfortable with him there, like being kept company by a distinguished guest who never speaks."

"Quite," agreed the imperturbable Holmes.

"Well, Mr. Holmes, Doctor, as you observe, today is Tuesday, the twenty-first, and this Friday is my turn to escort the Lord Protector's cranium down to the banquet hall and pass him off to Dr. Shelley, our Master of Romance Languages, and you see, it's that...like I said... Er, umm, the Lord Protector has vanished, box and all, from inside my locked cabinet!"

"Goodness me," I said sympathetically, though inwardly I found this fellow a peculiar one, as sheltered academics often were, dwelling as they did in an atmosphere of unchanging tradition amid class syllabi that swayed subject to subject with each passing scholastic season. The outer world was simply not like the one known to them.

Holmes though showed the gravest attentiveness and rose to place a comforting hand on Curtis' wide shoulder.

"Though you have borne it with admirable fortitude, I can well imagine the shock of your realization must have been grave," he told his client.

"Oh, it was, it was," the fussy librarian agreed.

"You said upon arrival that the head was missing," Holmes pressed him, "but to be clear, you have told us the box in which it was traditionally contained was likewise taken from the cabinet?"

"Yes," Curtis clarified, "all is gone, box and august contents alike!"

"Interesting," Holmes stated, and I gathered he saw significance in this fact. "Had the theft involved the item and not the box itself, assuming you had not peered within the box yourself since it came to you, the artifact could have disappeared at any hour since the conclusion of last month's banquet. As it is, we can narrow down the time frame considerably, since you saw the box there earlier yesterday, I presume?"

Curtis nodded, and said, "It was there in the foremost part of the day, but as I prepared to go home after overseeing evening study-hall, it was quite gone."

"I see," stated Holmes.

He then looked at my friend imploringly and asked, "Knowing your reputation from my avid reading of each new case to which the good Doctor sets his pen, what else could I do but come to you?"

"In that decision you were most wise," said Holmes.

"If I am forced to admit to Headmaster Pomeroy that I have somehow lost an artifact so beloved to our school, a secret possession known to none save the innermost circle of the school's masters, I shall be forced to resign and leave the place I love best in all God's world: my beloved library so filled with beautiful books... I will go forth in disgrace, like Cain, ruined, all the sacred trust placed in me in shown in vain."

"My good fellow," I said consolingly, "surely all is not lost."

He let his face fall into his hands, covering his eyes from the world, then added, "I do not say it would be an event I should survive."

"Now, now," I comforted, calling upon my best bedside manner, "be of good cheer, sir," "My friend is a wonder-worker who never fails to do his best for his clients, and Sherlock Holmes' best is a very great thing indeed!"

Holmes looked pleased, both at my words and at having a mystery to dissect at last after the tedium of his Italian vacation.

"Mr. Curtis," he began, composing himself to total gravity, "I fear I must ask you an unpleasant question, and I implore you to answer only after you have given the matter some consideration."

"Of course, of course," the stout-figured academic agreed.

He clarified: "Have you any knowledge of person or persons at the school who might wish you ill?"

"Certainly not," Curtis said at once.

"Do ponder a moment, sir. There are no grudges among the students, no rivalries among your fellow masters, no past slights, intentional or otherwise for which one might seek redress? No incidents of oversight for which you might, however unreasonably, be blamed?"

"A most adamant no to all of those, sir," Curtis maintained.

"And outside the school?"

"I do not flatter myself to think that in all my life of forty-one years I have never had an unpleasant word with another person, though as a rule I hold myself well-liked. My neighbor and I exchange roses from our gardens each summer, he growing white, while my wife and I preferring a variety with a pinkish blush. The Hungarian restaurateur next door is a charming man, and it is nothing save smiles of greeting and passing nods of hello there. Across the way is a retired vicar and the spinster daughter who cares for him. All is congenial in my domestic hemisphere."

"Then is there anyone who might envy your position, who seeks it for himself?"

"Mr. Holmes," he said, "I appreciate the nature of those questions and comprehend why it is you must ask them, but I assure you, in all of England you'd find no happier or more fraternal a group of men than those of us blessed to be on faculty at Saint Brendan's Academy for Boys."

"And among the students?"

"Oh," Curtis confessed, "the occasional bad egg seeking to make trouble among the good boys, certainly, but the students knew nothing of the cranium's existence. It was a most closely-kept secret among we of the academy's masters, and guarded as a strict matter of honour since the days of King George III."

Holmes considered this, then said, "Finally, given its nature and all which you have told us, I intuit you would rather that this disturbing theft be kept unknown from your fellows at the school."

"Yes," said Curtis. "If they suspect, well...as I've said, the loss would be crushing, and my shame all-but unbearable."

"Quite so," said my friend. "Then I shall not set foot on the campus as Mr. Sherlock Holmes, but as, let us say, your correspondent of some years, a Cornish librarian come to visit you and enjoy the campus tour you will give him on the morrow."

"Cornish librarian....? Curtis asked in a puzzled voice.

"Mr. Holmes is a master of disguise," I told him, catching on at once. "I think the identity of your illustrious guest, and the purpose of his visit, will be quite safe."

"Then it is wonderful!" Curtis cried, rising and pumping Holmes' hand before lending a similar service to my own.

"Til tomorrow, then, sir, and your visit from a *faux* Cornishman!" Holmes called cheerfully, as he showed Curtis to the door, hand between the shoulders of his massive back.

As we espied the scholar departing toward a waiting line of cabs, Holmes asked me, "Watson, have you ever heard of anything so singular?"

"Not in many years," I agreed. Then I asked: "Holmes, I sensed an honesty to him, but the cranium of Oliver Cromwell? Could it truly be the original item, or has this been a tradition rooted in someone's Tom-foolery?"

Holmes shrugged his tall shoulders and re-lit his pipe.

"The head of some luckless long-ago peasant passed off as a more prestigious one, you mean? I can tell you our fellow Curtis certainly believes it to be bona-fide. As for me, I withdraw my thoughts from conjecture at this point. All I know for certain is a client came to me for aid, and I have promised to offer my assistance. But I tell you, Watson, the thought that it is indeed so odd and august a relic from the Commonwealth....it stirs me.

I will in any event give this matter my fullest attention, you may be sure."

"Don't you always?" I said, making Holmes chuckle.

I remembered how in my own school days in Scotland my fellow pupils had delighted in deviling the masters, so I asked him: "Do you think, Holmes, it may have been taken by a student, intent on a prank?"

"I cannot yet say, Watson, though if so, how was it the student was privy to what the client has assured us was the most well-kept secret in the school, one he and those who knew of it had taken heartfelt oaths to conceal?"

"Well, yes," I muttered. Then I added: "Students know a great many more things about the management of a school than the masters would suspect."

"Yes, rather as servants know more of the lives of their employers than the employers would wish to believe," Holmes agreed.

"The knowledge of servants has been of use to you quite a few times," I reminded him, "and was the means of solving more than a few cases."

My mind flew back to a matter in Wiltshire some two years previous, The Case of the Wallpaper Stain, in which an under-house parlour maid had inadvertently revealed to Holmes certain habits within the residence that had resulted in him coming across a clue that solved the entire mystery as to the whereabouts of a five-year-old boy taken by his mentally-deranged former wet-nurse.

"You are recalling our little adventure in Wiltshire back in '92, are you not?" Holmes startled me from my thoughts by asking.

I demanded, "Yes, but how should you know that?"

"Well what else should you be thinking of at mention of a servant's intimate knowledge of an employer's habits?"

"Of course."

"Now, Watson, as I am sure you are required home for dinner with your good lady wife, I have a Cornish librarian to create from my store of paste-paint, wigs, and above all from my renown skills as an actor...."

"Then I shall leave you to the crafting of your illusion!" I said with a smile, as I retrieved my hat and made my way out, with a call of goodnight to Mrs. Hudson in passing.

In the morning I rose and breakfasted with my wife before packing a day-valise and making my way via cab to Waterloo Station. I knew it was ever Holmes' habit to test his disguises by playing various tricks of identity upon me, so I was on the alert that morning, and in fact did espy him ere he could do so yet again.

"Well, well," said I, "I think I have never seen a more Cornish-looking scholarly librarian as the one I see before me now."

"Whet? Whet say ye, ser?" the figure of the Cornish librarian demanded. "Ye address me with familiarity, ser, yet I am Mr. Jowan Jago, of St. Breaca's School, just off the overnight train from St. Ives th's very morning."

"Ah, very convincing, Holmes," I said with a chuckle, "even down to the Cornish accent!"

"A *west* Cornish accent, Watson, for I leave nothing to chance! And I thank you, for I have gone to some pains to make myself believable in this rôle."

"I don't think many at this school where we are traveling will doubt you," I assured him. "Did I not already know you myself, I certainly shouldn't."

A quarter-hour saw us aboard the train to take us up to the fertile downs of Suffolk, where St. Brendon's Academy was located just outside a village called Tawny, a settlement so old it was registered in the 11th century in the *Domesday Book*. As we rode, Holmes stayed in character when among others, but secure in our compartment, he spoke to me in his regular voice, telling me of certain readings he had undertaken in the night in preparation for the investigation ahead. Some of the titles he mentioned were a surprise to me.

"I can understand the study of Cromwell and the matter

of his long-misplaced head," I allowed, "and of referring to your guide to Suffolk, but consulting a monograph on the subject of woolen threads made in the mills of the north of England? In what way should that be of aid?"

"It may be of no aid at all, Watson, or it may prove germane. And if not today, then perhaps some other day, as knowledge is seldom completely wasted. In any event, we shall have to wait and see."

I said, "I have found it is usually wise to take you at your word."

The trip was not a long one and by mid-morning we had arrived at the station, where, the result of a telegram, Curtis, the client, stood waiting for us. After a polite greeting on both sides, Holmes said to him, "Be mindful to remember that to all outside eyes I am your correspondent, the head librarian at the Longacre Academy in St. Ives, Cornwall, and this is my friend, the physician Dr. James Hamish."

I chuckled, for 'James' and 'Hamish' were respectively my Christian and middle names.

"I understand," Curtis said solemnly, "and I shall endeavor not to break character. Regardless, though, I cannot tell you with what relief it is I see you come here."

He took us upon the route Holmes had spoken of the day before in the moments of our earliest meeting, passing as it did between the alleyways of several buildings, and taking us past the spicy scent of the Hungarian restaurant, leaving me still to marvel at how Holmes had spoken of these things with such accuracy the day before. Curtis then guided us on foot up to the school along a straight road that fit well into the flatness of the Suffolk countryside, finally coming to the wrought-iron gateway that led up long and formal approach to St. Brendan's Academy for Boys, where he was among the masters.

To my eyes St. Brendan's was revealed to be a gray-stone structure built, I would guess, in the late 17th century. Its single tower of about fifty-feet in height looked sedate and pleasant, and the whole of the grounds was pleasing to the eye. I could see why Holmes' client loved it here and was so stricken by the thought that the scandal of the missing remains might compel him leave, for the academy was all things a scholar might wish for in his life.

Holmes asked if there had been any new developments in the matter, and Curtis informed him there had been none, and that thankfully the matter was still a secret.

In due time we were lead across the verdant lawn and up the paving-stone path toward the entrance to the school, and as we did so our paths crossed those of a tall man with iron-gray hair and mustache, perhaps fifty years of age. He had huge shoulders, a confident air of authority, and, I noted in my doctor's eye, the beginnings of a goiter soon to hang low over the front of his neck, doubtless to the eventual amusement of future students.

"Dr. Osborne!" Curtis called in a jocular tone, "may I present my day-guests, Mr. Jowan Jago," he said giving the Cornish name Holmes had created for his identity, "and Dr. James Hamish, his physician. Gentlemen, this is our good deputy-headmaster at St. Brendan's, Dr. Jabez Osborne, who is filling-in for Headmaster Horace Pomeroy, while that gentleman is on a semester's sabbatical, studying linguistics on the Isle of Man."

The deputy-headmaster, a taller fellow even than Holmes' six feet, and broader than him by a larger measure still, bowed low and in a cultured Midlands accent uttered, "Gentlemen, I bid you welcome to our school!"

"Deputy-Headmaster Osborne," I allowed, perhaps putting on the Scots a little more than was my wont.

"Good to meet ye at last, ser," Holmes said, the west-Cornish accent he'd affected, thick as sea foam, "I 'ave heard much of ye and of St. Brendan's in my correspondence with yer Master of Books 'ere."

"Then I am flattered, Mr. Jago," replied Osborne, "though I confess this meeting to be the beginning of my familiarity with you, sir. I am at a miss as to why our worthy librarian never mentioned your acquaintance."

His hazel-colored eyes went curiously to Curtis, who allowed that mention of the correspondence must have slipped his mind, then as a change of subject hurriedly explained that the two of us were touring the library on a stopover on our eventual trip up to Scotland.

"Edinburgh," I put in, mentioning my birth city.

"A fine place, that," the towering deputy headmaster said, seeming to accept our story at face value. He then graciously bade us welcome once more, and invited us to take our supper in the dining hall with the other masters at seven, for which we thanked him and rather gratefully prepared to make our parting while our cover was little the worse for wear.

"There'll be turtle soup seasoned with sherry and tarragon," Osborne cordially called back to us before he, too, walked on.

"I don't believe he suspected a thing," Curtis squealed with pleased laughter. "You are good, Mr. Holmes, completely convincing in the part!"

"Thank you, I have long worked to become so," allowed Holmes.

Though Curtis, perhaps mutually caught up in the rôle he too was playing, would have happily bestowed on us the full tour of his beloved library, Holmes reminded him of the true purpose for our presence and informed him it was his study, where the theft had taken place, that interested him more.

"Of course, of course," the Master of Books agreed. "We'll go up at once."

Curtis took us down a well-lighted hallway, where busts of Shakespeare, Plato, and Pallas Athena sat atop marble plinths here and there, past classrooms where boys either sat in silent study or from which voices of teachers echoed out, going over Latin verbs, or the causes for the Danish invasions in the time of Alfred the Great.

Then in a moment ill-timed for our purposes, classes were dismissed, which resulted in every door bursting open and a rush of gray-uniform clad boys shoving and jostling one another, chaos instantly rampant, all order dismissed.

"Toot-toot! Mind your starboard, Mr. Curtis!" one boy cried out as he came up from behind, rushing by the three of us at a full-tilt.

"Manners, Arkfield," Curtis growled at the fleeing boy, "or it'll be points from Hastings House!"

"He's a funny-looking chap," another of the boys called, stopping a moment to tilt his head toward Holmes, who'd been affecting a stoop in his shoulders.

"Never seen *him* here before!" a second boy agreed with his friend's evaluation. "Maybe he's to be our new Anatomy Master, for he certainly looks cadaverous enough!"

"On your way, Owens, Stanhope!" Curtis said sternly to the pair, sending the laughing boys trotting down the hall.

"Things seem to have changed since my own school-days," I noted, dismayed at the disorder of class' end, and at the familiarity with which the pupils were addressing one of the masters.

"Oh, it is the way of boys," said Curtis apologetically, as he dabbed at his brow with a handkerchief.

A second wave of young men scurried past us in a burst of rambunctious bodies crammed into the stampede-filled halls as we helplessly pressed ourselves to the side to give them egress.

"Hiya, Curtis, sir!" called one roguish blond boy in passing, clearly, one of the leaders, I judged, of the cliques among the student body. "Be sure to tell your guests to be on the watch for the Black Saxon! I heard him moving about last night!"

"Cheek, Miller, cheek!' Curtis called after him, though the high-spirited blond boy was already bounding away, obviously less than intimidated.

"Not, er, the most sedate of young men, these," Curtis apologized, clearly embarrassed over displays we'd witnessed. "Headmaster Pomeroy has been strict in academics, but allows the pupils 'free reign' as he terms it when not in class. It is not, ahem, how I would see the school run, and should Deputy

Headmaster Osborne take over one day, not how he would have it either, I assure you."

"Mr. Curtis," I asked, "what is this 'Black Saxon' the boy, Miller, bade us be careful of?"

"Oh," said Curtis, "in so old a place as this, well over two-hundred years, it's unavoidable there be a legend of some resident spirit, in this case a ghost from the Dark Ages some of the boys claimed to have seen over the generations, a sort of shadowy black vapor wearing a *spangenhelm,* and chain mail. It keeps the boys amused to frighten one another with colourful tales of this Black Saxon terrorizing the unwary in dark hallways, and taking small objects that belong to others, then leaving them to be found in odd locales, like atop the grandfather clock in the study hall. Nonsense, of course, and I've certainly never seen this mischievous specter in my tenure here."

"Indeed," replied Holmes.

Could stories of this ghost be connected to the taking of Cromwell's head, I unavoidably wondered, *perhaps a mischievous prank gone too far?*

We went up a curving staircase, passing portraits of seventeen former headmasters, the first few clad in the great powdered wigs of their era, for this was clearly always a Tory school, til we came to a tall, thick door, past which lay the offices of the faculty. A sign on the door itself was captioned:

NO UNACCOMPANIED STUDENTS PAST THIS POINT

Curtis's own room possessed a large window, and was open to the light from outside. The office contained a desk, two chairs, a shelf lined with an eclectic collection of books, and against the wall was the cabinet from which the cranium of Cromwell had disappeared, mahogany storage box and all.

Wasting no time, Holmes let his eyes pass from one end of the cabinet to the other, then knelt, and removing a magnifying lens from his great coat, peered long and hard at and into the lock on the front of the cabinet's glass doors.

"Most curious," he uttered, "most curious indeed, and at the moment I do not know what to make of the story I see told here in miniature."

"Yes?" Curtis said, nervousness punctuating his tone.

Holmes informed him: "To my eyes it is obvious a theft was carried out with a duplicate of your own key, Mr. Curtis, for however carefully-formed the duplicate of an original key may be, it will often leave a mark upon the interior of the lock which the original will not. Sometimes the markings are faint, sometimes they are easily discernible, and this, gentleman, was no skillful duplication, but a rather clumsy one that clearly incised the lock's interior with a notable striation. However there is more. Above the marks of the fraudulent key, and therefore coming into things later than its own use, I see signs of a lock-pick being employed, also by an inexpert and clumsy hand. Sir, I tell you, your cabinet has recently been violated by not once but twice, and not merely by one individual, but by a second."

Curtis took this news with speechless dismay.

Rising back to his full height, Holmes asked, "Think carefully now, Mr. Curtis, who else has had access to your cabinet key?"

"Why, no one!" Curtis cried, aghast. "My keys are never out of my possession. I even lay them at arm's length on my bedside table when I sleep, and our bedroom door is kept locked, as is the outer house door itself. I tell you also that while I am a deep slumberer, my wife is a somewhat delicate one, and would awaken at the slightest sound of intrusion, as would our adopted poodles, Juliet and Héloïse, who occupy the lower end of our bed. No such theft could have happened in our house."

"Then another place, another time?" Holmes pressed. "It is at the very core of the solution that this problem be answered."

Curtis stood looking perplexed, his mind turning over the matter until he said, "There was one recent occasion, but it is so unlikely as to be barely worth mentioning, and it was but a minute, perhaps not even so long as that, til they were back in my hand, a means for duplication nowhere about us."

"Ah-ha!" Holmes cried. "So we have it. Be so good as to tell me all…"

"I won't believe ill of him, though," Curtis pledged. "I speak of my friend of some years, the Botany Master here, Mr. Victor Thatcher."

"And how did this Thatcher come to have your key?" Holmes demanded.

"It was right after the big rainstorm a week or so past. Thatcher sometimes walks in with me of a morning, and many a pleasant talk have the two of us known during our strolls to the school. He had been away in Brighton, at a gathering of botanists, as I remember, and was just back. That morning there was a large limb that had fallen off a sycamore tree that stood along the path, and so we were obliged to go a different route, a detour of some ten minutes that involved us making use of the stepping stones that have lain there in the little creek since time immemorial: centuries, I doubt not. He bade me go first, so the stones would not be rendered slippery by his own passing."

"And the keys?" Holmes asked, nudging him onward.

"At the last moment Thatcher said to me, 'Daniel, better give me your key ring as well, for if you were to fall in, it might be lost.' It was a valid point, I am a clumsy fellow, so I did, then I passed carefully across the stepping stones in half a minute, and he tossed my keys across to me at once, then threw me his own to safe guard, then likewise stepped over, and we were back on our way, continuing our discussion of the works of Alexander Pope, and came to the academy before eight o' clock. It was the exchange of a minute, Mr. Holmes, he'd have had no time to make this duplicate key you speak of."

Holmes smiled indulgently for a flicker of an instant then set his face back to seriousness. "Mr. Curtis, being an honest man, I see you have no knowledge of how one might render a means of ingress when in a hurry. Allow me to demonstrate. Watson, if you'd be so kind as to pass to me your key to Baker

Street...?"

I complied and handed over my own ring, which also contained the keys to my marital residence, and my Harley Street surgery.

Holmes took the key he sought and from his own pocket pulled a lump of a peculiar sort of stiff white wax, which he pressed atop the key til a perfect imprint was left behind. He then dropped the wax back into his pocket and handed my own key back to me.

"Done in the blink of an eye," Holmes said. "And from this imprintation a copy, inexact though effective, can be made. It is a thing of ease."

Curtis looked both awestruck and stricken. "But...even if the scenario you describe is possible, why would my friend have done such a thing?"

"There I do not yet know," Holmes admitted, "but that is the thing I intend to learn. This Botany Master, Mr. Thatcher, he is here on the grounds?"

Curtis glanced at the clock on his wall and said, "He is a creature of regular habits, and usually takes a stroll out to the herb garden he maintains in raised beds near the woods."

"Then let us await him there," Holmes instructed.

Out in the hallway Holmes again became the Cornish bibliophile, stooped and on the cusp of man's aged years, and Curtis skillfully played along with the ruse as more rowdy students passed by, but out on the lawn he set aside all pretense and reverted to his identity as Holmes' client, and assured us again that it could not be as Holmes thought, that his colleague Thatcher was as earnest a gentleman as could be met anywhere, and a true friend.

"If that is so," said Holmes, "then I shall know in a matter of moments."

We were in place at the herb garden, a series of raised beds crafted from evenly-cut white stones, covering perhaps fifty square yards, and across the green, as if on schedule, the botany master cheerfully strode, brass-capped walking stick in hand.

"Ah, Daniel!" he called. "Scuttlebutt has it you are showing a Cornish visitor and his Scottish doctor friend around the grounds today. A pair of Celts brought to our Anglo-Saxon oasis of learning!" He made a bow to us, which we returned, and said, "Victor Thatcher, botany master at our fine academy, at your humble service, gentlemen."

Instead of replying in his guise as the Cornish librarian, my friend lost his stooped posture and gave the new arrival a piercing glare as he told him: "And I am Mr. Sherlock Holmes of Baker Street, London, solver of crimes, and the worst foe any criminal might find upon his trail."

For an instant the expression of shock on Thatcher's face was complete, then he sighed and held up a hand and commented, "Say nothing more, Mr. Holmes, for it is with relief that I will come clean. It is true that I am proven stained by dishonor, though when I tell my tale it may show I am perhaps not the utter villain the evidence might at first suggest."

I for one was surprised at how quickly the matter was unraveling, and had expected greater machinations would be required to elicit an admission of guilt.

"Victor, have you done this thing then?" Curtis demanded, injury in his tone as he began to wring his hands.

"Daniel," the botanist said, "I will tell all, though I must ask, how on earth did you know the Lord Protector's head had been removed and returned?"

"Returned?" I exclaimed.

"Watson," stated Holmes, "it is as I had begun to suspect the instant I spied those later markings left by the pick used upon the cabinet's lock. We have the dark workings of a second thief in this case."

The unwelcome words hung in the air until Holmes said: "Mr. Thatcher, you employed a counterfeit key, I gather, created from a wax impression surreptitiously made when you cajoled my client out of its possession just before he crossed the stepping stones some days ago?"

"I admit I did so," Thatcher said, looking ashamed.

"But I am correct in my belief that you no longer have the artifact?"

"You deduce correctly, sir, I do not, for as I said I returned it to Daniel's office, though deep is my shame to be exposed for the dishonorable thing which I have done in removing it even for a short time."

"Then it will come as a surprise to you to hear that the object in question, the alleged head of the Lord Protector of the Commonwealth, is missing?" Holmes quizzed him.

Thatcher's face registered shock. "Missing...? That cannot be. I put it back, I assure you. My intention was never to steal it, I..."

"It is time for you to tell all," Holmes said sternly, interrupting Thatcher's near-babbling.

"Of course," Thatcher agreed. "Then if you will permit me, here are the facts..."

Thatcher's tale was indeed one of dishonor, yet not so black a stain as it might at first have seemed, for his story was that some weeks previously he had taken a holiday to Brighton, and there attended a conference for botanists. Many of the attendees there known to him personally, or by reputation, and he described it as a great pleasure to meet like minds and exchange talk of their mutual field of study. A number of newly-discovered floral specimens from the tropics were displayed for them all to marvel at. After the second day's lectures, Thatcher had strolled upon the promenade in Brighton, and outside a tent there, there saw an advertisement for a slideshow depicting highlights of an American museum on the island of Manhattan, a place dubbed "The Cabinet of Professor Mullhausen."

Thatcher paid his shilling's admission, and looked on at projector slides of wonders both brilliantly remarkable, and starkly disturbing. He saw the stuffed body of a three-headed lamb, and the suit worn by the notorious poisoner, George Weaver, at the time of his hanging. He saw gallstones whittled into figurines of the Last Super, and tusks from a Columbian mammoth. He saw slides of a twenty-foot king cobra suspended in formaldehyde, of fleas dressed as if for a wedding, and of a cat-mummy from the deserts of Egypt. There were oddities of virtually every description....a Bible that had stopped a Confederate bullet at Gettysburg, hair from the beard of Abraham Lincoln, and a meteorite that had fallen onto a schoolhouse. And there was the mummified leg of the great American pioneer and Indian-fighter, Solomon York. It was while peering at the image of the mummified leg flickering against the tent wall that a strange notion struck him, not yet what it would become, but taking root and awaiting full germination.

After the slideshow, Thatcher spoke a moment to the proprietor, an American impresario of perhaps thirty-five, who introduced himself as Captain Gordon H. Tallyworth III, though he felt this was no doubt a stage name. This Tallyworth said he was an associate of the great collector of the weird, Professor Mullhausen, back in New York, and that he was taking glass slides of the Cabinet's collection on a British tour.

Thatcher chatted with him a moment, discussing the items he'd seen, and telling of his own profound knowledge of botany.

The charismatic showman indulged him in conversation for a moment then said, "Ain't too much call over our way to see vegetation in our Cabinet, Mister, though we're always in the market for something unusual that might have an appeal to the public. If you ever come across a man-eating plant, well, we'll pay you top dollar for that!'

He cordially slapped Thatcher on the arm and laughed, preparing to move on to the demands of the after-show, but Thatcher found himself saying, "And what would you pay for a wax replica of the mummified head of Oliver Cromwell?"

The words stopped the American, who paused and gave Thatcher a peculiarly penetrating look, and Thatcher said he knew that under the man's fancy suit he was a slick street barker akin to the infamous gypsy carnies. Still this so-called Captain

Tallyworth smiled and asked, "Tell me now, friend, just what would a fine botanist like yourself know of such an oddity as that?"

Remembering that he was bound by his oath of honour to the academy, and surprised to have heard himself say anything, Thatcher stammered and said, "If such a thing were to exist, how much would it be worth?"

"For a thing like that? A replica taken straight off the original?" the American laughed coarsely. "For a thing like that, why five-thousand dollars!"

Thatcher knew enough of conversation rates between US dollars and pounds-sterling to grasp it was a princely sum to an academic such as himself, and grew dazzled for an instant. With so much suddenly come to him, he could invest for retirement, and once his teaching days were behind him, take the voyage to the Nile Delta he had always dreamt of, and collect plants \ along its waters. Oh, he felt a tempting ambition begin to tremble inside him.

The American stared hard, then said, "You know something, don't ya, friend?"

"I made a deal with him," Thatcher admitted, causing poor Curtis, at my right, to sigh deeply. "But not the one you might be thinking, no. This Tallyworth, he told me he worked with a sculptor in London who could create the most convincing wax replicas, and for just the right to let his friend measure the head of the Lord Protector, and photograph it in preparation for his work, he'd pay the $5,000.00."

"Or thirty pieces of silver, perhaps?" Holmes charged.

The deal was struck. Thatcher made it clear he would not reveal where he obtained the head, though he would deliver it to Tallyworth, who would meet him in the company of the sculptor who would render the likeness. Tallyworth would pay the money, in cash, and the cranium could return with Thatcher to the academy, none the worse for its adventure, and no one at St. Brendan's would have to be any the wiser.

"But, why, Victor, did you take it during my time of

possession?" Curtis demanded. "Why not wait until you had it in your own office in three months?"

"Alas, because, Daniel, the American would be sailing for home in less than a fortnight, and our arrangement needed to be immediate so the sculptor in London would have time to do his work."

"And so you came up with the plot to craft the impression of your friend's key, then make off with the skull," said Holmes in summation.

"I did take the artifact from my friend's office, yes," Thatcher told us, "and did carry it home with me and lock it in my own writing bureau, but by all that's sacred, I swear to you I could not do the rest I'd planned. I desired the money on offer, certainly, but as I lay awake on the night before I was to travel and meet the purveyor of oddities, my conscience got the better of me, and the next morning I put the Lord Protector back into place while Daniel was occupied in the library, hoping he was never to know it had ever been gone. I never made my way to London for the meeting with the American and his sculptor friend."

"I doubt very much there ever was a 'sculptor friend,'" Holmes informed him, coolly, "and it is fortunate your conscience forestalled your journey, for had you kept the meeting, I've little doubt the artifact would have been taken from you, either by subtle subterfuge or outright robbery. It was possession of the actual artifact which interested this so-called Tallyworth, never the chance at a copy, for it is lurid spectacle that these vulgar American pseudo-museums display to the curious masses. A wax figure would have been of little value, but, ah, the actual head of Oliver Cromwell? Oh, New Yorkers with morbid interests would have lined up and down the block to see that, and what could the school have done when it learned its most honored endowment was publicized as among the exhibitions in an American cabinet of curiosities?"

"Oh, dear me," Thatcher groaned, seeing for the first time the true nature of the situation.

"You were a fool," said Holmes, "though you inadvertently bested your foe for a little while by not proving a greedy one as well."

"By Heaven, Victor," muttered the client, Curtis.

Holmes asked, "On what day did you return the object, Thatcher?"

"The very next morning, Thursday."

"And it was two mornings ago Curtis discovered the cranium was missing, Assuming you speak honestly to us, Thatcher, as I believe you have, then the final theft of the object was between Thursday evening and two mornings ago. Three full days for the American to do his work and lay hands on his prize."

"Oh," Thatcher vowed, "but it couldn't have been the American, Tallyworth, for I did not tell him where the Lord Protector was kept!"

At this Holmes truly let loose a laugh. "Are you so innocent a soul, Thatcher, to believe this oily showman would not have taken pains to locate you? You told him you attended a botany convention, that you were a teacher of the subject at an all-boys' academy in Suffolk, and that you were returning the next day. You might as well have led a sharp character like him straight to the school itself, for in the end, it seems you did."

Silence followed this summary of unwelcome facts, til Holmes announced, "The unskillful lock-picking on Curtis' office cabinet which resulted in the head of Cromwell vanishing to its present whereabouts, I perceived at once was the work not of an adult but of a boy of middling height, and left-handed. I saw this as more likely than it having been a man of so short a stature, especially as there are so many boys hereabouts."

"One of the *boys* did this?" Curtis exclaimed. "How did he even know the artifact existed? We do not share our secret with the students, only among the school-masters, and each of us is sworn to silence!"

As if dealing with a child, Holmes gazed at his client, then said with a mingling of patience and condescension, "My good

Curtis, the boy knew because the American scoundrel sent him after it. Now, I require the both of you to think of any left-handed boys in attendance here, with the most likely at the top of the list. Call them up to your study and confront them, not over the theft of Cromwell's remains, make no mentioned of that, but with suspicion of an unspecified lesser crime."

"Oh," said Thatcher, "now that is a time-honoured tactic among headmasters and teachers to learn of random wrongdoings, I assure you."

"Interview the boys one by one," said Holmes, "telling each that you know what he has done, and that you are giving him a final chance to confess ere you lay the matter before the stern graces of Deputy Headmaster Osborne."

Within a moment, speaking together, Curtis and Thatcher had compiled a list of some six boys known to be left-handed, and at the head of the list was none other than Miller, the blond boy who had called out to us so saucily in the hallway, bidding us beware the school ghost he dubbed the Black Saxon.

"Holmes," I said as we walked back from the garden under the gray stone arch of the old school proper, "I wonder if this Miller *is* this 'Black Saxon,' terrorizing other boys for sport?"

"If he is, it is no concern to us, Watson, for we seek a real world crime, not a disciplinary matter in this ivy-bedecked environment of academic rules and patent un-reality."

Twenty minutes later the spirited blond boy, Miller, stood with jaunty confidence before the two masters, and listened as Thatcher followed Holmes' script and sternly bade him admit what he had done, lest he face Osborne, the deputy headmaster, and possible expulsion.

The boy grinned fearlessly at first, until Curtis spoke up for the first time and said to him, "If you are expelled from here, Thomas, I imagine your father will send you to Buckinghamshire, and the rigid order of the military academy."

At that Miller's expression changed to seriousness and he conceded. "Very well, sirs, I will come clean."

For a moment hope brightened the masters' faces, til

Miller said, "I confess it was I who took Valentine Rolland's boater hat, sirs, before the outing into town last Friday. I'll return it, sirs, and receive my licks for it."

"You took Rolland's boater...?" asked Curtis, confused.

"Yes, sir," said Miller, his eyes darting with confusion between the teachers. "To leave it someplace funny and make him think it was the Black Saxon. Isn't that what this is about? The hat, sir?"

"He knows nothing of the matter," Holmes, devoid the faux Cornish accent, told Curtis. "Send him on, bring in the next."

"Return the boater at once, Miller," Thatcher called after him, relief already returning the boy to his sneering cockiness ere he even passed out the door.

Over the next hour, four more boys were brought up and each was challenged as to his culpability for an unnamed rules-violation. Three pleaded total ignorance, one admitted to cheating on an algebraic examination, but none proved to be our culprit.

Holmes had joined the rest of us in showing indications of frustration, til finally the sixth boy was admitted to the office. His name was Herbert Maines, a thin, mousey child of ten, and the student Thatcher and Curtis had unanimously deemed least likely to be capable of the action. Yet upon sight of him something changed in Holmes, who smiled knowingly and with what I discerned as visible relief, he stepped past the two masters and said, leaning low toward the lad:

"Young Herbert Maines. My name is Sherlock Holmes, and I know about the box in the master's cabinet, and I know exactly what it is that you have done."

In a trice the boy's composure collapsed, and like Thatcher before him, he admitted everything. As for motive, he explained:

"I am not from a rich family as so many others here are," he said, defiance and anger joining the tears forming in his brown eyes. "My father is clerk to a proctor in Ipswich, and struggles to keep me here at St. Brendan's. I have always wished there were a way to lighten his burden. That was my only goal, sir!"

"Herbert, how did you come to meet the American man?" Holmes asked him, patience now in his voice. "And I bid you, tell me no lies, for I shall know."

The boy narrated: "I have no friends here, and often am alone, lacking money to go into town with the other boys on our half-afternoons there, and it was as I was walking by myself on the oak path on the afternoon of the Friday cricket match against Albans, that a man came up to me. He was smiling and spoke in a friendly way, though his accent was terribly grating, like an American's or some such."

"Yes," Thatcher and Curtis joined me in spontaneously agreeing.

"He said he could see my uniform was bought second-hand, and my state a friendless one, and that I was not like the other boys, the richer ones who had it so easy. He seemed to know all this about me right off, and the way he said it was soothing. It made me want to listen."

"Because he is a perceptive chap, this fellow," Holmes told the boy, "schooled on the streets of New York, where he long-ago learned to con many who are older and wiser than yourself. He has made it his life's practice to study others for personal gain, and he studied the students here, you see, and marked you, like a lion marks its prey. The rest was merely waiting til he could speak with you and turn you toward his purpose with his showman's guile. But go on, what was his promised enticement if you did as he said?"

"Five pounds, sir, if I brought a box back to him from Mr. Curtis' office. More money than I'd ever seen! He gave me a lock-picking set, showed me for a few moments how to use it, and said there was nothing to picking a desk drawer, then told me if I brought him the box I'd find there, unopened, for I was never to peer inside...."

"He guessed you'd be so frightened you would cry out, or tell what you'd seen," Holmes provided, "queering his ambitions."

"Well, he said if I got this box at my first chance and brought it to him any evening that week, where he'd be waiting, he'd give me my reward."

Five pounds, I thought, was an enticing sum on the one hand, but such a small price for asking a boy to risk so much.

"What did you do next, Herbert?" Holmes asked him.

"I took the lock picks in their little cloth pouch and went back inside the school, feeling excited, proud someone trusted me, also frightened, but during the evening when most others were at study hall, I made my way to the door we're never supposed to pass beyond without a teacher. It was all shadowy and I kept thinking about the ghost called the Black Saxon, how so many tell me they've seen him.... But I made it to Mr. Curtis' office, and I knelt in front of his cabinet, then took the picks like the American man showed me and I worked at the lock. It wasn't easy and I kept imagining I heard someone coming. Right when I was ready to give in, I heard a snap and pulled the doors open, then took the box, and at the arranged time, which was the same time any night of the week in case it took longer, I sneaked out of the school with it, and met the stranger where he said he'd be."

"And how did he seem to you? Holmes asked.

"He grabbed the box and opened it, and a strange expression came over him, like he couldn't believe what he was seeing, whatever it actually was. He never even looked at me, just thrust out a five pound note and hurried off into the woods. I never saw him anymore, just came back in, scared, knowing somehow I was going to get caught, but these past two days, they went by and nothing was said about any theft, so... I wondered if I'd gotten away with it, sirs. I wondered til I got called up here today, and then I knew it was curtains for me. And what will my father say? What will he think of me now?"

With that the boy, who had til then kept his composure, broke down sobbing.

"Gentlemen," said Holmes, "in this humble office we have a pair of guilty souls, one a dishonourable botany master, the second a lonely boy enticed to theft. As we all will agree, I believe, that retrieving the....*item*, before my client, the only innocent party in this sordid business, should face ruin, I say we swear young Maines here to secrecy, and that you give him your mutual word that since he came clean with us, he'll face no punishment for what he has done."

The assurances of confidence were given by both parties, and Maines, looking shaken but, I thought, five pounds richer for all his wrongdoing, was allowed to proceed back toward his poetry class, his eyes red with tears. Yet at the doorway Holmes stopped him and asked. "One last thing, Herbert. Where precisely did the meeting with the American take place?"

"In the woods down by the old Benedictine oratory, sir. The stone ruins."

"I know the place!" Curtis and Thatcher called out in sequence.

Holmes waved the boy, Maines, on and said, "Gentlemen, we may yet learn something at the scene. Guide me there."

Together we progressed to the woods near the edge of the school grounds, where there stood a roofless stone structure about the twice the size of my bedroom back home. I judged it had been constructed long ago as a place of solitary prayer by the aforementioned Benedictine monks, who'd once owned great stretches of land in the county, only to fall victim almost overnight to Henry VIII and his policy of monastic dissolution.

Holmes held out an arm, indicating the three of us were not to follow, then carefully stepped into the ruin, and after a moment paused and glanced down. I saw that on the ground were the butts of several cigarettes, and a small matchbox with the cover bent in on itself. With a pair of tweezers pulled from his greatcoat pocket, Holmes lifted up the printed matchbox and looked closely at it.

"Ho! Our American quarry has either been exceptionally careless, or had the foresight of cleverness and has left behind a false clue, for as you can see this matchbox advertises none other than the famed Sullivan Arms Hotel, in Brighton."

From his pocket he extracted a small case and dusted the matchbox with a black ash-like powder. "Ahhh," Holmes marveled, "a print!"

He held the box up to us and remarked, "Whether we shall indeed find this showman in his tent at Brighton, still displaying his vulgar slides, or whether he has left the Sullivan Arms and now seeks a ship to take him home to America with his ill-gotten prize, we have his fingerprint, and he cannot conceal himself from us, wherever he may roam. I am not above chasing him all the way to America, though I fear that outcome would be too late to prevent catastrophe for you, my good Curtis."

"No," said Thatcher, "I'll never allow my friend to fall into disgrace for what I have set in motion, nor would I have had you never arrived to investigate this matter, Mr. Holmes. Daniel, I vow to you with all the force of whatever honour you think left in me, I would have told the deputy headmaster before letting you be blamed, and I will now, if it comes down to it."

Thatcher's words had a remarkable effect on Curtis, who had theretofore showed a certain cool distaste toward his former companion, but at that his face softened and he held out his pudgy hand.

"Victor, I cannot know what drove you to such a mad scheme, but I accept you never meant me harm, nor would I have come to harm save this American scoundrel betrayed you as well. Whether or not it will yet be possible to bring this sordid mess to a good outcome, know in any event I forgive you heart and soul."

The pair shook hands long and hard.

"Gentlemen, however glad one may be for this reconciliation," Holmes stated, "action must now follow, and swiftly! The two of you should return to the school and keep up the pretense that nothing is amiss. I do not think the boy, Maines, will confess his misdeed to anyone, so there is yet hope this may be resolved as we would wish. But, Watson, we must hurry!"

Within an hour we were in town, where the railroad depot

proved to possess a telegraph, which Holmes used to send word off to a friend of his, Inspector Phineas Collins, of the Brighton Police.

"Watson, if this scoundrel has not yet fled the country, we may yet have him before sundown."

Strange it was when all my instincts prodded me to seek the fastest route to Brighton, to sit idly about with Holmes, taking refreshment in a tea shop, til finally a local boy returned with a most welcome telegram in hand.

It read simply:

HAVE HIM. COLLINS.

At these tidings, Holmes emitted a cheer. "Watson," he veritably chirped, "Fortune smiles upon us!"

The remainder of the case can be brought to a conclusion rather abruptly, as these matters sometimes are. Upon receipt of the telegram, Holmes and I boarded a train for Paddington Station, and on from there to Brighton, and were met upon our arrival by Inspector Collins, who would prove to be a fresh-faced young man, newly promoted to his position, grateful to Holmes for his assistance on the matter of a cheque-forger some months in the past. He guided us back to the station, where inside a cell sat a somewhat handsome, if hard-featured, American man just this side of middle years, well-dressed, but with a rat-like shine in his all-seeing eyes.

On sight I found I did not like him, though as he spoke I discerned he held a certain sarcastic charm.

"Oh, and who is this now?" the man called out in his nasal American accent. "Are you my lawyers finally? If so, tell these madmen police I did not walk out of any restaurant without paying my bill! By the Eternal, I am no pauper who need flee the cost of a meal."

Collins shrugged and said apologetically to Holmes and me, "It was all I could think of to hold him, doing a dodge on a restaurant cheque."

Holmes asked for a few moments alone with the American, and when he had them, he said, "'Captain' Tallyworth, I presume? My name is Sherlock Holmes, a private consulting detective, though being a foreigner, you may or may not know my reputation as a perceptive man, so allow me to give you a demonstration of my powers."

The man frowned in puzzlement and began to wear a disdainful smirk, though that would fade in a few seconds' time as Holmes told him:

"You come from a rather rough portion of the island of Manhattan, likely the Five Points, where you frequently went hungry as a child, causing that distinct nutritional deformity of your teeth known as 'shelled enamel.' You left home at about age ten, resulting in the availability of better food, giving you growth to the un-stunted adult height you attained. Had you stayed in your original dire straits, this would not have been so. You entered into rough work there, probably as a bouncer in tradesman's bar, and as a result of this, fisticuffs were a way of life for you in your past. Much to your pride, you have a small chunk of someone's tooth subcutaneously suspended in the second knuckle of your left hand."

The American's eyes dipped involuntarily toward the hand Holmes mentioned.

"You walk with inserts in your shoes to add some slight measure to you height---"

"Now just a moment...!" the man burst out, offended to have this detail spotted.

"Come, sir," Holmes chided him, "anyone with an eye half as trained as my own can perceive that trick of vanity."

He continued: "In New York you live in a flat which faces the sunset, staring into which as you watch the evening streets has given you the habit of undertaking a faint squint as your natural expression. You are in the practice of cleaning your nails with a pen-knife, which has resulted in the tips of your nails displaying a minute upward tilt."

He again gazed at his hands.

"Furthermore, you have a secret child, a little daughter, for whom you retain affections, yet do not wish her near you, so, alas, she is being brought up by others elsewhere in the city."

"Some matters are private!" the American thundered. "How the blasted devil did you know that?"

"Because, sir, you have enough affection for the child to still be wearing in your buttonhole the paper flower she made you on your last visit with her ere your departure from America, yet you did not bring her with you as it might be expected a father would."

The man placed a hand over the paper flower, as if something about it pained him, and our eyes had no right to see it. "Leave her out of this," he said. "The arrangement is best for her, given the life I lead, though I admit her absence causes me no small grief. But when the devil am I getting out of here, Mister?"

"I sense a defiant stubbornness remains in you," said Holmes, "not as yet an acceptance that in me you face one from whom there is no possible escape, rendering cooperation your only option. So shall I go further? There are still tiny details I could mention from my insights into your person, such as you sleep only on your stomach, you like to dust your hands with talcum powder, and feel annoyance that you have not been able to do so for a number of hours now, due to this confinement I have so effortlessly set upon you."

"All that's true enough," the American called Tallyworth admitted. "Now how about you tell me what this is about, and what business the likes of you have with me?"

"Patience, sir, patience, for I have but one final observation."

"What, more parlour tricks?" he laughed with hollow haughtiness. "I'll tell you, I oughta offer you a job back in New York. Pass you off as a mind-reader."

Holmes lit a cigarette and said, "It is just this. Several nights ago you bribed a student at a country boys' school in

Suffolk, convincing him to commit a theft on your behalf. The theft of an object which.... Ah, yes, I see from your expression, there is no need for me to describe this hidden object aloud."

The American looked keenly at Holmes, his face now set less in hostility, and more in caution.

"I done nothing like that," he said, his accent slipping, becoming less the respectable New Yorker, more the fast-talking roughneck from the Five Points he'd been long ago. "I bought somethin' rare down in Brighton and paid for it square to take home to my boss Mullhausen, in New York, and I defy you, Mr. Sherlock Holmes, with your second-rate deductions and insinuations, to prove I done otherwise, no-how!"

"Paid for?" asked Holmes.

"You're tootin' right, *paid for*, bought off some fella name of Thatcher."

"You made this purchase here in Brighton?"

"Yup!"

"Then you have, I presume, a bill of sale?"

"Mister, in my business I find it better not to deal with no bills of sale. Now I won't be saying nothin' else til I get a lawyer, and that's the story I'll stick to when I get my him in on this and sue you good and proper-like!"

For an unpleasant instant I considered the man's story. What if he was telling the truth, and Thatcher, the school botany master, had deceived us one and all, and we here in Brighton had left him back in Suffolk to make his escape with Cromwell's head?

Holmes, though, smiled disdainfully. "You may get away with telling a great many lies in your professional life, sir, or shall I call you 'Captain,' deceiving your paying customers that a common monitor lizard dyed cherry-red is an infant dragon from the mysterious Orient, or a bit of paper-mache forms an Andean sky-mummy, but you cannot mislead me no matter how hard you try. Aside from the testimony of witnesses, one a boy whom you involved in your crime, an automatic three-year extension of the sentence you could receive, let me add,

I discovered your place of concealment in a Medieval oratory, which to your eyes may have seemed but a roofless little structure of no historical importance."

The man swallowed before he said, "Yeah, so what?"

"I also have this." Holmes held out the matchbox and said, "With your fingerprints left conveniently upon it."

"My...what?"

"What, in your business you've never heard of a fingerprint? Suffice to say it is something which proves to me that you were on school grounds, a place you insinuate you never were, hiding and waiting, smoking several cigarettes of the variety matching those currently in your breast pocket, *Captain*."

The American who called himself Tallyworth touched the cigarette case under his clothing and then looked annoyed with himself for doing so. He seemed to reach an inner resolution and said, "I ain't no captain, and you know it. And outside the oddities-business my name ain't Tallyworth, it's Ulysses Boyle, a cholera orphan from Five Points who done his best to take that grand name given him by a mother he don't remember, and make good in a hard world. And so you know, I pay for my daughter to be brung up right, with respectable people, to get her a good start in the world. Better than I could give her."

"Yours was an ambitious rise, I don't doubt," said Holmes, "yet it comes to this. If you purchased the item as you say, in Brighton, you'd have had no reason to be on the grounds of the school in Suffolk, concealed and waiting for a rendezvous with the small boy who was so shamefully your partner in crime, though your presence in the oratory does rather corroborate the story that boy gave when I interviewed him. He whom you bribed to carry out your plot to steal a school's most valuable treasure."

Boyle's perceptive eyes looked away from Holmes in defeat and he said, "I really would've paid that Thatcher fellow his due if he'd played fair with me, just like I paid that boy at the school when he done me square. When Thatcher didn't keep his word, well, I couldn't let what he was offerin' just slip away. Not a thing that could be worth 10,000 paying visitors the first month alone..."

"So many as that?" I quizzed him from across the room.

"Mister, ya got no idea how willing and ready New Yorkers are to look at something crazy. They'll cough up anything. Hey, now," Boyle's eyes lit up and he gazed hopefully at Holmes, "if I happen to give back the---"

"The 'thing'," Holmes interjected, jerking his eyes toward the door, where Inspector Collins may or may not have been listening. "No need to put its true name to it. The 'thing' suffices here."

"Yeah, all right, if I give back 'the thing,' and get on the ship for New York I was plannin' on being aboard tomorrow anyway, could we, just maybe, come to some deal between us...?"

"Will I let you walk away, you mean?" Holmes finished.

"Well? It's not a bad bargain we'd strike, all things considered," Boyle offered. "I keep my word, you keep yours, everybody gets what he wants, and everybody walks off none the worse for the experience."

I suspected it was what Holmes had wanted all along, sparing as it did the secret of the academy's treasured artifact, and protecting his client's good name and honour.

To the American behind the bars he said: "I believe the good Inspector Collins *might* be persuaded to forget the matter of the, oh, what was it, Watson?

"An unpaid restaurant bill," I provided.

"Yes," said Holmes, "that is should you return the item and hastily depart from the country."

"Mister," said Ulysses Boyle, his tone somehow back again to that of 'Captain Tallyworth,' a New Yorker with some culture behind him, "as we say back home, ya got yourself a deal!"

The promising young Inspector Collins of the Brighton police, who'd done Holmes such a good turn in bringing in the man on whose trail Holmes had set him, did indeed find it in him to forgive the apocryphal matter of the unpaid restaurant tab, and we were soon lead to a small suite in the Sullivan Arms Hotel, near the waterfront, where among several valises and crates packed and ready for a voyage across the Atlantic, was a mahogany box about the size of...

Well, a human head.

"You win some, you lose some," said Boyle. Then he pointed and said: "There's the cursed thing you're after. It would've brought the right sort of spice to our Cabinet back home, which I own thirty percent of, by the way, and drawn in visitors by the gobs, but turns out it did me no good and I hope never to set eyes on it again."

"I think that a likely scenario," Holmes mused. "Now, Watson, it is our professional duty to make certain what this man claims to be inside the box truly is what the box holds. As a doctor I leave it to you to render your professional verdict."

He stepped aside and with a certain relaxed contentment began to smoke.

Somehow something inside me hesitated to open the box, though I had witnessed far more lurid sights, both in my medical career and in my time with Holmes. With a deep breath and a steady hand, I lifted the lid and peered inside at a shriveled, time-darkened face which seemed to stare eyelessly back up at me. I observed the nose, which appeared broken, the brittle dusting of whiskers on the discoloured chin and cheeks, the natural result, sometimes, of continued growth in the days after death. Above all else I recognized the face from portraits I had seen a score of times in various history classes from my time as a boy in Scotland.

"Holmes," I stated, raising the amazing object out of the box and into the air, "I give you what is in my medical opinion, likely no less than the cranium of Oliver Cromwell, the Lord Protector of England!"

"Ho!' said Holmes merrily. "Then against very steep odds, Watson, we have done it!"

"So you're both satisfied," said the seemingly irrepressible Boyle. "Now you mind shovin' off from my room so I can have some peace and quiet before I go get on that boat?"

The morning saw us back in London, tired but triumphant, the mahogany box in our possession, and a jubilant Mr. Daniel Curtis notified and on his way down from Suffolk. His arrival around tea time brought on a sincere pumping of our hands in thanks and the sort of happiness only the most welcome relief can engender. It was the thing which I knew brought the greatest professional satisfaction to Holmes.

"I shall never be able to sufficiently discharge my debt to either of you!" Curtis cried as he veritably cradled the box in his arms, rather like it was some beloved child.

"It was a worthy case," said Holmes benignly, "and that is reward enough."

"Along with your fee, of course," Curtis said, reaching toward his inner coat for his chequebook.

Holmes told him: "Not this time, I think. Not when solving this meandering misadventure has presented so many pleasant privileges to my theretofore neglected brain. It is rare in my profession to be able to truly set matters completely a-right, and the feeling is itself a deep reward. Take your prize back with you to your school, Mr. Curtis, and enjoy tomorrow's banquet among your fellow masters, with my compliments."

Holmes' magnanimity left the man speechless, but he nodded and bowed and an instant later was out the door, his formerly heavy step light, the much-desired mahogany box tucked into his plump arm.

"That was rather good of you, Holmes," I told my friend, feeling a deep satisfaction myself. "I think this was a fine case, indeed, for all ended well for everyone involved."

Holmes lit his pipe and looked away from me before saying, "I saw an example of the best in human behavior from that man, Watson, when he forgave the friend who'd stood to injure him so fully. It was, I think, the least I could do to allow him to keep something so trivial in comparison as his money."

"Would that Thatcher fellow truly have spoken up rather than let Curtis be blamed by the acting headmaster of the academy?" I asked.

"So the client seemed to believe, Watson, and it is not for me to second-judge an erudite bibliophile such as himself. I believe their friendship will survive, and perhaps even be deepened by the concerns they endured in this matter."

"Ah," I said simply.

We both sat quietly a moment there inside 221B Baker Street in our favourite chairs, the hour nearing when I would need to return home to my wife, my thoughts turning, though, to old times, past investigations undertaken by Holmes and me, and somehow I thought Holmes' mind might likewise be leaning in similar directions, til as he smoked he broke the silence and said:

"The past is past, Watson, and it does a man little good to tarry there too long. Now pray that our next case proves half so momentously rewarding as this pleasant adventure...."

Sherlock Holmes
and
The Case of

Moriarty's
Betrayer

C. Thorne

THE CASE OF MORIARTY'S BETRAYER

"You feel absolutely nothing beyond the ordinary this morning?" I asked Holmes.

"And why should I?" the great detective replied, as he skillfully applied larch rosin to the strings of his beloved Stradivarius. Under his hands the violin glowed with a golden-red hue in the sunshine streaming in through the window above the bustle of Baker Street.

It was three minutes before eight on a morning of bright

skies, and for my part I felt my gaze captured by the ever-advancing hands of the clock, quite perturbed by my friend's seeming lack any expression of awareness of what the hour would bring, so I said to him, "Because, Holmes, in less than five minutes a man shall die."

"Men die in London at every hour of the day and night, Watson. It is the result of a shared condition philosophers dub mortality."

"Yes," I pressed him, "but this man is to be hanged on your evidence."

"You refer to the former stockbroker, Preston?"

"Is there another man to be hanged today because you apprehended him?" I demanded.

"None I am aware of save Preston," he said without sarcasm.

"And nowhere does his fate infiltrate your thoughts, even now?"

"A man who poisoned his own grandfather for his inheritance, then tried to frame his brother for the crime?" Holmes asked me. "It would seem the world might be a better place without such a one in it."

"Well, perhaps so, yet---"

"Is it your concern that my evidence was faulty? I assure you it was not, and I am satisfied in every particular as to the man's guilt. He even readily admitted his culpability, if you remember."

"I have no doubt of his authorship of the crime," I insisted, "or the justice of the sentence, but, Holmes, are you not in any way to react to what is about to occur not ten miles from here?"

"My role in that sordid matter, Watson, was to investigate a suspicious death, which I did with excellence, thereby freeing an innocent man from an undeserved doom, while identifying the party who was guilty of the actual crime. What happened afterward in the halls of British justice went on without my involvement."

I looked at the clock, one minute til the hour, and

said truthfully, "I don't disagree with anything you have said, Holmes, but are you not compelled to take note of the time and reflect, even momentarily, that a man is to die because of your actions, however righteous they were?"

"My actions, you say?" He seemed puzzled by this suggestion and asked, "*Should* I have some concern, merely because we arrive at a certain hour, Watson? I bear this Preston no special enmity, nor have my thoughts dwelled on him since the conclusion of the case, finding it hardly a remarkable one, considering he left his fingerprints upon both his grandfather's bedside water glass, and the package of strychnine from the garden shed."

"Well I assure you, it has been in my own thoughts today!" I said rather forcefully.

"Ah, but you, Watson, for all that I find extraordinary about you, are in the best sense, a *normal* man, and a doctor at that, so it is in your nature to think firstly of others. My own outlook is considerably different, for as I have often told you, I am but a brain, and all the rest of me merely an appendage. I *think*, Watson, I do not *feel*."

"Yes, but---"

Thundering out across the streets of the city echoed the bells of Westminster, signaling eight o' clock, interrupting whatever it was I was about to utter, and Holmes listened for an instant, then remarked, "Well there you have it. In any case I perceive all is finished for the parricide Thornton Albert Preston, formerly of Longacre Road, Essex. *Requiescat in pace*. May we now move on?"

Betraying no further apparent thought on the matter, Holmes went back to work on his priceless Stradivarius, and I sighed and shook my head, perturbed less in memory of a murderer who deserved his fate, and more out of having failed yet again to understand the ways of my friend's unfathomable mind, deciding that he was one who lived entirely in the present moment.

◆ ◆ ◆

The remainder of that fleeting morning I barely remember in retrospect, though my day-notes show that it saw me out about the town, seeing to several small cases, one involving a baby girl with the croup, another a septuagenarian with a carbuncle in the unlikely spot of her toe, though well I remember the state of Baker Street when I returned for my midday luncheon.

Upon opening the door I found Holmes in the midst of vigorously pacing the floor, his attention turned in pseudo-monomaniacal fashion to a crisp letter he clutched tightly in his long hands, his expression one of utter focus, a glee burning like an inferno in his eyes.

"Holmes," I called, "what is the matter?" As he did not reply, I cried again: "Holmes!"

"The matter?" he finally answered, not breaking his jarring pace as he trod from the window to the wall opposite. "Nothing whatsoever, Watson," he answered, "all goes extremely well."

"Then what is in that letter that makes you devote such energy to its contents?"

He halted and seemed to re-gather himself, picked up the pipe he'd left inside a dish on the table, then cried, "Watson, it is glorious! A traitor in his midst at long last. My many efforts to reach into that accursed organization may finally have borne the first promise of fruit. It is a challenge, my correspondent says! A contest to judge my worthiness. Fail in his quest and he will find no reason to put his trust in me and shall not become my informant. Succeed, however, and he vows he is my man, and highly-placed on the inside at that!"

No more enlightened by this answer, I demanded, "Whose man? What challenge? Holmes, what is this?"

Looking away from the letter at last, a contented smile

upon his lips, his eyes all but blazing with a manic excitement I had little seen since the days of his cocaine addiction, Holmes exclaimed: "Who else and none other, Watson! It seems Professor Moriarty, to whom we were introduced by name in the case you dubbed 'The Slain Newsman,' at last has a weak link in the iron chain of his nefarious organization!"

He stopped to puff at his pipe before telling me: "I perceive our letter's author is a right-handed man, hardly unusual, that he is a chain-smoker who was brought up somewhere in the north, possibly Manchester, though has dwelled in London for some many years. I would judge from the pressure of his pen that he wrote this at his leisure, no rush, little fear of apprehension, perhaps after several previous draughts, and that he is perhaps thirty-five, judging by the formation of the letter 'f' in his note, for an older man would still use the more Georgian style taught in our government schools until forty years ago, which sees the bar of the letter drawn in a more rigidly level fashion---the straight, the narrow, closer to Godliness, children were then told. The paper, you see, is neither fine nor flimsy, the black ink is commonplace Stark's, available almost anywhere, but if you note the faintest odour of rosemary on the paper, I tell you this is because the writer stored it in a desktop where a nosegay was kept, hinting that his workplace, or perhaps his lodgings themselves, rest in an area where the air smells less than fresh. That could be any number of places in the city, but my suspicion is this challenge to my powers was composed near the runoff of the ancient River Fleet, where warrens of criminals are to be found in an area literally 'thick with thieves,' this agent of Moriarty being on-hand to govern them as a seneschal governs the serfs of his prince. He has standing in the invisible empire indeed! I feel our fellow is a man with some intelligence and personal authority within Moriarty's ranks, but that he labours under conditions that are less than to his liking. As for his motivating grievance, I cannot yet say, though it must have been considerable for him to take on such a grand risk."

"Grievance?" I asked, slightly overwhelmed by this burst

of information cast toward me like a sudden rain-shower.

Realizing my bewilderment and his exuberant oversight, Holmes handed the letter to me, so I set down my medical bag, and with great curiosity read:

Mr. Sherlock Holmes,

I am unknown to you, sir, though we have met, just once, in passing, which was no accident, for you are watched, and I have numbered among the watchers. I have heard of your efforts to breech the Professor's network, and while til this time I never dared act against my employer, I now have reasons, of which I will not tell here, to wish the fall of the man I have served these six years, namely Professor James Moriarty.

I reveal to you that I am high in his army, close to his most trusted right hand, Billy the Fowler, and to prove my words I offer you this: the Professor knows about your work against his interests on Mulberry Road. I trust you know of what I speak, and that I shouldn't own this fact were I not, as I claim, among the Professor's chosen few.

He likewise knows it was you who foiled him in the aftermath of the break-in at the Earl of Balmourne's townhouse in Belgravia last August, which was done on the professor's orders by a team of burglars hand-picked by him, straight out of his own training program he dubs the 'academy.' It was then that he began to take hard notice of you, Mr. Holmes, and he is a deadly man to cross, as you have done more than once. That you still survive is something I cannot quite explain.

If I am to risk my very life, which I would be doing if I were to become your eyes and ears from inside, I have to know you are worthy not only of my confidence, but are such a man as can work to topple the Professor and his criminal empire, which stretches into every neighbourhood in the city, and much farther beyond besides.

So to that end, I propose a contest in the form of a quest. Three clues must you seek today, one leading to the next, the last of these telling where to find me for a meeting which I will keep, if I see you there. But as this is to be a race, time is of the essence. Fail in any stage of my challenge, and I will disappear back into the underworld this very night, and you will never hear from me anymore.

If you hold yourself man enough to claim the prize I offer, I submit to you:

Look for the first clue in an unseen basket, near the shadow of an ersatz tear shed to the beloved of Wallace's Hammer.

Until tonight, or nevermore, sir, you may dub me:

Moriarty's Betrayer

Dazed, I paused after reading the letter, and called out in something approaching a state of awe, "Holmes, could this be genuine?"

"Oh, it is no fraudulent lure, Watson, but quite the authentic article. Who but a trusted lieutenant of the man I have named as my most worthy and ardent foe would know of my careful trap on Mulberry Road, or be aware that I foiled the Professor's crew in the matter of the Earl of Balmourne's townhouse in Belgravia?"

That was a crime I had dubbed "The Adventure of Osiris' Pearl," intending to add it to the published records of our cases, til Holmes forbade me, citing the need to keep his role in the matter out of the public's attention, telling me it was part of his plot to set a wide noose and bring in far larger prey than a gang of house-breakers, however skilled they had been.

"It is the apprehension of their unseen master which draws me, Watson," had been his summation of the aftermath of the incident.

I asked, "What then of this first clue? 'Ersatz tear'? 'Widow of Wallace's hammer'? And how may a basket exist and be 'unseen'? Shall we have a smoke and ponder it a while?"

Holmes smiled. "No need, Watson, I grasped in an instant the destination to which the first clue referred. The 'ersatz tear' I would argue is Mr. Edward Middleton Barry's modern-day replica of the monument to Queen Eleanor of Castile, beloved wife to King Edward I, foe to Sir William Wallace, and oft dubbed the 'Hammer of the Scots' for his wars against your native country."

"From my school days I know of him only too well," I said with irony, thinking of how an Englishman's hero could be a Scotsman's villain.

"Edward had monuments to his late wife erected across the kingdom in the 13th century, and Barry's substitute for the original---hence it is 'ersatz'---adorns Charing Cross station, so it is there that we must go. As for a basket and how it may exist 'unseen,' that I think we shall have to discover for ourselves when we reach the site."

"That is all quite remarkable deduction, Holmes," I offered, meaning it sincerely.

"It was elementary, Watson," he said, drawing on his pipe, "nothing more."

"This challenge, though, is set up in the form of a race," I said. "It startles me that you have not departed already."

"Come now," he said gravely, "do you think I value your company so little? Most assuredly, I was waiting for your return."

That my often cold friend would offer such an admission was, I confess, edifying to hear, and I was at a loss for words until I simply said, "Thank you, Holmes. I shall go by your side to anywhere this adventure might take you."

"You are a splendid, stout-hearted fellow!" Holmes cried, pleased, his spirits as high as a hound's on the trail of its quarry. "Let us together seek this most coveted prize!"

With that he grabbed his Ulster coat off the door-side stand and another instant found him tromping down the stairs, doubtless thinking only of the adventure ahead, til suddenly he froze and turning to me called back, "Watson, I think it best that bring your army revolver."

We hailed a hansom outside our door and proceeded the two and half miles, across Marylebone and Covent Garden to the grand edifice of Charing Cross station, finding the Gothic memorial we sought rising upward into the air in a series of tiers, coming to a sharply pointed steeple that reached skyward, as if it were a finger indicating toward Heaven itself.

"A touching monument to love and loss, even across six centuries," I remarked, staring at the object before us, towering some forty feet above the well-trodden pavement. "But where is its shadow? The mid-day hour is not particularly helpful there. Had we better wait for the afternoon, Holmes, when conditions are more conducive to the growth of shadows?"

"A shadow..." My companion in this adventure looked around us and sneered in dislike of being halted by an impasse. He uttered, "No need to tarry, Watson, clearly it will grow in an easterly direction as the overhead sun takes its labours to the west."

He gazed eastward, as did I.

Around us passed a veritable horde of mankind, entering and exiting the vast reaches of Charing Cross, the odour of train engines biting at nostrils, voices a swirling cacophony as the masses passed us, but there was at this mid-day hour no obvious shadow to be found.

It was then that Holmes asked, "I wonder, is this reference to a shadow too literal, Watson, and do we seek a metaphor instead?"

"A shadow as a symbol of human darkness, perhaps?"

"I wonder...."

It was at that moment I saw Holmes' sharp eye turn to a tiny drama enacted some fifty feet from where we stood. I noted his attention was focused upon a well-dressed man who passed by clutching the handle of a valise, a clear sense of gladness in his countenance, seeking, no doubt, the path back to his home. Yet quick as a flash, a little girl, no more than seven, passed close to the man, and fast as a striking snake, her tiny hand flashed out, carefully seizing the man's pocketbook, which she tucked into her sleeve, before advancing a few paces, and with equal care and economy of motion, passing the pocketbook to a slightly older boy, who, without pausing slid it into his waistband, before melding into the crowd, retreating at a rapid speed.

Holmes!" I cried. "Those urchins have robbed that man. We must intervene!"

My friend raised his index finger into the air and said, "No, Watson, I suspect we have just beheld a drama arranged for our benefit, if to that fellow's detriment."

"But mustn't we come to his aid? He doesn't even know he has fallen victim to a crime!"

"At times a general must sacrifice a soldier to attain a victory, Watson, and judging by the quality of that fellow's attire, he can afford to lose whatever small sum was to be found in his change-purse. No, what we saw we were meant to see."

I fell silent, unsure what to add to that.

"Watson," Holmes said with a tiny smile playing at his mouth, "do you know the popular Cockney slang for a young girl who is a pickpocket?"

"I do not," I admitted.

"It is a 'shadow,' Watson."

"The shadow near the ersatz tear!" I cried. "Holmes, the monument is 'ersatz,' as it is not the original, it is a 'tear' since it mourns a woman's loss, and the girl works as a pickpocket here, meaning she is a shadow."

"*The* shadow, Watson, the genuine article. We have seen a true master at work, for if I am not mistaken we have looked upon 'Merry Moll O'Sullivan' at her craft this morning, and it is she whom we are surely meant to find. Come, Watson, let us meet our messenger's agent."

By this time the child dubbed Merry Moll stood rocking on the heels of her bare feet, leaning with her back to a wrought-iron fence near the station's outer terminus, and she stared straight at us with a piercing cockiness as we drew near, then grinned a knowing smile of mockery and welcome before she halted our approach by pointing toward her left, where about fifteen feet away another girl, younger still, sat crow-legged on the pavement in a filthy sack dress, a basket containing half-wilted flowers nestled pathetically between her soot-blackened feet.

No sooner had I turned my eyes toward the flower girl than I looked back to where Merry Moll had stood, only to see the space she had occupied but an instant before was now empty, and she nowhere in sight.

"She's vanished!" I exclaimed. "Shouldn't we find her?"

"It would be to little avail, Watson, for that child is known to me by reputation and is no less a master of her criminal art than Mozart was in the nobler field of music. I've no doubt it will be an impressive career she'll own in the underworld before her own eight o' clock arrives one day. Doubtless she has hiding places scattered about Charing Cross Station, and probably many friends to aid her. It is likely she gazes out at us from someplace nearby, even as we speak. Besides, her role in our quest today is finished, and it is with that flower girl that our time here shall conclude."

With that, he strode over to where the sad child sat on the pavement with her half-dead flowers, her body thin, deprived of all apparent vitality. She looked up, her face dirty, her hair tangled into braids that looked a fortnight old, and with a shock I spied the fulfillment of final hint of the clue: she was blind.

....in an unseen basket....

"Merry Moll says I'm to give you this," the girl said with lank disinterest in the matter, producing from her skirt an envelope, crisp and white and starkly contrasting the filthy little hands that offered it.

Leaning down, Holmes took this from her, then turned his back, tearing it open at once. I, however, reached into my pocket and handed the flower girl five shillings.

"Do get yourself a blanket, child, and something to eat."

"Can't," she answered simply, "all I make I owes to Billy Bowers, what pulls my leash, see. He owns me."

She slipped the five shillings into her skirt and went back to staring sightlessly out at the passing crowd, leaving me to shake my head at the cruelty of street life, while wishing I had a loaf to bread to give her directly. Her state was one of slavery as surely as if she wore chains, I thought, sighing. Knowing I could do little for her in what was doubtless to be a short, hard life, I turned back to Holmes, who studied the second clue, his face given to a frown of engrossment.

"What does it say," I asked, as, still looking only at the paper, he began to walk away from the grounds of the station.

"Less than the first," he said harshly, before handing the letter over to me.

All I saw upon the page was this: *To fight your next battle, seek the bones of a cavalier whose attire was a cape of blood.*

"To whom does this refer?" I asked, my spirits falling.

"That is the question," he replied tersely, clearly annoyed. "History…." He threw out his hands. "I know of it only as it bears directly to my profession. Ask me to name the butlers in half the great houses in the city, and I could do so without pause, for they might one day prove of use to me, but question me on when the Battle of Flodden was fought, and I could not tell you."

1513, I thought, being a Scot, though I suspected what he said was true, for while my friend's knowledge of many subjects was most profound, I doubted very much if he could have told me which party was currently in power in Westminster, let alone cited from memory the man who fit this obscure reference from the mists of time.

Holmes stood rooted to the ground, his eyes turned skyward, and I could see behind his gaze that formidable brain was turning, parsing through the mountain of facts it contained, seeking some clue to the reference on the paper.

For my part, I feared I was to be of little help, for all I knew of cavaliers was that they were royalists during the civil war of some two and a half centuries previous. And one with a cape of blood? What did this even mean?

"I believe the best course of action here, Watson," Holmes said at last, "is to confess myself at an impasse, and consult with one who stands learned on matters of history. I have in mind one

Professor Emeritus R. Jeremiah Axton, of the Corbyn Library, formerly known as a profound and erudite lecturer, now given to spending his days laboring to complete his *magnum opus* on the Stuart kings, ere the heavenly trumpet summons him to parts unknown. He is to be found each day across town at the library itself. Let us hurry!"

Dashing to acquire a cabriolet to take us north, Holmes lit his pipe, and explained to me *en route* that the Corbyn Library was a private institution, its membership historians who paid rather exorbitant subscription fees to access its famed archives, wherein were stored papers dating as far back as records themselves were kept here upon our fair island.

"Perhaps a fair warning, though, Watson," Holmes said somewhat amusedly, "Professor Axton and his fellows, who have collectively been of use to me in my work on several occasions, are men in the tradition of those eccentric academics who dwell in a figment of the world, their true homes the pages of books, each more used to the company of long-dead personages from history than the presence of living men in general, and men from beyond their library in particular."

"I know the sort," I assured him. "Men who reside bodily in the here and now, but their minds are kept inside the books they treasure."

"Precisely," Holmes concurred, blowing out a billow of smoke. "And in Axton's case, it is thusly to the extreme."

In good time the cab brought us to Hampstead in the northwest of the city, just off Willoughby Road, where I saw that outwardly at least the library was less the grand repository of knowledge Holmes' words had led me to expect, but rather an unassuming three-story square structure of brown brick with a slate-topped roof. It little resembled a library as I thought of one, and more some lugubrious meeting hall of a secret society left over from the Georgian period.

I was soon to find this was precisely what it was.

"The Corbyn, Watson," Holmes said stolidly. He emptied his pipe upon the cobbles and handed our driver his fare before hopping down and taking to the walkway with me by his side. At the last instant he offered a final admonition: "If you must speak at all once inside, Watson, do remember, the cardinal rule is *sotto voce*."

Holmes did not knock, but opened the thick black door straightway, to reveal a dim foyer with a floor done in mosaic tiles depicting a Roman motif of Janus, perhaps original, and around the walls hung a number of paintings of white-wigged scholars from ages past, members, I judged, for I sensed the library was venerable. At the desk sat an old man who with his graying side whiskers and fierce close-set eyes somewhat resembled a badger. Still, when he spied Holmes his face lit up brightly and he called out cordially in a soft but reaching whisper:

"Bless me, is it Mr. Sherlock Holmes returned once again to our illustrious collections. Welcome back, sir, most grandly, welcome back."

"I thank you, Mr. Perceval Wade-Roberts," Holmes replied, with an equal stillness to his tone, "and may I present my esteemed colleague, Dr. John H. Watson, MRCS."

"A pleasure, Doctor," allowed this Mr. Wade-Roberts, with a tiny whisper. "And may I say that any friend of Mr. Holmes is more than welcome here at the Corbyn. Why we owe much to Mr. Holmes, who recovered for us, at no charge whatsoever, our most prized volume, an illuminated Book of Psalms, presented in 1511 as a nativity gift to Queen Catherine of Aragon, by King Henry VIII. Mr. Holmes was, in an inadequate show of our scholarly gratitude, made a lifetime peer of our learned brotherhood."

"It was," whispered Holmes simply, "a most satisfying case, and the collective gratitude of so distinguished a gathering of historians is its own reward."

"Such humility," Wade-Roberts beamed.

"But may I say, my good sir, you really should not skip breakfast in the mornings, for it is, as Watson reminds me during my own frequent abstinences, the most important meal in one's day."

"Wha-why...Mr. Holmes, how should you know I have not yet broken my fast?"

"Simplicity itself, sir, for your shirt front betrays no indication of your having tucked a napkin into it, as I know a well-mannered individual such as yourself would have done upon dining."

Wade-Roberts released the quietest peals of amused laughter I had ever heard uttered, then re-gathered himself after moment and said, "You are indeed most correct, but come, Mr. Holmes, I will take up no more of your time. Are you here to access our archives today, or is there some manner in which the brotherhood of the Corbyn may be of assistance to you?"

"I seek the expertise of Professor Axton," Holmes told him in a quiet voice, "concerning a matter I believe might fall within his purview."

"Ah, yes, yes, that good and worthy gentlemen is indeed in attendance today, as he is most days, laboring on his great work concerning the Stuarts. Allow me to lead you to him. And I bid you remember, without exception, speech is prohibited within the reading room."

Mr. Wade-Roberts departed from his sprawling desk and guided us into a large room, lined with heavy oaken shelves crammed with book after book covering a panoply of topics of historical research, from the rude days of the ancient Britons, to the minutes of Parliament's latest session, and as we walked, not a word was spoken in a place so still I imagined one might hear the breathing of a mouse. So serious was the rule of silence that when we at last came to be in the presence of the man we sought, one Professor Axton, it was by the hasty scribbling of a note that Wade-Roberts reached out to him, sliding it onto a desk at which sat a wizened man with a long snowy beard and the thickest of glasses, a number of books and a stack of writing paper before him.

Surely this man is part wizard, I thought, taking in Axton's peculiar but somehow fitting appearance, amid his perhaps overlong-worn clothing and his ink-stained fingertips.

Upon glancing at the note, Axton looked up and saw Holmes, making his bushy eyebrows lift in profound delight, though he made no sound, merely composed a reply, which he held out to Wade-Roberts, stating: *Have I a moment, you ask, sir? I have not just a moment but many to spare for this most worthy gentleman.*

Rising to the sound of protesting knee joints, wince of discomfort briefly upon his face, Professor Axton left his papers behind and with the aid of a cane, its handle darkened by long use, walked slowly with Mr. Wade-Roberts, Holmes, and myself, out of the reading room and into a small meeting area on the opposite end of the foyer. Here, with its tall windows and long meeting-table, I took it, speaking in low tones was permitted, for at once Axton said:

"Mr. Sherlock Holmes! I do say, a long-overdue pleasure it is to see you again, my good sir. It is not for just anyone that I would leave the company of King Charles I., purest of heart of all the Stuarts. I have spent my morning in his royal presence, researching the little-studied influence of merchant factions upon the Long Parliament. But for you, to whom so exceedingly much is owed by all of us here in the hallowed halls of the Corbyn, I have all the time in the world!"

"I suspect I shall not require so great a quantity," Holmes replied, "though it is with ready thanks and free acknowledgment of your erudition that I bring an historical puzzle which may be of interest to you."

"Splendid, splendid!" Axton replied quietly, rubbing his liver-spotted hands together and emitting a rasping sound which registered all the louder in so still a place. "Oh, and whom have I the honour of meeting in you, sir?" he asked looking toward me.

"Dr. John H. Watson, MRCS, at your service, sir," I introduced myself.

The aged scholar nodded. "A pleasure, a pleasure. And do I detect in your voice, sir, a hint of the homeland of my beloved Stuarts?"

"You do, indeed, sir, for I was born and raised in bonny Scotland."

"How enviously wonderful," he said. He then turned again to Holmes and inquired, "And what is this puzzle from history you say you bring?"

"It is a clue to a mystery I seek to solve, Professor," Holmes said, removing the note from his pocket.

Axton's eyes squinted as he peered through the thickest spectacles I had ever seen, and read: "*To fight your next battle, seek the bones of a cavalier whose attire was a cape of blood.*' Well," he summed up after a moment, "it doesn't say much, does it, gentlemen?"

"Precious little," Holmes admitted, "and time is of utmost essence."

"Ah, that I understand as only an old man may. Still, you spied the word cavalier, and thought of me," Axton noted, chuckling, the sound a wheeze in his throat, "and wise you were, for I do not augment my own reputation to say few men know the age of the Stuarts more completely than myself. Yes, the mention of a cape of blood…it stirs some memory. Indeed…yes, yes, I have read some footnote that beckons my memory…"

The professor leaned onto his cane, and one could see the wheels of his mind veritably turning behind his bottle-thick glasses, til at last a light seemed to flare in his rheumy eyes.

"Ah, yes, yes!" he cried in his standard whisper, "of course! 'Upon a great black warhorse he rode, wearing a cape dyed brightest red, as if soaked in enemy blood, and it trailed behind him so that no eye would miss his presence.' It is surely he of whom your mysterious correspondent speaks!"

"Whom?" pressed Holmes.

"Sir Gaspar Coventry," Axton explained. "I knew there was

something. At Balliol College, Oxford, where I took honours in '40 for my dissertation upon King Charles' trial, a most unfair proceeding, I tell you, I read of one Sir Gaspar Coventry, a third generation Huguenot, much devoted to his king and cause, who rode most viciously against the Roundheads, his belt stuffed with a brace of pistols, his sabre flashing at Puritan necks on a half-dozen battlefields, before he was finally felled by Cromwellian grapeshot at Naseby in 1645. They may have shot him from a distance but it was said few could stand against him in single combat, poor fellow. But tut-tut, those who live by the sword, you know."

"Sir Gapsar Coventry," I repeated to myself, tasting the name. Could it be the man whose grave we sought?

"Yes, yes," Axton confirmed, "why that worthy cavalier is not more remembered in these modern times, I do not know, though perhaps my prejudice in his favour does run deep, for I am an unapologetic Royalist at heart---though completely impartial in my scholarship and writings, I assure you."

"Oh, undoubtedly," Holmes agreed soberly, no mockery in his words. "There was mention of his bones, Professor, so where might one find the grave of this dashing cavalier?"

"Now that," Axton admitted, "is beyond my immediate grasp."

My spirits plunged, til he added, "Though nowhere else in this sceptered isle is more likely to contain that knowledge than our sacred Corbyn, and I know where to begin our hunt. Come, gentlemen...."

With a reminding finger laid to his lips, Axton shuffled with his ancient cane back into the stacks of the reading room, pressing deep until we came to an ill-lighted recess near the far wall, obviously a little-visited archive, the volumes there clearly seldom-read. Stumbling toward a shelf about shoulder-high, Axton put his face close to the spines, silently perusing the titles, til with a nod of satisfaction he took one down and jotted onto a scrap of paper:

It will be here if it is anywhere. Now may Fortune herself smile upon our search.

He took a step back and opened the book, bound in leather so old it had darkened, and its innermost pages yellowed with time. With utmost care, Axton turned to the old concordance and ran a finger downward til he grinned with victory, setting a feeling of utter relief into my own heart.

Holmes leaned close and I saw him soundlessly take in the name 'Coventry, Gaspar.'

With a rapid but oh-so-careful flip toward the book's midsection, Axton found the referenced page, and unable to resist any longer, I too moved to my friend's elbow and read:

....the great and worthy Cavalier, Sir Gaspar Coventry, who was awarded his spurs by none other than Prince Rupert of the Rhine, and who fell at Naseby among so many of his brethren, lies buried at Saint Godwin's of Aldersgate, beneath a modest stone upon which is carved a pair of crossed pistols....

There it was! I thought, resisting an urge to shout in triumph, a mortal sin in this place, I knew.

We made quiet haste back out into the reading room beyond the foyer, where Holmes thanked both Professor Axton and the library's secretary, Mr. Perceval Wade-Roberts, for their assistance, then drawing me by the elbow, strode back outside, where I saw the steady glow of the noontide, which marked the start of our quest, had given way to a more westerly light.

Hailing a cab, we were soon on our way to Aldersgate, far across town in the East End.

"Double your fare if you have us there within an hour!" Holmes promised the cabbie, who in reply whipped the sturdy-looking bay to a fair approximation of a trot.

"Watson," he said to me, eyes bright and penetrating, his love for the pursuit at a fevered pitch, "I know not what awaits us, but surely it is not grave robbery itself, for our writer would know the impossibility of desecrating a burial in the middle of London, and by day, no less."

I cried, astonished: "Do you mean to say you would consider plundering a grave if the hours were more conducive to that wicked pursuit?"

He peered at me with an amused expression and admitted, "It would not be the first time if I did so, nor would I let the repose of mere bones stand in the way of the target I so diligently seek."

I was left to ponder this confession while for the remainder of our breakneck journey, Holmes smoked in silent contemplation, probably thinking through the possibilities ahead, and seeking the next course of action.

◆ ◆ ◆

In just under one hour we arrived in the streets of Aldersgate, much of the district in the shadow of St. Paul's mighty dome, til we made our way at a more deliberate pace to the church of St. Godwin's, a Medieval pile of stone with its copper roof long since gone green, streaks of lime-colored residue staining the once-fine outer walls. In its yard, lay a small burial ground where neglected headstones sat tilted in the shifted ground, their lettering gradually wearing smooth, consigning the occupants to the equality found in anonymity.

Holmes leapt from the cab and handed a generous recompense to our driver, before plunging through the yard's creaking iron gate, rust eating away at its one-time blackness. Paying little attention to me as I raced after him, Holmes hurried from row to row, glancing wildly at whatever was still legible among the long-ago names inscribed on the solid mass of each antique headstone, yet it was I who found the one we sought mid-way down the second aisle, closest to the church itself.

Seeing the crossed pistols I cried out, "Holmes, I have him here!" I pointed at the stone, which read:

Sir Gaspar Coventry
1624—1645
Nec hostis umquam virtute superavit;

Nullus amicus unquam fortitudinis suae cor negavit.

"'No foe ever bested his courage,/No friend ever denied his bravery of heart.'"

I just had time to translate this aloud before bursting over and bodily moving before me, Holmes smiled and said:

"Take note, Watson, of that small disturbance of the soil at the grave's foreground. No larger than a hand, it is at least a fortnight old. This testifies that our letter-writer was no spontaneous correspondent, but has been planning his defection to our cause for some time."

Down on his knees in the dirt, amid clusters of weeds and the residue of years, Holmes scooped out the soil around the disturbed place til underneath the slight depression in the earth, he pulled out a glass vial, no larger than his middle finger, sealed at the top with a cork, slightly moistened by its time under the consecrated soil.

I marveled at our unlikely discovery, as Holmes plucked free the cork and tipped a small, rolled note onto his palm. It read:

If you have made it this far, Mr. Holmes, you own my admiration as one with a worthy intellect, and I lay but one further challenge before you ere you learn of where I shall be waiting for our meeting---or not---this night. To this end I bid you, to find my upcoming location, travel to where a man, half-named for a bird, saw the sneezes of the sun. There beneath a crystal sky, shall Lady Rubiginosa, with hair aflame, grant you the revelation of where I will await you this night.

I found I did not wish to move a muscle, and felt no more encouraged by seeing Holmes' face take on a sneer of frustration. Finally, he stood and walked pacing in the confined space of the aged burial ground. As he did the bell tower behind us struck four, and I glanced back to see the sun was now low in the western sky.

"Holmes..." I began, only to have him quiet me with a waved hand.

He paused beside a headstone that time had worn smooth as slate, and finally said, "Of course! Hurry, Watson, we have only an hour til it closes!"

He took off through the groaning gate and into the lane beyond, I at his heels. "Before what closes?" I demanded.

"Why, Watson, it is as obvious as any schoolboy's lesson. What is the sneezing of the sun?"

"I...know little of astronomy, Holmes."

"I hazard it is a phenomenon known as a solar flare, great dashing plumes of fire which rise like demons off the burning surface of the sun itself, Watson, held by some to disrupt telegraphy, and even transfer their burdensome effects into the human mind."

Waving down a cab with almost violent gestures, he leapt in, leaving me to scurry up beside him, barely touching the seat before we were on our way, the cabbie heeding Holmes' urgent cry of, "To the Crystal Palace!"

We had miles to cover on our journey south, the setting sun behind us, the traffic of the impending evening clogging the streets and making our trip back across the heart of the city a far slower affair than our earlier excursions north and east. As we journeyed, at times plodding along, at others achieving a decent clip, Holmes explained his reasoning, telling me:

"Watson, it took me a moment to pierce this code, but there were, in fact, two items which dissolved the riddle. Firstly, the name of the lady, do you recall it?"

"Lady Rubiginosa," I said at once. "She is Italian, I presume?"

"The word is Latin, Watson, and is the scientific name for a rose."

"A rose? Then the crystal sky is a hot house, of course! But there are scores of greenhouses in the city, so how do you know our final clue lies inside the great crystal palace itself?"

"Via the first part of our hint! Where 'a man half-named for a bird, saw the sneezes of the sun.' In the eighteenth century, the astronomer Sir Edmund Dunfinch, whose name, as you see, is half that of a bird, used to gaze into the heavens with his telescope upon the grounds of Penge Place Park, where now sits the Crystal Palace."

"Brilliant!" I exclaimed.

"The poor man, Watson, ended his days half-blind from all his gazing at the sun, though he did become the foremost authority on that heavenly object, and regarded it as a fair trade. His theories on solar flares did not gain confirmation until the middle of the present century, long after his passing in 1797."

"So it is amid roses growing in the Crystal Palace that we seek the final prize, that being the time and location of our meeting!"

"If we make it, Watson, if we make it...."

Indeed, I saw his reasons for concern, for the structure closed promptly each day at five, and we were still some distance away, with the first shadows of evening gathering in the low places, and filling the alleyways.

As if some cruel fate were aware of our need for urgency, and determined to vex us, we had no sooner crossed the bridge to south London, when ahead there was a crashing noise, and a number of barrels spilled off a lorry, rolling into the street, making pedestrians scream, and horses on both edges of the lane shy and swerve aside. A constable with a large belly and stern eyes promptly appeared from someplace nearby and halted traffic in all directions while workmen hopped off the lorry and began to laboriously load the barrels back onto the vehicle, granting its sweating dray horses a moment's relaxation.

"This will not do!" Holmes snarled. I thought for a moment he meant to urge the driver to push through the congestions, despite the constable's command, and I think he considered doing just this, but finally he barked, "It is but nine furlongs, Watson, we must make a run for it!"

Leaving it to me to pay the driver for his unfinished service, I rushed to catch up with Holmes, who moved as quickly as gentlemanly dignity would allow, the coat-tails of his Ulster trailing behind him, as he varied his pace from a rapid walk to something not unlike a canter. Even at his heels, I was soon exerted, as I had not carried on such a fast march since my army days. While I was not lacking in conditioning, Holmes' lean figure cut through the distance, growing farther ahead of me til he glanced back and called:

"Watson, I shall await you there!"

Then he hurried onward, soon lost to my sight amid the late afternoon throngs.

I admit I slowed slightly and allowed myself to catch my breath even as I faithfully pushed on. I was bolstered by seeing the great gleaming Crystal Palace ahead of me, beyond a surrounding dirt track, where several gentlemen were in the process of galloping their prized horses.

I was all but spent from the strain of what would have made a perfectly pleasant stroll but which was taxing as a run, and just as I was no more than a hundred feet away, Big Ben thundered out its notice that five o' clock had been achieved.

To my frustration and near-horror, I saw a blue-coated man at the entrance close and lock the doors, re-opening them only to allow a trio of aged ladies to exit, with a tip of his hat to them.

"Please, sir," I cried as I reached him, "I must be allowed inside to join my friend. It is a matter of some urgency, I assure you."

The man was ginger-haired, and while his freckled face betrayed nothing of tyranny, and much of open friendliness, he still said, "Sorry, aren't I, sir? The rules are I shut these doors with the chime of five o' clock, and admit no one after."

"But my friend is inside!" I protested.

"If he is, he'll soon be out again," the man said, kindly enough. "We don't keep anyone locked in for the night."

"Have you heard of Mr. Sherlock Holmes, the detective?" I demanded.

"Oh, indeed I rightly have," the man answered brightly, "and enjoy reading about his cases, don't I? 'The Yorkshire Train

Robbery' is my particular favourite. Never guessed how that would end!"

Flattered as I may have at by his mention of one of my narratives, I still said, "Yes, well, my friend who is inside happens to *be* Mr. Sherlock Holmes, and I am Dr. John H. Watson, author of those same accounts!"

He gazed hard at me, skeptical and amused. "Truly now, you say, sir? Well that is a marvel, isn't it? Never thought to meet you, and wasn't half-sure you weren't made up, like. But still and all, unless you happened to be the Prince of Wales in person I don't think my job could stand to let you in after hours. Not with my boss! Come on, be a good fellow and wait over there for your friend, and then call again tomorrow at nine when you'll be duly welcomed back."

Seeing the man meant every word, I had no recourse but to follow his advice and stand a distance off in the park, watching the doors for Holmes' reappearance. The sky darkened, and at last the doorman set off away from the building, but called to me in passing, "Begging your pardon, Dr. Watson----if that's who you truly are---I fear you are mistaken, for it seems your friend must not be inside, as I got the all-clear from the night watchman, meaning there's nobody left in there but him and the floor-sweepers."

I felt a fright then, a recognizable jolt that split me head to feet, and I hurried back to the Crystal Palace itself, cupping my hands to my face and peering into the vast, darkened interior of this glass-walled wonder of the age.

"Hoping to find me still within, Watson?" a familiar and most welcome voice called from behind me.

"Holmes!" I cried, relief all but overtaking me. "You are a sight for sore eyes. But I did not see you come out."

He shrugged, feigning indifference, but nonetheless betraying pride, "I know ways to pass in and out of a place less obtrusively than most."

"And the location marked by the third clue," I said excitedly. "Did the garden of roses reveal where we are to meet

Moriarty's man?"

"Blackfriar's Bridge, at nine o' clock," he said with a cool eagerness. "I find it an ideal spot."

"That is splendid!" I told him, as we walked from the park, a far distance from our familiar haunts north of the Thames. "You have achieved the fulfillment of this fellow's tests, the quest is done, and a well-earned reward awaits."

"Then why at this late hour, Watson," he asked, "do I now find myself so uneasy about this business?"

"You suspect a trap?"

"One always must suspect a trap in a matter as serious as this."

"But you do intend to keep our rendezvous, don't you, after we worked so hard to find the meeting spot?"

"Do *I* intend to? Indeed, beyond question, I will go there. Shall *we*, however? Watson, I would prove a false friend were I to allow you to plunge with me into such potential danger, for with every passing moment my senses warn me more strongly of a danger, which in my eagerness to solve the mystery, I have so far ignored."

"Holmes, naturally I will come, I---"

"Think for a moment of what a perfect point of ambuscade a bridge makes. A man could be trapped with no escape were a foe to block the pathway before and after him. And with the swift-flowing water below, what more ideal place could there be to dispose of someone, either alive or dead?"

I felt a mortal chill at his words, and confess I had likewise been so swept up in the thrill of the quest that I had little paused to dwell on the promised interview ahead, and how this might all prove a trap.

"So what shall you do, Holmes?" I asked.

"I intend to alone, well-armed, and in disguise. It shall not be Sherlock Holmes who sets foot upon the bridge, but a white-haired costermonger, slightly the worse for gin, who staggers across on his way home to the south bank. Should my reconnoitering eyes spy danger, it is the costermonger who will continue on toward the south. Yet if all seems well, I will keep my meeting with this correspondent, and hope he is who and what he claims to be, a potent weapon to use against his one-time master."

"And I?"

"I well know your faithfulness of heart, Watson, and that you would not seek to leave me in the lurch, however much I might try to reason with you. Thus I have a task for you that should yet aid me tonight."

"Anything and gladly!" I vowed, glad to have some rôle to play.

"Just before Blackfriars' Bridge, lies a small hotel, known as the Bainmoor."

"I know of it."

"Go there and take a room on an upper floor which faces the bridge, then darken your surroundings and wait, looking out beginning at half past eight. Should you spy anything suspicious, such as a gathering of likely-looking sorts lurking out upon the bridge, I wish you to turn on the lights of the room. If I see this, I will not approach the rendezvous, but rather return to Baker Street, where you can join me in due time."

"I understand," I said, more than willing to play the part of lookout.

"And something else, if you find nothing suspicious, then stay in the dark and watch me on the structure. If you see me meet but a single man, and all looks well to your eyes, do nothing more, but if I am followed by those who seem intent upon my harm, I charge you with a more difficult task."

"Naturally I will rush out to your aid!" I promised.

"No," he said, "it will take more than that to dissuade Moriarty's assassins. Again, do nothing unless you see me set upon, or unless I lift one of my hands high above me, a signal to you that danger threatens to overcome me, and only then do I wish you to open the window and with all the vigor that lies within you, begin to shout a cry of fire! There is no other word in the lexicon so guaranteed to draw attention and bring men running by the dozen. In the midst of a gathering crowd, surely even the cut-throat minions of the Professor would hesitate to spill blood, and in the confusion I might affect my retreat."

"A daring plan and a desperate one," I said in summation.

"Is it one to which you feel prepared and worthy?"

"Holmes, of course," I said, "though I'd still rather go with you and face the danger man to man."

"I know you would, Watson, and for that you have my eternal thanks. Never has any fellow had a truer friend."

To my surprise he reached out and clutched my hand, a rare gesture from him, who, I knew, seemed averse to human contact. I sensed then something I had never before encountered in Sherlock Holmes...the signs of worry, and detecting this frightened me all the more.

Although I was left with deep trepidations, I did as Holmes instructed, and as he returned to Baker Street to affect his disguise and arm himself for whatever lay ahead, I made my way to the Hotel Bainmore, a clean place, though unprepossessing and given to admitting a clientele made up of respectable though not wealthy tradesmen. I had no difficulty in obtaining the room I desired on an upper floor, facing the bridge, the north entrance of which lay some fifty yards before me.

I felt a desire to hasten time itself, and advance through the hours which separated me from the nine o' clock rendezvous.

Outside the night was dark, though punctuated at regular intervals by gaslights, so that I could perceive the bridge without difficulty, its span crossing the Thames alternating between segments of shadow and oases of illumination around each gaslight mounted on the outer walls.

I took no dinner and soon felt the unwelcome pangs of hunger, as I'd had nothing since my modest breakfast, but gave little thought to this as I took up my place in a chair just far enough inside my darkened room to readily watch the bridge, but be unseen in return. To my eyes nothing seemed suspicious as time ticked by and eight-thirty came. I saw a few people step upon Blackfriar's and pass across, some going north, most to the south, a few lingering a moment to regard the flowing river, but none staying overlong. All seemed well to my probing eyes, though a nervous anticipation gripped me as nine o' clock neared.

Then a strange thing happened. It was at ten minutes before the hour when I saw a short man in dark attire walk to the mid-point of the bridge, and using a long tool extinguish several of the gas lights in their fixtures, creating a cocoon of darkness near the bridge's centre, before he in turn passed across and was lost to my sight somewhere on the south bank of the Thames. This could be no coincidence, and my heart began to race, wondering what this portended for Holmes' fate.

It was precisely one minute before the hour when I saw a tall man with stark white hair and the clothing of a decent tradesman, a costermonger, certainly, pass down the street and take his entrance upon the bridge, moving toward the southern terminus. I felt sure this was Holmes, so closely did it match the description of his proposed attire. Still, I marveled that I saw so little to prove it was my friend out there, for not only the appearance, but even the stride of the individual was unlike the confident steps that were the trademark of the proud consulting detective.

And then as this figure was about a quarter of the way out onto the bridge, I saw another man approach from the opposite bank. I could make out little of the specifics of this person, only that he too was of taller than average height, his clothing dark, his stride neither fast nor slow, confident nor hesitant. Save for these figures the whole of the eastern face of the bridge was now empty, as the distance between the two closed and I saw each enter the space where the lights had been extinguished, creating an area of darkness about a dozen yards across

The men stopped about six feet apart and I saw a conversation transpire, stretching into a minute, then a second, and all the rest of the world itself felt very away as I concentrated on the interaction before me. And then it was done. The figure who had come from the south turned and went back in that direction, while Holmes likewise returned to the north bank, his steps now more regular, and despite the disguise I saw him undertake the pace I knew, his familiar, almost arrogant stride.

But what had happened?

I could stand the suspense no more, and grabbing my coat, I left the room and hurried down the stairs and out of the hotel. Conscious that Holmes had given me no instructions about when and where to meet him, I pushed forward til I was near his side, only to be told, "Keep walking and do not look at me, Watson, there is danger to you in pausing here."

"Holmes," I said heartily, "I am relieved you are well!"

"Do I seem so, Watson? I am in fact as of this hour a man under a conditional sentence of death."

"But your meeting!" I exclaimed. "Your correspondent!"

"Dead."

This news struck me like a blow, for after our quest I almost felt as if I knew this nameless man, and demanded, "Then who was it on the bridge?"

"My greatest enemy, Watson, the enemy of all men who live in harmony with civilized laws, and wish only to dwell in amity with their fellow man. One who is evil embodied."

"It was *he* who was out there?" I said, marveling at the weight of this horrific fact. "Then, Holmes, why did you not seek to apprehend him? I know you have collected some evidence on the fellow and his far-reaching criminal activities."

"Because, Watson, I was anticipated, and you were not the only watcher this night. He assured me he had five marksmen concealed about the vicinity with rifles trained upon me, and I believed him. Had I moved on him, I'd have not lasted an instant before I felt the kiss of lead."

"Then why was he there?"

"To speak to me in the flesh. To deliver a message that my would-be ally was dead, and that if I wished to keep my meeting with him, I should try the floor of the river near the docklands. Moriarty claimed I have thus far entertained him with my pursuit of his organization, comparing me to a lone fox who seeks to turn upon a pack of hounds."

"Good Heavens!" I uttered, quite shaken. "He was ahead of us at every step today."

"Yes, I confess he is as adept in his dark arts as I am in those which bring evil into the light, and his resources are far greater than my own. Yet if he sought to dispirit me, he achieved quite the opposite, for I half-suspected from the start that the demise of our potential friend might prove the end-point of our quest, and possibly the ending of me as well. Instead I find our foe elected to stretch matters a little farther between he and I, so that he might meet me tonight in our correspondent's place, and thereby to demonstrate that he knew from the first that he had been betrayed, and by whom, but he allowed his minion to lead me on my pursuit before he culled his ambitions, because Moriarty claimed it amused him to see us scampering about London, lead on like marionettes by a doomed man's puzzles."

"Chilling! He was watching us the whole time?"

"So it seems, Watson, though I was cognizant of our surroundings and never saw any sign of him or his many eyes, which are everywhere, and that should say all one needs to know of his skills, and the breadth of his reach. The underworld of London is, I admit, his kingdom."

My spirits were in flux, discouragement owning me for the first time on an adventure which had begun amid such hopefulness. "Holmes, these are grim tidings," I allowed, "for we have been out-danced at every stage in this sordid affair, and how might anyone ever hope to overcome a rival of such seeming omniscience and might?"

Holmes frowned, and inquired in a quiet, serious tone of voice, "Watson, do you judge me any less formidable than this man?"

"I don't doubt you match him in brilliance, nay, exceed him, certainly, but you lack his resources, and his evil heart."

Holmes did not reply for an instant as we continued on foot toward Baker Street, the walk suiting my mood of dejection, but at last he answered, and in his voice was a confident determination that reversed some of the hopelessness which had overtaken me, for with a steadiness hinting at depthless determination, he declared:

"Professor Moriarty's confidence was misplaced! By not killing me tonight, Watson, he missed his sole chance, for unbeknownst to him in his hubris, I very nearly have him ensnared, and as of this hour the curtain rises upon his final act...."

Sherlock Holmes

and
The Adventure of

The
Séance
Society

C. Thorne

THE ADVENTURE OF THE SÉANCE SOCIETY

G o backward in time with me, if you will, to the last
days of the winter just past, and picture what I
describe, for something very close to this scenario
once took place.

Imagine that there is a girl, very pretty, young, her dress
costly, her hair a champagne-colored cloud teased high above her
head in a Parisian manner, and she is sitting at a round walnut
table in a darkened room in a manor house in the countryside of
Wiltshire, her face alternating between a strange blankness and a

quality of concentration, even exertion, as though she were holding an unseen rope and pulling something from a great distance away. Perhaps let us envision her dragging a reluctant man toward herself, causing her face to alternate between paleness and a flushed red. She draws deep and frequent breaths and her hands clench and unclench, almost as if telling of pain. Twice as you look on, her chin drops to her chest, and her head lolls, only to snap back upright. On her brow rests the faintest glisten which catches in the glow of a single candle near the table's centre.

She is a prodigy, and among the best in all of England at her controversial trade of clairvoyance.

Though the girl was born in Yorkshire, and had once known hardship, money is now ample in her young life and the life of her mother, a woman who is an older version of the girl, and is presently occupied in standing nearby, nodding to her daughter's whispered words, her own eyes riveted on her child, a suggestion of a smile on her lips, and in this dark room in a manor in the Wiltshire countryside, incense swirling through the air, this girl, barely seventeen, is telling of a thing she had never seen with her own brilliant blue eyes, as a well-dressed man with a scar over his lip sits across from her, his own gaze hot, unblinking, listening as impressions of an occurrence from some two years before actively form in her third eye.

"They have walked into the cell," the girl tells the man, "which is a room painted white, no bars, and three guards are there with the man, none looking him in the face, or meeting his eyes as he....I... try to tell them, even now at the last desperate hour that they are wrong, I am no murderer. Three men come through the door... the death squad...the man in front is short, fat, hard-looking, he is the hangman, and he turns him....turns me...around so that he is behind me, and he has bound my hands... They do not pause, they are leading me out through a door in the back wall which another guard opens, his eyes not meeting mine and I am telling him, telling them all, 'I am innocent! I did not do this thing! He lied! The detective from London lied!'"

"And what do they say?" asks the man with the scarred lip,

breaking his silence of some minutes' duration.

"Nothing..." says the girl with pain in her voice, "...nothing... they don't care. Through the door where they are pushing me as I try to resist, still begging them to listen, telling them I am not guilty of the crime, I see it now, the death-room behind the white cell, it is only a dozen steps to the gallows, not a stand to be mounted, but a wooden floor with the trap door in the centre, a rope hanging from an overhead beam, the noose bound like a waiting snake at its bottom."

"Good," utters the man, whether to the girl or the air of the darkened room one could not say, "good...a snake, a good image. And next?"

The girl pauses and her head begins to shake from side to side, as if the vision before her tightly-shut eyes is horrible for her to behold, harder still to speak of.

"There is a vicar there," she cries out, "with white hair combed to the side in a long part which shows a strip of pink scalp, and he is as hard a man as any of the guards... He opens the Bible to a page he's had marked with a strip of black ribbon, and he begins to read as the guards move swiftly at the prisoner...at me, binding my legs with a leathern strap, and move me over the hatchway in the floor. They are like a team, well-oiled, long-drilled, and one shoves a hood over my head, so for an instant all is darkness, darkness, darkness, then the muted light from the single barred window high above comes in through the canvas sack which covers me."

"What do you do?"

"I scream, I panic, I twist my body, but I cannot move with their hands restraining me. 'Please,' I say over and over. 'He was wrong, the detective was wrong! Please just look at the evidence again!' But no one listens, or even cares. The fat, short hangman fits the noose over my neck, I feel his breath on me, it stinks of onions, and then he steps away. I feel a scream bubbling up from my lungs, and the vicar reads: 'Our Father, who art in Heaven—'"

The girls emits a shrill scream as her entire body jerks within the chair, and her mother flinches and places a hand over her heart, but the man with the scarred lip stays still, and after there has been silence for a quarter of a minute, he asks: "Yes?"

"The trapdoor fell open under him...me. I died. And now my ghost seeks him out."

"Who?" asks the girl's mother, her voice trembling in sympathy with her own quivering body.

"Why, my betrayer, Sherlock Holmes, of Baker Street."

Across the table the man with the scarred lip smiles.

◆ ◆ ◆

As cold rain fell steadily outside the window which overlooked a soggy Baker Street this day, and the air inside swirled with a mist of tobacco smoke, Holmes' posture showed the little-disguised contempt he felt for our long-expected visitor that inclement March morning. Several times he had 'hmmphed' at various statements the visitor had made, all of which that gentleman, for his part, overlooked and merely continued on with equanimity. Holmes was by no means an easy man to know, and there were certain sorts who brought out the most difficult side to him, with those who suggested the world operated on other than knowable principles of rationality being high on that list.

As for me, I quietly listened and took my usual notes on the consultation, and said little. It was an interview custom-made to elicit incredulity, yet the man who was speaking to us seemed most sincere. He was tall, about fifty, professorial in mien, his manner of speaking educated and direct.

Holmes, though had had enough, and clearly regarded ten minutes invested in the man to be more than ample.

"Sir," he stated, bristling and impatient, " you sit here in my parlour and take up my time to tell me a story only a fool would embrace, yet without evidence you expect me to accept your tale and govern myself according to some farcical scenario. And, I might add, it is an insulting notion to suggest that I would lend my reputation to such a cause as *spiritualism!*"

"I am not unused to scepticism, Mr. Holmes," replied the man, still calm even in the face of this outburst, "as are all members of the British Séance Society. We have long met with reactions of ignorance from the uninitiated into the reality of mediumship, and have endured ridicule, dismissal, even persecution by those whose minds are tragically closed, yet I confess I had heard you were a man who governed his life on the weight of evidence, facts, investigation, all of which I come prepared to provide you, and so I confess myself aggrieved and disappointed by your rather mundane response."

"I am sorry to disillusion you, Mr. Hilltower," Holmes said, sounding not sorry at all, "but I have neither inclination nor willingness to dedicate so much as a minute of my valuable time to pursuits which I know shall only profit those, like yourself, who attempt a nullification of reality. I declare your work illegitimate, your results ersatz, and your claims today contemptible in the extreme!"

Mr. Hilltower said: "Might I remind you, sir, that during the time you undertook this investigation into our cause, your fee would of course be paid in full by the British Séance Society."

Annoyed, Holmes replied, "Money is merely a tool, and as I have enough for my needs," he waved a hand dismissively, "it does not itself in any way motivate me."

I saw the duration of the interview had very nearly reached its premature end and could feel Holmes about to gather himself up and show his visitor to the door, when amid the patter of rain on the window-glass, Hilltower uttered a name which had the profound effect of freezing Holmes cold, and seemingly changed the entire trajectory of the morning.

"Willoughby Slade."

Holmes stared at Hilltower for a number of seconds, and I saw his body become tense, then I think only by the intervention of a deliberate action did he relax himself, and though his eyes became hardened, now less arrogant than openly hostile, he demanded, "Pray, having polluted our environs with that name, you must continue."

"I see the name is known to you," Hilltower said, and now he too changed, less one come hat in hand to seek Holmes' services, and suddenly one who perhaps saw he had gained a toehold in his climb.

"And why should it not be known to me," Holmes said, "as it was I who gathered the evidence to send that odious murderer of innocent children to a deserved death on the gallows?"

I did not have to search my mind for the name, for I remembered it only too well. Two children, a girl of six and her four-year-old brother were found drowned in a pond in rural Lincolnshire nearly three years before, and while the matter was dismissed by local police as an accident, Holmes, upon reading of the day-old tragedy in the newspaper had become focused on the detail that based on tracks found at the bank, someone had come upon the children's bodies in the pond, yet left them there without raising a cry.

Upon reading this that day he had cried out: "No one would conduct himself in such a manner, Watson, and the county police are great fools for thinking otherwise! How they could see such a detail and conclude what they did strikes anger in my heart, for the tracks are far more likely to belong to one whose presence in the situation hints at a far darker involvement. To Lincolnshire I shall go, and see justice is found for these infants, whom I suspect, were cruelly slain!"

And to Lincolnshire we did go within the hour, arriving by the afternoon, which saw Holmes alone and uncompensated soon lying down in the fetid mud beside the pond, examining the scene of the drownings, and finding the strong suggestion that his instincts had been right. By evening his investigation had become focused on a watercolour artist, up from London, a certain Willoughby Slade, who was leasing a cottage there. Holmes' confrontation with the man had been most interesting, as I had never seen one look more guilty, or fly into such paroxysms of hostility were he innocent, as did Slade. It would soon turn out that he was a man of vile, indeed unspeakable, habits and attractions, and inside the cottage were a number of indecent sketches made of the lost siblings, along with a vial of laudanum, which would be found in the children's stomachs, showing, Holmes proved, they had been drugged when they met their death."

"And what of it?" Slade had roared at Holmes and the local sheriff, a plodding man whose determination to see justice done far outweighed his talents for investigation. "Who is to say the brats did not wander off tipsy from having broken into my cottage and drunk laudanum on their own?"

"For the inconvenient fact," Holmes had said squarely, his eyes staring at Slade full of venom and righteous fury, "that the dose my chemical analysis has shown present in the children would have rendered them insensible, unable to walk any distance at all on their own. They were carried to the water, and cast in."

Slade steadfastly denied all, both that day and at his trial two months later, where Holmes' testimony upon the evidence against him—his tracks on the bank, the sketches of the children which no decent or moral man would ever make, the children's fingerprints in the cottage, and Slade's fingerprints upon the buttons of the children's clothes, and finally the brand of laudanum within the cottage matching the composition of that in the children's stomachs—all served to lay out the scenario that Slade, fearing apprehension for his crimes perpetrated upon the innocents, had arranged their drowning, confident it would be taken for an accident, as it nearly was.

The county judge, Mr. Justice Hugo Fatherton, Esq., had seen it fit to condemn Slade to the gallows, where six weeks later, still refusing to admit his guilt and make peace with man or God, he swung for his infanticide, and good riddance to him, I'd felt then, as I still did that morning at Baker Street, for few Holmes had pursed in his career had ever deserved their fate more. So, to hear the name now, two years later, in our very parlour, brought a reaction in me as it did in Holmes...

"Mr. Hilltower, please," I spoke up, "in what connection do

you bring that tainted name to Baker Street today?"

The man, who styled himself Chief Minister of the British Séance Society smiled, for he was no fool, and I saw he felt he had set his hook at last.

"Dr. Watson," he said gravely, "one of the Society's most skillful mediums, Miss Adelia Markham, talented far beyond her scant years, has on several occasions of recent vintage had Mr. Willoughby Slade manifest from 'the other side,' and speak through her. Indeed with each subsequent occasion of his contact, his presence grows stronger, and it has of late become the case that Miss Markham is beset by the spirit, which stays close to her now at all times, seeking her attention and pleading but one thing each time she allows him access to her talents."

As Holmes sat silently, smoking and looking toward Hilltower with eyes like a viper, it was I who inquired, "And what is it this girls claims he pleads?"

"His innocence," Hilltower said.

"And what, specifically, is it that brings you here, sir?" I asked. "Neither Mr. Holmes nor myself are in any way proponents of mediumship as advanced by your society."

The man said simply: "I come as a courtesy."

"A courtesy?" I repeated.

"To deliver to Mr. Holmes a stark warning, and to offer him a chance to right a terrible wrong he did in naming Willoughby Slade the killer of children, and clear this man's name, so that his spirit might find peace, and move on, for to be held earthbound by some unfinished business is a terrible fate for the departed, one of unceasing torment and woe, to speak plainly. And I can think of no condition more horrid than to exist disembodied, barred from ascending to paradise, while one's family and friends live on in the physical world each day, thinking him a murderer of innocents."

Here Holmes actually brayed a shrill laugh. "Your philosophy is as mad as you, sir, as is the charge that this despicable Willoughby Slade was innocent of anything save all human kindness, for seldom have I met a more selfishly cruel man than he. I have known immoral sorts, yes, but rarely one whose utter disregard for others stood so clearly revealed as it was in him. Upon the fact of his guilt I would stake not merely the whole of my considerable reputation, a thing marred by no flaw when it comes to my pursuit of truth, but my own life as well."

"Mr. Holmes," said Hilltower seriously, "I find that is exactly what you stake, for the ghost of this Slade has often been around you these last years, seeking your harm, wanting revenge upon you, and ghosts can be daunting foes, for they dwell outside time itself, and have ways to gradually sap the vitality of the living. I doubt not he will eventually harm you, perhaps fatally, such is his rage and sense of feeling entitled to justice. But I speak not merely of your life which is staked, sir, but your immortal soul, for think on the karmic burden that awaits one who sent an innocent man to his death, after stealing away from him all shred of his reputation. Only by clearing the honour of your victim can you—"

"My 'victim,' you say?" Holmes cried, rising and throwing his long pale hands violently into the air. "Enough of this! I have no more time to waste on such claims suitable only for the gullible and imbecilic. Based on the hysterical prattling of some young girl, you would seek to set aside the due process of British law under which this Slade stood convicted? Watson, kindly show this charlatan to the door! I will be in my room!"

He marched with keenly abiding anger from the parlour into his bedroom, and shut the door so forcefully behind him that I doubt not it rocked the dishes in Mrs. Hudson's kitchen down below. A moment later and he was vigourously performing a Braham's piece on his Stradivarius, drowning out all else.

While I had little regard for Hilltower's claims, or indeed the entirety of the spiritual movement, which was making a comeback after fading in popularity in my adolescence, I felt embarrassed that a guest at Baker Street, however unwanted, would be shown such discourtesy.

"Mr. Hilltower..." I began awkwardly, only for him to hold up a hand.

"It is all right, Doctor, for I am well-used to such receptions, though rarely do I receive them from one who should by all rights stand invested in heeding our medium's warnings."

"You had sought for Holmes to come to the Society's headquarters in Wiltshire," I said, recalling the facts stated at the interview's start. "To help you prove the truth of spiritualism."

"That is true, it was one of my purposes, though not my primary one, which was the warning I revealed at the interview's end. I have come to believe, after long presence in Miss Markham's séances, that Mr. Holmes has indeed sent an innocent man to the gallows, and that he is in great danger from a ghost starving for revenge upon him. If I cannot have Mr. Holmes' aid in helping us legitimize our movement through his investigations verifying our legitimacy, then for my part I would still seek to benevolently help him remain safe from a vengeful spirit's would-be harm, and likewise help this spirit move on and find peace, by seeing his name cleared before the eyes of the world."

Hilltower had a way of speaking that was calming, rather like a doctor I had known in medical school in Scotland, who often sat at the bed-sides of dying patients, and merely through the serenity of his voice instilled in them a sense of peace. I considered what he said, but had to conclude that it was not for me to instruct my friend as to how to proceed, nor was spiritualism something I felt inclined to grant much beneficence of opinion, for as a doctor I had seen many people die, but had never once seen a ghost appear afterward.

"I am sorry you have come all the way from Wiltshire for so little, Mr. Hilltower," I said, offering him my hand, which he took, "but based upon his response, I do not think Mr. Holmes will be able to give you the assistance you seek."

"Or accept the life-saving assistance the Society offers in his present state of dread danger," said Hilltower with what I perceived to be genuine sadness, and at that instant I realized that whatever the truth of mediumship, the man stood convicted of its reality, and was himself no hollow prophet.

"Goodbye, Dr. Watson," he said at last, as I held open the door to our rooms. "I promise you, despite his rejection of us, we at the British Séance Society shall still do all we can on Mr. Sherlock Holmes' behalf, and he will find our doors always open to him."

And with those mysterious words of promise, he set off down the stairs, and, as I mistakenly believed then, out of our lives.

Yet fickle time was to prove me very wrong.

A fortnight was to pass, and while Holmes never again mentioned Hilltower's visit or the case of Willoughby Slade, I admit both drifted into my own thoughts as I made my medical rounds, for they seemed somehow to hang in the air, unfinished and vexing, so that especially as I lay down for sleep the parting words of Hilltower turned over in my thoughts.

...we shall still do all we can on Mr. Sherlock Holmes' behalf....

My own sentiments, however, were to matter little, and the event which motivated Holmes' to involve himself in the affairs of the Séance Society came about quite unexpectedly, for on a morning which marked fifteen days since Hilltower came to 221B Baker Street, my eyes took-in an article in the morning paper that jolted me with shock, and I cried out, "Holmes, it is an outrage! You must have a look at this!"

Seizing the paper from my hands, Holmes scanned the article, and I saw his eyes smolder with irritation at what he saw.

"Watson, they are like biting flies, Hilltower and his ilk, for like disgusting insects they nip at one, seeking droplets of life-blood."

When Holmes cast the paper down onto the tabletop, the headline lay open toward me glaring:

Famed Detective Sherlock Holmes Sends Innocent Man To Gallows?

A thin, frightful smile played out on Holmes' lips as he recited the article. "'Convicted on the word of an amateur...' 'Fairness ill-served by allowing one outside the police force to interfere with the workings of justice...' 'A reasonable doubt surely remains in the minds of all men who review the unfortunate case with an open heart....'"

"Terrible!" I confirmed, angry on his behalf.

He sighed, "Ah, Watson, it is not difficult to obtain an alliance with a venal journalist, as this society had clearly done, but still, to see such slander in a paper like the *City Herald*, it lowers one's faith in the integrity of the press. "

A press which had generally treated Holmes rather fairly, I thought. "What does it mean?" I demanded.

He sounded amused as well as annoyed when he answered: "I assume that in the face of my cold rejection, Mr. Hilltower and his 'British Séance Society' have taken it upon themselves to," he shrugged, "declare war on me."

"To what end?" I asked.

"Publicity?" he offered. "An effort at the validation of their nonsense in the public eye, attainable by posing as an agent of common good and taking on a case I don't doubt the press may well seize upon with further headlines in days to come, resulting in a cry uplifted in the cause of a man duly convicted by jurors after a fair trial, a child-killer, suddenly elevated to the status of faultless martyr. The scandal here is not a miscarriage of law, for none took place, it is that such a warping of truth could ever be possible."

"And the brunt of the charge, I am sorry to say, Holmes, appears to be aimed at you. How unfair that they should put you on the defensive."

"On the defensive, Watson, because of this article in a

second-tier rag?" He laughed genuinely and deeply there. "I do not go on the defensive, my friend, I bring to mind the Duke of Wellington's maxim, which brought such woe to the cause of Bonaparte, chiefly that when peril rises, strike at its heart!"

There was something cheering in my friend's forceful declaration, and I trusted that whatever his next step, one might almost have felt pity on the Séance Society for casting down the gauntlet as it did, and therein stirring the frightful ire of Sherlock Holmes.

"Do you know the saying 'be careful what one wishes for,' Watson? I shall indeed go to them, as they wish," he said, laying out his plans to me, "it is what they want, and what I shall give them, dulling their guardedness and allowing them to think they have lured me in and bent my will to their desires, yet from inside I will prove their worst nightmare, and their undoing. Kidnappers, housebreakers, blackmailers, have I dealt with by the score, yet in those instances it was not personal, as these frauds have rendered it by smearing my good name. They have no understanding of what they have done in besmirching me so publicly, Watson."

"They have certainly made an enemy beyond their conception," I agreed, glad to see Holmes step into the fight.

"Let us make our preparations!" he cried, eyes flame.

The rest of the day I saw little of Holmes, who had taken up his hat and stick by the door and told me what he set out to do in the immediate sense needed to be undertaken alone. He spoke of sending Hilltower a telegram, informing him that he was at last accepting his invitation to come to the headquarters of the Society in Wiltshire, and beyond this, I was unsure of his intentions.

For myself, I went out on several medical calls and

returned for dinner to find Holmes already back at Baker Street, smoking, looking pleased with himself in a way that reminded me of a tomcat who'd at last caught an elusive blackbird. He ate heartily, tucking in with a ravenous glee, laughing easily and well, telling me his day had included some marvelous successes, which he left unnamed, and bidding me to be ready to leave for the countryside around seven the following morning, should I wish to journey with him.

"You may sure I do," I confirmed, "for I'd not miss this undertaking for a lairdship and a castle."

He laughed at my Scottish expression, his spirits truly boisterous, and took to his violin after dinner, inviting Mrs. Hudson up to hear him play, and so jolly did my friend seem that I could not then have guessed at the deadly seriousness with which a portion of his day had passed, unseen by my eyes, nor would I know of it til near the case's conclusion.

When night came on in earnest, I retired, bidding Holmes a pleasant slumber, only to learn that he would be "sitting up a while" and contemplating certain matters he'd uncovered that afternoon

It was to my surprise that I awoke after dawn to find him still in the chair, in the same pose, still smoking, his features rapt, as he bade me good morning, and rose at last to disappear into his room and ready himself for the trip ahead. How he managed such feats of deprivation, yet showed himself so little the worse for them, I have never been able to grasp, as a man or as a doctor.

"We may be there more than a day, Watson, I do not yet know," he called to me through his closed door, "so do pack accordingly."

In my own room I took his guidance and prepared a valise before returning to the parlour, there to see my friend still buoyant with energy, not only ready for whatever the day held, but by all signs exuberantly welcoming it.

"It shall be a delightful trip, this upending of my self-appointed enemies!" he promised, as he set off down the stairs, crying out a goodbye to Mrs. Hudson before he hurried to the street in search of a passing cab

◆ ◆ ◆

The train journey to Wiltshire was not a pleasant one, the incessant rain leaving little to see outside the windows, including the area around Stonehenge, which we passed, and the air felt damp and close inside the car. It also took longer than was forecast, owing to a delay at the terminal ahead of us. Arrive though we did in due time, to find a red-trimmed carriage awaiting us, adorned on its sides by a crest with which I was momentarily unfamiliar, til I saw it was a coat of arms loftily claimed by The British Séance Society.

"Goodness me," I remarked to Holmes, "they even style themselves as possessing an award of arms."

"As it happens, they do," he answered knowingly, "owing to their involvement with the dowager Countess of Strysedale, who has sworn to all her noble friends that the mediums within the Society have placed her in regular contact with Lord Mitchell, her late husband, who passed in '81."

"A Countess? Really?"

"It is the nature of this society to seek out the famed and moneyed, and draw them into their fawning embrace. Yet for ordinary folk associated with the group, it is more a life of drudgery and empty promises. Take note, Watson, how they tried to draw me in two weeks ago and add me to their collection with that visit by the 'Chief Minister,' Hilltower, and his offer of promises of revelation and prominent standing on one hand, his subtle threats to cause me trouble on the other. They are, for all their honeyed ways, a vindictive lot, and you see from the paper what my rejection has stirred in them."

"I do see that now," I agreed. "They truly longed for your aid in validating them."

"Oh, it was their fondest hope that I should be taken in and would soon radiate praise for them, making headlines, and granting them all the more acceptance in society. They have also sought connections with half the note-worthies of London's salons and stage, and as the Countess shows, they are not unconnected to the titled."

He said all this while waiting for the porter to deliver our luggage, and as we did, the red-livered coachman from the Society, a tall, chestnut-haired lad of about twenty or so, as fine as any coachman in a ducal household, waited patiently, only to lose his composure to surprise when Holmes trod past him without a glance, and summoned a common Surrey-cab from the line drawn up outside the station.

"Moreland House," he commanded, an instant before the jolt of the humble Surrey's rough start rocked us both back in our seats.

It amused me to see the face of the young coachman, doubtless among the minions of the Society, when he perceived that Holmes should prefer a rickety conveyance over a fine carriage as good as that of any gentleman.

"Begging pardon, sir," said the driver of our Surrey, the tones of the West Country booming in his voice, "but it hain't called Moreland House no more. Not since them lot took its lease, a gift from a wealthy gentleman is what I heard. No, now it's termed 'Rising Dawn'."

He spat out the side of the Surrey, showing his thoughts on this.

As we were traveling along at a decent but not notable pace, the carriage from the Society drew up behind us and easily passed us by, the coachman showing off how fine his matching horses were, and went far beyond us, no doubt to arrive well in advance and deliver the news of Holmes' recalcitrance, and the slight it implied.

"Bad lot, them folk," said the cabbie, nodding his head toward the rear of the fine carriage which was drawing away from us by nearly a furlong's distance.

"Are they now?" asked Holmes, cordially, all ears at the man's statement.

"Aye, not good Christians as they aren't, not the whole lot of 'em. Doing those séances there, and all manner of people coming forth to see the mediums there with their unholy arts, talking to them what's dead." The man shuddered, and were he of the Church of Rome I've no doubt he should have crossed himself.

"So you believe, then, that their powers truly extend to speaking with the deceased?" Holmes inquired, politely.

"Them, what's dead, you mean? Oh, aye, I do at that. Some folk in this world, well they're liars, 'tis true, pretending at such craft, but them as lives at the manor house...nay, they do the devil-arts sure as they claim, and I'll tell you how I know...."

"I should be obliged to hear," said Holmes with easy politeness.

"Well, sir, it's like this. Last May Day my sister-in-law, Maude, she who has but one eye, come over asking for my help and my two oldest boys' help in beating the bushes for her neighbour's little boy, Danny, he was called, so drop everything we did, and set out among all as live in this part of the county, you see, and spent all day, we did, looking for the child through the oat fields and in the hollows, but couldn't find him nowheres."

"Terrible business," I commented.

"One of the gentlemen up at the house what used to be Moreland and now is Rising Dawn, Hilltower his name, he comes down from the manor with a young lady and her mother walking beside him, Miss and Mrs. Markham, and pleasin' to the eye, that girl, the mother not half so bad herself, and she went up to my sister-in-law's neighbour and she says, "Let me have something that belonged to the boy.' So young Danny's mam, she done this, giving this Miss Markham a woolen scarf the boy liked to wear in the wintertime. I seen with my own eyes how this Miss Markham, she held the scarf right close and pushed it even into her face, like to smother herself, then she looked back out again, and her eyes, sir... I swear as a Freemason and Christian, her eyes like to have been glowing like they had blue lights inside them. She took to stumbling and nearly fell, but the mother, she steadied her, then the girl, she say, 'The child is still alive, but hurry! Look in the old dry well in Hammond's Bottom.'"

"And was the child discovered there?" I asked, as swept up into the driver's narrative as was Holmes himself.

"We all set off at a trot, must've been near on two-dozen of us, and near falling over we was by the time we got there, it being three miles away, farther off than any of us had thought to look for the boy, and the girl's words were true, as at the bottom of the dry well he lay, alive down there, but had cried hisself to sleep so that for an instant we took him to be dead. Down his pa went on a ladder and brung him up, and the doctor in town seen to him, said his arm were broke, and his collarbone too, and the tale came out from the boy's lips, saying as how he was trying to look over the side when down he fell into the pit. Well, all's well what ends well, and that boy is still alive and kickin', a year older now and hale as you please. Had that girl from the manor house, Miss Markham, not said what she done, well, it'd be his little bones laying down there in the darkness, and none of us ever the wiser."

I thought on all this and said, "If a child's life was saved, why is it you think their practices evil?"

The man shook his head, whipping his shaggy brown beard about and said, "Better mayhaps down there he stayed, for sometimes it's a soul's hour to go in God's mysterious plan, hard though at times it be, and it were the devil's powers that girl used to find him, for no Christian would have used such means as talking to spirits. No, sir, if you mean to go to that cursed house among them people, and many do, I can tell you, famous people as well from London, and Paris and America, too, well, just mind yourself, is all I'm sayin', for there's nothing holy under that roof, not among that kind."

For emphasis he spat again.

I turned thoughtful at the man's account, but Holmes seemed as cool at heart as he had been all day, his mood high, and with a smile he interrupted my contemplations by pointing to a line of apple trees, which merrily dotted a pleasant field by a distant grange.

Seeing me distracted, though, he said in a voice too low for the driver in the front bench to apprehend: "That stunt was an educated guess bolstered by a run of luck, Watson, doubtless augmented by a good local atlas in their library which showed the nearby well. They have no more preternatural powers than does a common housecat, I assure you."

Likely he was right, but the first crack of wonder appeared in my mind, as it often did when we faced brushes with the unusual, for it seemed to me no small thing to correctly name the location of a missing child on the first try.

◆ ◆ ◆

A little over an hour after departing the train, we reached the manor house re-named Rising Dawn, and Holmes paid the driver generously, being told in return:

"Remember, sir, on your best guard here among this sort."

With a tip of his well-worn cap, the driver departed with noted haste, and we were approached by a welcoming committee, led by the smiling and impeccably dressed Hilltower, who had previously visited us at Baker Street. On either side of him stepped a lady, one quite old, her hair a frizzy gray mop, a trio of gaudy rings on either hand, the second middle-aged and dressed in the plain, severe style of a country schoolmarm, her hair so black I suspected it dyed, pulled back from her brow in a tight bun.

As two decidedly tall young footmen in red livery came forward to take our luggage, Hilltower called out as he drew near, "Mr. Holmes! Dr. Watson! I cannot tell you how it does my soul glad that you have come at last, per our heartfelt invitation!"

He extended his hand, which I took, but he received only a nod from Holmes, who declined the gesture. Pretending not to notice or at least to care about this rejection, though surely his companions had observed the cut, Hilltower went on.

"Gentlemen, may I introduce two of our Society's most noteworthy mediums. On my right is the delightful Madame Bajusz, the Seer of Debrecon, Hungary, consultant to the Hapsburgs, here among us for a four-week engagement. Her claim to fame, I confide to you, is to have brought forward in the presence of his aunt, the Grand Duchess Maria, the manifested spirit of Archduke Rudolf, who last winter took his own life, amidst a broken heart. It was through her," he said leaning forward with an air of imparting a secret, "that the *truth* of that tragedy was revealed."

As if on cue, Madame Bajusz uttered in a thick Slavic accent: "Possession by a malignant entity."

"Yes, quite," agreed Hilltower, all but glowing with delight at her words.

He turned next to the other lady and said, "And to my left is Miss Rosemarie Curlow, the Vestal of our society, whose great feat at age thirteen, namely correctly identifying sixteen of seventeen random objects set before her on a table, while blindfolded, is still spoken of in tones of deepest awe in spiritual circles. The powers of both ladies are most acute."

"Madame Bajusz, Miss Curlow," I said, bowing to each.

"Doctor," said Miss Curlow with a curtsey.

"Sir," replied Madame Bajusz, more gravely, her unblinking eyes boring into my own, as she turned her head in an odd manner which somewhat reminded me of a lizard.

"Such is our hospitality here at Rising Dawn," declared Hilltower, "that even before we settle you into your rooms, we shall provide a quick demonstration of the ladies' keen abilities, a taste of what is on-hand here within our Society."

Holmes looked bored, but smiled condescendingly and waited, yet it was not to be he of whom either woman spoke.

Turning to me, Madame Bajusz, her words so heavily accented that they were almost a puzzle in themselves, said, "Dr. John Watson, son of a stark land, your path in life has been an unlikely one, taking you far from the green land where you were born. Yet there will come a day when you will rue ever leaving your native town, for I see in your future a great love which is to be marred by unspeakable tragedy. Not yet, not for a while, but it lies before you, like a great tree fallen in the road of your life."

Mockery in his voice, Holmes said, "Might such a vague exercise in seer-ship not be fitted to the circumstances of any life?"

Hilltower did not rise to this taunt but smiled sadly at me by way of commiseration, and said, "Dear me, I was hoping for some better news for Dr. Watson here. My apologies, Doctor, I recoil from those words as much as you do. Perhaps Miss Curlow shall foresee something better in your future to balance out Madame Bajusz's lugubrious sentiments."

He nodded toward Miss Curlow, who abruptly seized my hand, though rather than staring at its wrinkles like a gypsy palm reader, she shut her intense eyes and said, "The energies of Mr. Holmes are too closed off to readily pierce, as he holds his secrets well, and I cannot read him, for I let the unwilling remain shielded out of courtesy. But you, Doctor, ah, I, too, see it, the tragedy my colleague foretells. I see its nature, though through a glass darkly, and intuit that it is not one but twin tragedies which await you, falling together, two losses, each terrible on its own, yet together...nearly enough to break you. You shall persevere, but remain evermore a changed man.

Without warning she released my hand, clacked her tongue, and as if overcome drew a deep breath before re-opening her eyes, which seemed pierced with sadness. "I am sorry," she said softly, "it is a heavy thing to foretell cruelties which await a man with a soul as kind as your own. I will not name the approaching sorrows, as the shutting of Pandora's Box is ever the gods' greatest mercy."

And with that, she turned and walked rapidly away, and though it may have been a pantomime, as Holmes would later assure me it was, citing the ill-explained vagueness of the words, I would swear that her departure was as unexpected to Hilltower as the rest of us, and that it displeased him to see her go, and ran counter to his plans.

"Yes, well," he remarked, his bonhomie temporarily sidelined before he forced the aura of welcome back onto himself, "such is the life of the psychically sensitive, gentlemen, theirs is a world of ever-intruding knowledge, not always pleasant to discern. Whatever it was Miss Curlow prognosticated on the heels of Madame Bajusz here, Doctor, know that time, I have found in my research, is not a straight line, but a river, with many small streams feeding into it, and many opportunities to change direction."

He let his words settle an instant, then announced, "Now, gentlemen, please allow the Society's excellent housekeeper, Mrs. Buck, to show you to your rooms. They are side by side in the north wing, as I hoped might meet with your wishes. Again, we are glad you are here, and til dinner, I bid you adieu."

"Oh," he said turning and adding after only a few steps, "and I should bid you, if you hear any noises of the supernatural in the night, do ignore them, as the spirits here can be noisy, but mean us no harm. There is an Elizabethan lady in particular who enjoys her nocturnal strolls down the long gallery."

"I shall indeed disdain any would-be ghosts I perceive," replied Holmes, who had been silently observant since our arrival.

Hilltower smiled weakly, nodded, and went on his way.

A serious-looking woman, nearly six-feet in height and mannish, though somewhat pleasant in her countenance, stepped forward and offered her greetings in a husky voice, saying, "Gentlemen, I am Mrs. Buck, housekeeper here, and I will take you upstairs, as Minister Hilltower directed. If you'd be so good as to come with me."

We were led past a double line of gathered servants, on-hand to greet our arrival as if we were guests of honour on a par with an Earl, and taken into the grand foyer of the manor, Rising Dawn, where a mural commissioned long ago depicted a hundred riders participating in some mythic hunt. The house was Tudor in outward design, though its interior bore the hallmarks of remodeling at some point in Georgian times, when many colourful Whig house parties were doubtless held on-site.

Miss Buck took us past a substantial library and a number of lower-floor rooms she dubbed "shrines for nonphysical communication," and as she led us along she remarked proudly on one feature or another of the house, and stopped before an ornate parlour of which she said:

"This, sirs, is a site of an event in history as momentous as the discovery of the New World, or the harnessing of electricity, for it was in this room a mere five years ago, that our beloved Madame DuMont, a physical medium as opposed to astral or ethereal, produced from her extended fingertips the first sample of ectoplasm ever harvested, and chemically verified."

"By whom was this dubious substance verified?" Holmes asked, making scant effort at politeness.

"By chemists at the Royal College of Sciences, Cambridge," she replied, causing Holmes to raise an eyebrow, this being not, I took it, the answer he had expected.

"This ectoplasm of which you speak, are samples of it still on the premises?"

"Indeed, sir, several, all bottled and kept preserved for later study."

"And may I, for instance, be permitted to make a study of this arcane substance? I do have no small background in chemistry."

It surprised me to hear Mrs. Buck reply, "I should think that would be possible, though it would require Minister

Hilltower's approval, of course. You will find he is most open, as are we all here, for we desire nothing so much as full scientific recognition of our work, and of the worlds beyond the visible one."

"And this Madame DuMont," said Holmes, "is she, too, by chance on-site?"

Mrs. Buck sighed and said sadly, "The dear lady is no longer physical."

"She has died then?" Holmes pressed.

"We do not say 'die' here, sir, for it is an outmoded term of less enlightened ages. We, through our research and open-minded study now understand that we are all beings of energy which dwell inside a body, and when the soul sheds the body, it merely moves on without any loss of personality whatsoever into another dimension, like a butterfly from its cocoon, the physical plane being merely one among an infinitude on which we all might—and will—dwell."

"How fascinating," Holmes said with a droll disdain out of keeping with the housekeeper's dutiful steadfastness, for Mrs. Buck seemed ungiven to contention, and did not rebut his overt scepticism, simply led us the final distance in rebuffed silence.

"Your rooms, gentlemen," she announced at last, "suites 212 and 214—there being no 213 to be found here owing, of course, to the ill-humours of numerology, and the unluckiness of the number thirteen. I trust you will find your lodgings comfortable, but as Minster Hilltower's guests, you must, of course, make any request you wish to add to your comfort. Extra pillows, coverings, anything you might wish from our library, you have only to ask, and it shall be brought to you. Dinner is at seven, vegetarian only, as meat interferes with the purity of the vibrations here, and you are both, of course, most welcome to join us, or a tray can be sent up to you, at your discretion."

I thanked her heartily, for so far we had encountered nothing but courtesy at Rising Dawn, and it began to gnaw at my conscience that we were there in an adversarial capacity, however justified it may have been.

"And are we required to stay in our rooms til dinner?" Holmes asked, having in any case no intentions of doing so, I felt sure, for I knew his dislike of rules was profound.

Mrs. Buck gave him a glance that made me wonder if she thought he was jesting.

"Mr. Holmes," she told him, "this house is an open area in its entirety, save only for those spaces occupied by other guests. Anyone within may go wherever he or she wishes. There is nothing concealed here, sir, and no hierarchy to subdivide and stratify. Even Minister Hilltower is but first among equals in the Society, proclaiming that in the far-seeing eyes of the divine creator, we are all children, equally beloved, if not equally endowed in our gifts."

Having said this, a sentiment I took it she truly did believe, she smiled, and went on her way.

As he watched Mrs. Buck take her leave and descend the grand staircase at the hallways' middle, Holmes said to me:

"Ah, Watson, the denizens of this place have let their minds be re-sculpted to another's purpose, that devoted lady most surely among them. She, I perceived hails from Kent, and retains the classic heightened 'r' of the county, and wears, I've little doubt the black of mourning in her heart, still marking after some years the widowhood which drove her into the arms of the Society, where she received false hope from the mouth of some medium. She is an unhappy woman who has channeled her grief into her work, and is to be pitied."

"Your hypotheses?" I asked.

"The clues are all there to be seen," he replied, "and stand most telling. She is a soul seeking a comfort which no church has provided her."

He then turned serious and said, "I don't doubt every room in Rising Dawn is designed for eavesdropping, which doubtless aids the quality of the 'revelations' the mediums here make during the paying guests' séances, so do be careful what you say in unguarded moments."

With that caveat, he entered his room, and I my own,

finding it large and comfortable, with a great four-posted bed rising on one end, and a writing table beside a vast window, well exposed to outside light. It was possibly more grand than any room I'd ever stayed in, and left me, a simple doctor from Scotland, feeling quite humbled.

Yet if the lull of comfort inclined me to be in any way sceptical of Holmes' claim, I soon felt myself a fool for it, as not ten minutes later, he knocked on my door and walked quickly through my suite, and pointed upward from the south corner to a vent above my bed. He placed his fingers over his lips, then moved to a window frame, where a pipe, seemingly of no purpose, was concealed behind the folds of the drapery, descending from an opening in the ceiling, and ending at face-height above the floor. These were eavesdrop points, just as he said, and I felt a sense of affront rise in me.

But then in the face of my outrage, Holmes shook his head and said, "Though they may make convenient use of them we cannot blame the Society for their presence, for none of these constructions are new, but date, I judge to the building of the house some three centuries ago."

"For what purpose?" I demanded.

"In researching the history of Moreland Manor, to call this pile by its proper and longstanding name, I learned that in Tudor times, it was the abode of Sir Wilmont Carver-Gaston, a spy in royal service, who pretended sympathy with the Catholic cause, and invited Papists here under the pretense that they would be free to speak openly of sentiments they may have concealed in other environs. All revealed here was all then sent in code to London where Sir Francis Wallsingham, Queen Elizabeth's famed and efficient spymaster, awaited it."

"He betrayed his own guests?" I asked.

"Most assuredly," answered Holmes.

"But can we know the present occupants here likewise employ these old venues for eavesdropping?" I asked.

"Certainly, and they may have even chosen the house for those very reasons, though I understand it is held as a gift in perpetual trust, and was not selected by anyone in the society. I confess it hints that perhaps clandestine oversight is not their primary occupation, Watson."

"Then assuming they do not truly possess the arcane powers they claim, and did not come here simply for the ease of listening-in on their guests, they are acquiring their knowledge somehow," I stated, puzzled and wondering about much.

"They have their methods, and as I often tell you by way of explanation in the case of my own powers of observation, once a feat is revealed, it may be counted on that it usually shall prove less impressive than the original mystery made it appear."

Shifting to a new topic, Holmes said: "When dinner comes, I shall find myself not hungry, Watson, though I bid you, go if you desire. I shall be taking the housekeeper at her word, and making rounds to scrutinize the place, for there is much to be perceived, and secrets to uncover. Above all, do not forget, Watson, the Society is a force for human exploitation, and for supreme dishonesty, however it may at times seem below their outward smiles."

And without another word, he took to his heels and strode from the room, leaving me no closer to knowing the situation in the house.

◆ ◆ ◆

In the face of Holmes' remarkable self-control, I for my part was famished, and dressed for dinner and went downstairs at seven. The dining room was, I found, elaborate, and in Tudor times had once functioned as the great hall, where Henry VIII was said to have been a guest in 1530.

The fare was vegetarian as promised, but well-prepared and seasoned, reminding me somewhat of the cuisine I had encountered in Afghanistan. Dining with us amid the Society members were several other guests, including a famed writer from the continent whose identity I shall omit here, but whose name I assure you you would know, and two couples from London, somewhat moneyed and each hoping for contact with a loved one who had, in the terminology of the Society, "departed."

The first couple, a Mr. and Mrs. William Sullivan, of Mayfair, had received word a fortnight before that their eldest son, Marshall, had drowned while yachting in the Channel. The other married couple, the Hayes, had lost a granddaughter to typhus over the previous summer, and it was explained to me that Mrs. Hayes was none the closer to recovering from the loss, and held ardent hopes of being placed in communication with the child.

"If I can hear her voice again, Doctor," she said to me from her seat, directly to my right, "I may find a little peace, though I pray God take me soon, in any case, that I can be with little Myrtle again."

I knew not whether to pity this lady her hope, or feel sadness at her willingness to place her trust in those who, Holmes had vowed, were taking her husband's money for the non-existent service they provided.

Still, I listened as the continental writer, who was a not infrequent guest at Rising Dawn, spoke in his Gallic accent of some truly inexplicable, even miraculous, events which had come to pass at his late visits, with this being his seventh in five years

"Doctor," he said, his voice nasal but his English confident, "I have had several conversations here with my dear mother, eleven years gone, and my father, who went last year, as well as ancestors of mine from the time of the Capetian kings, and with a Roman man who once lived nearby, all cordial and all benevolent in their advice to me."

"That is a remarkable conviction," I said.

"It is," he agreed, "and yet I feel myself no fool for holding it, as I know I have likewise received messages in the form of puzzling clues which seemed merest nonsense at the time, but which were later to be validated. The most impressive of these came from my first wife, who died in the train collision at Staplehurst, which nearly cost the world my late friend Mr. Dickens, who, alas, has not seen fit to communicate here with me. At the time I was given the clues, I thought the message some scrambled gibberish, as you say, but a year to the day later as I was walking through *le Parc de la Tête d'or*, in Lyons, there I saw a little girl of about four playing with a wind-up jack-in-the-box, and she was chanting the same merry, nonsense syllables which the medium, Senora Hernandez, had told me, singing out: *fa-dee-fo-hi-de-ho-see-mee-jo-fo-fo.*"

"That is odd," I allowed, quite truthfully.

"Odd?" he said. "Don't you grasp the significance, sir?"

"Perhaps I fail to at that," I admitted.

"Ah, you Scotsmen are so grounded, I know," he chuckled, unoffended by my lack of insight. "The child was my *wife*, Dr. Watson, reincarnated, but recalling the code she'd sent me through Senora Hernandez, from the other side, just before her rebirth!"

"Dear me!" I exclaimed at the account. I knew the writer was hardly an unintelligent man, and yet, his claim defied rationality.

Perhaps seeing some unintended hint of my scepticism, he continued: "The child's hair was the same shade my wife's had been, her eyes so similar, even the same pattern of freckles sprinkled about her cheeks, all evidence she had taken on a new body! Miraculous and overwhelming it was!"

"As the miracles of mediumship often are," Hilltower called from the head of the long, ornate table, having been listening in to the writer's tale. "My hope, Doctor," he said, " is that you and Mr. Holmes, however mercenary and uncooperative he may plan to be—oh, yes, I know he is angry with us concerning that unfortunate article, not our doing, I assure you, a reporter came and gleaned what he should not, rascally man—come to see we are genuine here, and the powers of the psychically gifted are as real as, and no different from, the inborn talents of a composer or an artist, or a healer, such as yourself. I dare say if you let your mind be open during the séance tomorrow, you may see things here which convert you to a doctrine of *possibility*."

I felt all eyes turn toward me, so feeling uncomfortable, I said, "I will certainly evaluate any evidence I encounter."

"That is all that may fairly be asked of any man, Doctor," Hilltower remarked, and raised his wine glass in salute to me, only to be joined by all the others.

◆ ◆ ◆

When I was back upstairs close to nine, conversation having lingered long around the dinner table, I sought out Holmes to tell him of the experiences, and of who was also staying at Rising Dawn, yet I found him pensive and taciturn, his good humour of the morning dashed, his mania quite replaced by drear.

"Watson," he said, "this house is riddled with points of eavesdropping, as we learned so easily upon our arrival, yet in other respects..." he shrugged, "save for its obvious grandeur, my investigations show it to be for all intents and purposes, unremarkable. The library I found extensive and well-stocked, the workers here rather at ease, and happier than those at most country homes one might visit."

"And this displeases you, as you were hoping to find some definite proof?"

"Of course not," he retorted, "I should not expect things to be so easy. Yet I also found no secret doors, no hidden passageways, no sites of concealment where fakery might be undertaken in suggestion of the supernatural. I was even preparing myself to see flitting along my path, far ahead of me some servant in a bed-sheet, simulating the specter of great-great-uncle Elsmere or some such. But no!"

"Then might that also suggest something?" I posited.

Rather than answer directly, he said, gloomily, "Watson, there was an *incident* I have been left pondering and have yet to find explanation for."

"I can see it troubles you," I said, "care to share it?

Holmes leaned back in his chair and inhaled from his pipe, which had been sending the scent of cherry-tobacco into the air.

"There is a code, Watson," he said uneasily after a moment, "arranged between my brother Mycroft and myself. It is known to the two of us alone, and is a combination of letters, numbers, the names of several towns, and an animal. We created this code, rather a lengthy one, committed only to our memories, to be a means of absolute confirmation of identity and freedom of speech between us, offered only if we are coerced by some power which might have one of us in its hold."

"I understand," I said. "And what of it?"

"Downstairs, I was examining a room where séances are held, confident I should find all number of concealed arrangements lying in wait to fool the credulous customers who have paid for the services here."

"And you did not?"

"It was a room as plain and unaltered to such purposes as the parlour of Baker Street itself. A single table, ordinary wooden chairs, a fireplace that led straight upward, no hidden nooks, no peepholes, no wires to be tugged to ring concealed chimes or sway the chandelier overhead. Despite my expectations, I uncovered nothing out of the ordinary whatsoever."

I nodded, considering this in light of the confidence of the words spoken to me by the writer at dinner, and the story of the seeming miracle in the park in Lyons he'd shared.

"As I was about to take my leave and contemplate the meaning of the room being so clean, as it were," Holmes said, " I found myself in the presence of young girl, perhaps sixteen or seventeen, very pretty, her hair in a French mode, though I perceived from many signs that she was as English as I. It was, of course Miss Adelia Markham, of whom I have heard so much since coming here. She curtsied and made no introduction, trusting in the way of confident people that none was needed, but advanced on me, Watson, and on her tiptoes, for she was a petite creature, she kissed my cheek, and said:

"'I welcome you to Rising Dawn, Mr. Sherlock Holmes. I know tonight you stand an unbeliever in all that we do here in this house, where the extraordinary is commonplace, but tomorrow, when you hear out the spirit who has followed me about for some weeks now, demanding I tell the world of his innocence, a spirit who is standing here beside you now, as it happens, I think you may find yourself a believer, willingly or not, for it is you who obsesses him above all else. I speak of none other than Willoughby Slade.'"

"Oh, my!" I exclaimed.

"If she'd thought the name alone would unsettle me, Watson, she was mistaken, and I told her it would require an immense volume of evidence, indeed, to convert me as she hoped."

"What was her answer?" I demanded.

"She replied: 'I do not hope for your enlightenment, Mr. Holmes, I only can tell you from your own vibrations, and the guardedness you wear about you like an armour, that you are not prepared for what waits once the session starts, for you have never met a medium with half my powers. Minster Hilltower, who has traveled the continent for twenty years in search of those blessed with the Sight, tells me I am the most radiantly gifted he has ever known. Since I was a babe, spirits, good and bad, have always been drawn to me, and I see them at every hour, in every place. And just as this is said of me, so I can say of you, that of anyone I have ever met, sir, you have more energy around you than I have ever seen, both your own and....that of so many others from the *beyond*, both the merely watchful, even admiring, yet also the predatory and angry, all of whom are focused on you, friend and foe alike. So many, many, sir, look out at you, unseen, from the other side.'"

"That is an outrageous claim, Holmes," I said. "This girl must be utterly deluded as to her own powers!"

"I perceived many things about her, Watson. I noted that despite her having been coached in voice til she spoke with the polished sheen of a Duchess, she was born of much lower stock, and in Yorkshire of all places. I saw that she had not always enjoyed the comfort of the easy life she has here, and that she cherishes it as can only one aware that it might one day be lost. I saw she was greatly under the control of her mother, yet did not wish to be, and perceived she was both very sure of herself, and very frightened of a *person* whose identity I think I may be able to guess at. I found her an enigmatic sort for one so young, and I found myself pulled to her as one might be to a complex symphony, or a fine blend of tobacco. She is far from an ordinary youth, though not for the reasons Hilltower and his Society may think."

He elevated his pipe for emphasis as he said this last part, and I waited for him to say more.

"Above all, Watson," he continued, "I can tell you she is the focal point here, the prized showpiece in Hilltower's gallery, the rose in Rising Dawn's garden, and I think it is she who shall prove the cornerstone of the mysteries here, barely past the time of childhood though she may be."

"You speak of her as I have rarely heard you speak of another," I said marveling.

"But not lightly, Watson," he claimed, "not lightly."

He waited a moment in dramatic fashion and said at last: "She then pressed a sheet of paper into my hand before walking away with the rare grace of a doe, this child mostly-grown to womanhood, who has been rigorously schooled in certain graces by a domineering mother."

"What was it that she gave you?" I asked.

His hand unfurled and from within lay a small sheet of paper folded width-wise. I took hold of it and saw what was written in a scrawled, childish hand read: *33-120-B-W-P-R-9-9-9-V-Sarum-Knightsbridge-Plymouth-14-B-I-R-O-K-Colchester-22-Lion-Owl.*

My mind drifted for an instant to the sing-song rhyme

sung by the little French girl in the park in Lyons, as related by the writer at dinner, yet this was much more. "Holmes...?" I began, "is it the secret code which you arranged with Mycroft?"

"There are several mistakes, Watson, but part of the sequence is..." He released he admission with reluctance. "*Correct.*"

My head spun, a thousand unwanted notions of possibility rising in me despite my efforts to silence them, all shouting that it was real then, the mediums, their claims, the unseen other world, and all I could do was utter: "How...?"

He told me: "I know Mycroft would never betray any confidence we share, this one in particular, for that code could represent life and death to us one day. It is incomplete, true, and there are several errors, yes, but part of it is strikingly correct."

I felt the floor under me seem to rock, so filled with consternation and dismay was I. "Holmes," I demanded, "by what means has this been done if not by genuine mediumship? You must tell me, for to my thought this seems....!"

"Proof?" he said, supplying the word.

"How can one see it otherwise?"

"Watson," he began, "in that vein it might interest you to know the girl, Miss Markham, said one more thing before she left the room."

From his words I sensed that in this lay the heart of the gloomy unease which I saw had overtaken him, pushing aside even his vaulted self-confidence, if only for this moment of aftershock.

"What she said, Watson was: 'This comes from Anna, who hears only improperly, of course, and who begs you forgive her for not catching *all* of the code when you recited it in the hidden room at Whitehall, with Mycroft."

"Was that where the code was agreed upon between you? I asked.

"Yes."

"And who is 'Anna'?"

He drew a long breath and admitted: "My sister, Watson,

mine own and Mycroft's, who died when she was eleven. She had been deaf in her left ear, a fact few would even remember now."

Without realizing I was doing it, I slumped into a nearby chair, and for the next several moments I was lost in a befuddled shock so grasping that Holmes forced a glass of whisky into my hand and commanded, "Drink slowly, Watson."

When I finally spoke, I said, "It is beyond encompassing, Holmes. No man could guess at such a code. And in all our time together only once have you made reference to having had a sister, and never do I recall you speaking her name. Even I did not know it."

"Yes," Holmes agreed, his gaze slowly seeming to turn inward, "her loss was a tragedy from which my family never fully recovered. She was the bright star of my parents' existence, the youngest of we three and the only girl, as charming a child as ever could be. And her mind, Watson.....as brilliant an intellect, surely, as any man, perhaps outreaching even Mycroft and myself. She read Greek and Latin by three. By seven she was undertaking higher mathematics, and had outpaced several tutors. She would play a game with us, wherein she would set up some problem of logic, and challenge us to solve it. Sometimes we, though we were older than she, could not. We all doted on her, and we lost her in but a single day. She began the morning as healthy as could be imagined, yet by noon she confided to our mother that her throat hurt. It went morbid within hours, and she dead just before the stroke of midnight, gasping in her little bed. I remember only too well we were standing about her, and the doctor folded her hands across her chest, as the clock struck that dreadful hour. It was the last time, Watson, I ever wept. I do not like to think, even now, on that darkest of days."

"I can imagine," I told him, shaken by my reserved friend confiding so much. I paused in deference to all he'd said, then asked, "Holmes, you have placed her very existence in your past, and spoken of her but rarely ever since, so you not think it significant that she should be known to the girl, Miss Markham?"

He said nothing for a long moment, simply stared into the empty grate of the immense fireplace within the room, then he admitted softly, "Do I find it significant, you ask? Yes, Watson, I do."

Outside the window the moon came free from behind a fleecy cloud, and as if in pain, Holmes said, "Leave me, Watson, I require sleep. We will speak more on the morrow."

And so I left him still seated in the hard wooden chair, smoking, in a room swaddled in the unbroken darkness of night.

I slept uneasily, but the dreams I recall having were pleasant enough, a small surprise considering all that had transpired in the day we'd been at Rising Dawn, from the mediums' prophecy that twin tragedies would mar my path, to the many challenging accounts to which I'd been exposed by other guests, to Holmes own matter, which rose in prominence above all others.

So it was I went down the hall to his room in a state of expectancy and hesitation, and knocked timidly, only to have him open the door before me, dressed, shaved, and seemingly quite restored to vigour.

"Ah, my friend," he cried, "Do begin the day walking with me!"

He proceeded at a fine pace across the house and through the large outer doors, til he was on the lawn, and walked farther still, his pace increasing as he put distance between himself and the manor house called Rising Dawn.

I did not know what to say to him, only felt glad to see him more himself today, but found my own emotions still reeling in a state of near bewilderment. Was there truly supernatural communication going on here, and if not, how on earth was fraud being achieved if it had unsettled even Sherlock Holmes, who could see seemingly through any deception? It was all too much.

Yet when we were perhaps two-hundred yards from the house, out onto the beginnings of a rolling meadow, I received a veritable shock, for it was there that Holmes stopped and threw back his head, and to my astonishment let loose a solid laugh.

"Oh, Watson, Watson," he cried, enjoying himself in his mirth, "they really must think me well and truly fooled!"

"Holmes!" I uttered. "This rapid change in you....are you quite all right?"

"Rarely better! I perceive you ask this based on my words back in the house last night?"

"Er...yes," I confessed.

"Pantomime!" he all but shouted. "A little play put on for the benefit of whoever was listening in, as I can assure you, someone was."

"Well you certainly fooled me, Holmes!" I said, the faintest annoyance mixing in with my relief to find him back to himself: though perhaps in reality he had never faltered.

"Oh, I admit," he said, "the extent to which *someone* here has gone to try to undermine my confidence in myself is impressive, and the talented Miss Markham does know something about the art of dramatic self-presentation, all the more remarkable in one so young, but the very attempt to unsettle me was my unseen foe's undoing."

His face suddenly changed again, darkening, "Though to employ the device of my sister.... that, Watson, galls me, for her memory is sacred to me above all else, and I shall remember that trespass when we reach the apotheosis of this matter."

"But the code, Holmes," I said again, "that is beyond any lucky guess!"

"It is indeed, which should tell you something."

I searched the logic-centres of my brain for what this thing might be, yet came up short, so asked: "But how should such a thing as that clandestine code be acquired if it is as sacrosanct between you and Mycroft as you say?"

"Recall, Watson," he answered, "the multitude of opportunities the house presents for eavesdropping, and take note of all I said there. I took it as a matter of faith that we were being listened to at every moment, and so used the opportunity to prime our foe with a false expectation, planting the seed last night that I was teetering on belief, when in actuality I was not for one instant taken-in, though I wished it to seem so."

"Holmes, I know your love of drama and layered revelations, but I beg you, no more, tell me, how, then, did the girl, this Miss Markham, have the code?"

"It was an old sequence, Watson, not the current one, for the simple reason the former code was compromised when it was once overheard."

"By whom?"

"By several others, I would imagine, for January last, my brother Mycroft suffered for several days and nights from walking pneumonia, the result of being involved in the incident with *HMS McFarlane*, the warship which ran aground off the shore of Fife. It had been the scene of hidden meetings among top government officials, so naturally Mycroft took part."

"Oh, yes, I'd imagine," I said lightly, Holmes having told me of his brother's deep involvement in secret governmental affairs.

"The vessel was swept up in the sudden gale there, onto rocks, and though Mycroft made it to shore along with most of those aboard, he was exposed for several hours to the winds and rain. Being as stubborn a man as I, he insisted on returning to London, though he had a chill, and he tried to go on, only to fall quite ill in the days which followed. He was taken to St. James' Hospital, Kings Gate, where I visited him as his life hung in the balance for a number of hours, during which he rather unfortunately raved, saying many things, among them the code you saw written on that paper, chanting it over and over into thin air, unaware of what he was doing."

"The poor fellow," I said, knowing full well how the ravings of the feverish could reveal much that person might normally seek to hide. As I thought of the many sickrooms I'd been in while men called out in their delirium, my mind was also racing to grasp at the edges of the profound human drama unfolding at Rising Dawn, and pull them together.

"Upon his recovery," Holmes continued, "Mycroft and I devised a new code, which we hold in secret now, neither to reveal it, but someone took note of his rantings in his semi-conscious state, Watson, and somehow that information was acquired, and transported here, where there was an attempt to use it against me, and convince me of a thing I shall never be convinced of. And add to that the insulting audacity of naming my own departed sister as the source of the code!"

I watched as anger ran through him before he mastered it and returned to cool self-possession.

"Then would it not be a sound starting place to investigate who overhead this in the hospital room?" I suggested.

"Perhaps, Watson, except, I ask, could you commit to memory a string of seeming nonsense as was that code?"

"No," I admitted, "so I suppose I should have written it down."

"Exactly. And all my brother said in his unfortunate delirium was indeed written down by a government transcriptionist."

"Then that's our man!" I all but shouted, excitement growing.

"Alas, I know this individual, a Sub-Commander Herbert Fullerton-Barnes, a faithful officer in Her Majesty's clandestine services, as prudent and circumspect with his secret-keeping as any man alive. No, the code was not passed to the Séance Society by him."

I confess again my thoughts wanted to skip backward and assign supernatural agency to the matter, and in particular the fact that the code was only "half-heard" when its claimed source, Holmes' deceased sister, Anna, had been hard of hearing. But I did not give voice to these worries, only asked: "Then are we back to square one?"

"Hardly," Holmes said, "for I know how the feat was done, and in due time I shall tell you."

"So they are all frauds?" I asked, of the Séance Society.

"No, I think not," he surprised me by saying. "To be certain there are frauds here, Watson, but also true believers, and those who are self-convinced of their own paranormal gifts, however unfounded that conviction. When one seeks verification of a talent, one will go to great lengths to find confirmation for it. As for the clientele who come here, they, rather like the faithful who travel to Lourdes, are determined not to leave without laying claim to some justifying miracle, in whatever form it suggests itself to be. It is a sad business on the whole, and I think the Society is a conglomeration of quacks, frauds, charlatans, and those genuinely deluded by hope, with a free mingling of all types in between. Some I hold to be quite genuine in that they do not seek to misrepresent themselves, and tragically those types are the most easily fooled by those who profit by misleading them."

"Like Hilltower?"

"I am coming to see he is among the most credulous and hope-filled of all, nor is he as firmly in control here as circumstances suggest."

"Who is?" I demanded.

"Miss Markham, and her mother, whom I have not yet met. While they seem underlings to Hilltower, the 'Chief Minister' of the Society, and while Hightower controls much here in a material sense, I believe he has come to rely more and more on the claimed abilities of that charismatic girl, and a mother I believe we will find quite the manipulator."

"You spoke of Miss Markham being afraid. Whom does she fear?"

"Our unseen enemy here, Watson, who stealthily moves against us, but who unknowingly draws nearer to my net."

I thought on this, then spoke what lay heavy on my mind. "Holmes, I simply must say it, for all your dismissing what goes on in this place, there have been many vast coincidences among the claims of supernatural dealings."

Holmes shrugged, "Who is to say in the end, Watson, though alongside sheer luck I think a mixture of research into the lives of clients, guesswork, skill at observation, and simple manipulation of perception can explain much, if not perhaps all."

"So there *is* a gray area?"

"A small one, Watson, for life is a condition which holds many mysteries. I do not, however, say that the proclaimed mediums here possesses the ability to communicate with the dead, nor the dead to speak to the living. In all my life I have found no proof or even convicting evidence to suggest such."

"But have you ever truly looked deeply into the claims of spiritualists?"

He took on a distant expression before he confessed something to me I had not known, nor suspected.

"After my sister's death, Watson, amid the grief that overtook my parents and brother, and which, try though I might, even infected me, I had an aunt who was a devotee of such arts, and involved my parents for a time with a medium my aunt claimed was among the most adept at communication with those lost to our mortal world."

He turned away, a look of anger and sorrow finding its way to his face. "It was blatant fraudulence, of course, and Mycroft and I saw through it at once, the medium chirping out a stereotypical little girl's voice that bore no resemblance to that of my learned little sister, a trumpet sounding nearby, the table lifting off the floor, clearly by use of concealed wires.... It was insulting, yet for several weeks, my mother consumed all the supposed messages from Anna like a starving beggar would a crust of bread cast from a Lord's table, all to the tune of several pounds per session."

"And what happened?"

"Eventually my mother, even through her haze of grief, allowed herself to be guided by my brother and me, and we attended beside her and exposed the deceptions....which provided my first lesson, Watson, in the paradox that truth may at times be crueler than the lullaby of a fabrication, for, disillusioned, our mother dropped farther still into drear melancholy, and was gone within six months, her heart shattered by loss."

I stared at him, taking in this revelation and all it spoke of. "No wonder you hold spiritualists with such...well, with far more than the mere disdain I have seen you show for others you have pursued in the past."

"I despise them, Watson, and their vile art."

"And now someone is using spiritualists to try to wound you."

"It is so."

"Above all," I assured him, "I accept that Slade was guilty, and you shall never be proven wrong there."

"I thank you, Watson, for he was as guilty a man as ever I brought to justice. And now," he said, his desire to speak further depleted, "we have just enough time for a salubrious walk about the lovely old wood I spy ahead, and then, I believe we have a séance to prepare for, and a further demonstration of the undeniable talents—of a sort—of the charming young Miss Markham, who is absolutely an utterly remarkable individual, though likely to her eventual detriment."

Without waiting for me, he set off toward the trees at a rapid clip, his heart perfectly content.

Rather than go out into the house the rest of the day, I stayed in my room and wrote several letters to friends in London, and family in Scotland, and as the sky to the west took on a purple stain, as if from a watercolourist's brush, I rapped on Holmes' door, and found him seated on the edge of his bed, one leg crossed, his hands limply at his lap. He gazed up, and I knew he had long been lost in deep contemplation of the issues of the case, and strategies with which to overcome them.

"So it is time, my dear Watson," he said flashing a quick

smile and rising from his seat on the bed. "Have you girded your loins for battle, and set your heart upon the road ahead?"

"As ready as any old campaigner," I answered.

Holmes led me out into the hall and with no hesitation in his step, took us downstairs to the spacious room which by arrangement had been appointed for the event ahead, no less than a contest of logic and artifice, Holmes had dubbed it on our walk earlier in the day.

At the door to the room stood a young woman I had not yet met, short and broad at the hips, her face alive with fascination, and from this I took her to be one of the members of the Society, employed here in a capacity Holmes disdainfully dubbed "minions."

"Gentlemen," she called as we approached, "how glad we are all that you have come. I am Miss Renner, and Minister Hilltower has tasked me with showing you to your places."

"We are assigned spots then?" Holmes said almost mockingly. "We may not sit where we choose?"

"I am afraid we have found it aids the mediums, and their drawing of energy, if there is a certain prearranged order to seating within the séance-chamber."

Holmes was about to reply, likely with some sarcasm, when across the room, unseen my me to that point owing to the thick dimness within, Hilltower called over, "It's quite all right, Miss Renner, as Mr. Holmes and his friend are our most honoured guests today, we shall allow them to sit where-so-ever they like, save only the head of the table, where our medium herself shall be when she arrives in a few moments, still being presently involved in astral preparation."

He approached us, and extended his hand, which I took, and Holmes, again, found reason not to, in this instance diligently examining the floor under the table.

Hilltower laughed and said, "We in the British Séance Society do not employ trickery of any kind, sir. The flooring is quite solid, I assure you."

As if taunting him by rejecting his words, Holmes knelt

and tapped on the floor in several places. So it is," he agreed upon rising, "though I doubted this little. I think the art here at Rising Dawn is above the parlour tricks one might find elsewhere."

"Well," said Hightower his smile still in place, "I am glad to hear you say so. Soon I hope you may express the sentiment with stronger confidence. We mean, Mr. Holmes, to leave you convinced today that the strongest possible evidence exists that the greatest truth in all of life is that life has no ending."

Looking hard at the leader of the Society, Holmes replied coldly, "To that end, I bid you not to cling too tightly to your hopes."

"Oh, where Miss Markham is concerned, there is often very little room left for doubt."

"You hold her as talented as that?" Holmes inquired.

"For her age and relative lack of experience, she is a prodigy beyond precedent in my long career. The heights to which she shall ascend shall dazzle the world entire. Why, I do not doubt it shall be through her abilities that before century's end all of mankind are awakened to the truths we have so long struggled to impart. We stand, gentlemen, on the brink of a new age, and the sun is close to rising."

Holmes' face demonstrated what he thought of this, and without looking in the direction, he took hold of one of the fine chairs from its place around the table, and pulled it out before taking a seat. I chose the one to his immediate right, and waited.

As if on cue several members of the Séance Society entered the room, in an almost processional fashion, and took up places at, I caught at once, the four ordinal points of the compass, east, west, north and south. There were two men and two women, and each of the devotees wore, I noted, clothing of a different colour, corresponding, perhaps, to the direction they represented. One of the women had red hair worn loose, the other was older and her dark tresses streaked with gray. The men were both bearded, though one's beard was as long and full as a hermit's, though his grooming somewhat better.

As for Hilltower, he took a spot at the table's foot, and sat composed with an eager expression on his face. He appeared, I noted, like a man in church, about to hear some great sermon. I sought out mendacity in his eyes, and did not, so far as I could discern, find it. He was, I told myself again, a true believer....

"Are Watson and I to be the sole guests of the event this evening?" Holmes asked our host.

"It is an honour we bestow on you," Hilltower told him. "That way the energies may be that much more focused."

"Why is there a need for this 'focus'" Holmes asked, "when it was my understanding that the spirit of the man I allegedly sent innocent to the gallows stalks the young lady at all times."

"Unfortunately that is true," said Hilltower, "yet we thought it a courtesy that the accusations the departed shall doubtless make be unfurled without an audience to hear them."

"I," Holmes scoffed, "have nothing to hide in the matter of seeing justice done to a child-murderer. And if your concern for my reputation stands so keen, why did you feed the slanderous story to a newspaper reporter to publish before the world?"

"Again, Mr. Holmes," said Hilltower, appearing genuinely troubled by the broaching of the topic, "that was never our intent. We were as duped and misrepresented by that cad as you were."

"Somehow I doubt that," Holmes said. "But as it happens, sir, I believe your explanation, and do not believe the agent of the orchestration against my good name was yourself."

"I thank you," Hilltower told him.

"No," Holmes added almost lazily, knowing full well the effect it would have on our host, "I believe your Society is not as unanimously dedicated to the same function as you think, and that you have some within who are opportunists, laboring toward their own goals, including the undermining of my reputation in the public eye."

"That can never be," Hilltower thundered, showing a contrary emotion for the first time. "Our mediums should detect at once if there were...traitors in our midst."

"Poor fellow," Holmes chuckled almost cruelly. He added:

"It is of no matter, for what is done is done, and the last word has not yet been had."

Leaving our host in a rather more ruffled state than he'd been upon entering the room, all discussion was ended at this moment by the opening of the door to the foyer, and the entrance of a frankly beautiful woman of earliest middle years, her dress fine and fashionable, her hair coiffed, as if she had newly emerged from a dressers' salon.

Surely Miss Markham's mother, I thought, and my noting was confirmed as a few feet behind the woman came a smaller and somehow even prettier version of her elder, the supposed prodigy among mediums, Miss Markham herself.

Removing my eyes from the mother, I stared at the girl across the low lighting of the room and saw a good deal of confident self-possession in her bearing and even in her proud gaze. Here is one, thought I, who has become used to acclaim, even adoration. She is a star in her chosen firmament, one who holds herself to be on the brink of a fine future. I also thought of Holmes' suggestion that she should one day be her own undoing.

Hilltower rose as the pair entered and crossed the room to them. He kissed the hand of the older woman, and bowed to the younger. "Mrs. Markham, Miss Markham," he said almost fawningly, clearly delighted at their presence, glee bubbling in him, eager for what was to come.

"Minister Hilltower," said Mrs. Markham, and I detected a half-concealed touch of Yorkshire in her words, "you will be happy to hear that my daughter's astral energies *surge* today, and that the stars above are propitious for our undertaking, as is her every internal humour. She has refrained from speaking for much of today so as not to deplete her *prana*, and shall offer to your guests from London the fullest demonstration of her—" here she turned her face toward Holmes, "—*piercing* talents."

"Splendid!" Hilltower cried. "Then all is as perfect as one could ever hope."

He showed Mrs. Markham to a place just behind the chair

at the table's head, where she was to stand, then scooted the chair out for Miss Markham, and pushed it carefully in for her, less as like a host than some doting uncle seeing to a favoured niece.

In another instant Hilltower had returned to his own chair, and odd it was to see one so young at the place of honour at the table's head.

"Let there be silence," Mrs. Markham called out, behind her daughter. "Adelia's reach *outward* must not be disturbed at this juncture."

She retreated a foot away from the girl, who sat still as a statue in the ornate, carved chair, breathing deeply before releasing long, slow exhalations. Gradually, as if falling asleep, her eyes began to lower til fully closed, and her mouth fell open just a small degree, as if she were silently saying: "Oh." There seemed something of total relaxation coming over her, and in this state she remained for perhaps two full minutes, and within the room there was utter stillness.

It all vanished at once, as with a jerk the girl's body seemed to spasm, and her head fall against her chest, and then continue forward until it rested on the tabletop, her entire form as limp as if all life had abruptly departed her. Even her lips seemed to part, as if lost to direction, showing perfectly white teeth. Beside me I espied Holmes was watching carefully, though with an aura of evaluation rather than my own state of marveling at what I saw.

What came next was stranger still, for the girl began to fold upward, as if her body were being filled from the floor up, so that she rose back to a sitting position rather like a tube being filled with compressed air, or—-the uneasy thought struck me—rather like a cobra lifting itself from a *fakir's* basket.

Miss Markham, her eyes still shut, her face as limp as one trapped in deepest slumber, was now siting fully upright, and finally her fists contracted, the first movement of her hands in minutes, and her face contorted, as if in deep pain, so that she, eyes still shut, thrust back her head, and a little cry issued from her lips, like a gasp of one suddenly struck a shocking blow. Her head twisted in several directions, grotesquely, and finally came to be held erect and upright as normal, though somehow the pose of her head and her body was not entirely as it had been when first she sat down. It was, I noted with some involuntary disquiet, as if another person entirely sat there across from us, five feet away, and no longer the girl who'd daintily taken her seat in the chair

"My hands, Mother!" the girl abruptly gasped. "Secure them! It will be necessary for the detective's safety!"

I could not imagine what this meant, but the older woman then stepped forward and fastened cuffs onto either of the girl's wrists, a sight which discomfited me for being so wrong. As Mrs. Markham did so, two attendants from the Society left their places and moving with practiced order, fixed long bolts through cuffs of steel on the chair's legs, and into holes in the floor which I had not noticed, effectively imprisoning Miss Markham where she sat.

"Good! Good..." the girl exclaimed, her voice from far away as some struggle appeared to come upon her, her body rocking, almost convulsing, her arms yanking at the cuffs, making the chair groan against the bolts which held it fast to the floor. And then I felt my hair all but stand on end, for the sound which issued from the girl's mouth was truly among the most terrible noises I had ever encountered. It was all I could do to stay in my chair, the outcry motivating some call to action in me, to aid one who would emit such a pain-cry, or to flee, I knew not which. Holmes however continued to sit still as ever, merely watching... staring with a burning intensity at Miss Markham.

"You!" a voice as unlike that of a young girl as could be imagined broke out of Miss Markham's mouth. "You betrayer! You liar! You fraud! Holmes I speak to you! I so name you! You who sit here by me now, my murderer! My accuser! He who sent me to an undeserved death, when all my life lay before me, my prime just entered, my career in art as assured as God's own promise! I died, Sherlock Holmes, because you told the world your arrogant falsehoods, and I will destroy you as you destroyed me!"

Whether it was in the rules of the Society for a guest to speak at this point in things or silence was still the rule, the atmosphere in the room was suddenly shattered when Holmes laughed deeply and long, the sound contrasting the manic outcries of the girl across from us, yet somehow nearly as terrible for being mocking.

Holmes said, "If I thought it were truly the murderer Slade which sat across from me, I would expect him to know certain things, would I not?"

The voice raging out from within the girl roared, "Haughty man! I remember all things from my life, you murderer, and I know much from yours, for I have trailed you since the hour of my undeserved execution! I know where it was you went on that foggy morning last month, into the north of the city, and at whose grave you sat."

Holmes's eyes grew flinty, but he challenged, "Indeed, it seems *someone* followed me there."

"And shall I tell then what words you spoke to the raw rock of your sister's headstone? 'Oh, Anna,' you said while standing above that small grave, 'it is a hard world from which you were spared.' Those were among the words you said."

There was a certain dark joy in the tone with which the medium spoke this charge.

"You will have to do better than that," Holmes taunted. "If you claim to be Slade, tell me something gnostic from his past, something revealed which it might impress me to hear. Tell me the name of the woman in the portrait Slade entitled 'The Hidden Rose.'"

The voice laughed and said in low tones, "Oh, her? A diversion from my past. You'd have me put a name to that little rabbit I kept in her garret and speak of Miss Nan Owens, plain but fetching?"

"Indeed, I could scarcely describe her better," said Holmes, a light in his eyes. "And in the interest of fair play I might divulge now that I visited this woman the day before I departed London, having uncovered her existence long ago, in the time I was investigating Slade, before his trial. Hidden though he sought to keep her, her existence was not long a mystery to me, but then little to which I turn my mind ever is."

"And did she tell you how my death broke her heart?" the voice demanded.

"She did, and also how the lack of those funds deposited in her account each month from the time of Slade's 'keeping' of her as his mistress were sorely missed. Indeed her financial liberty itself was at stake, til another benefactor came into her life and offered the same allowance, save only that this party asked less of her than had the odious artist. In his case, he wished only for whatever secret and intimate details of Slade as might be known to her, all with a mind to building up a deep reservoir of knowledge regarding the late murderer. Whoever do you imagine this party might be?"

"What that trollop did after my life was stolen by you is of no consequence to me," replied the voice, though now I beheld some difference in it, a faltering of confidence, as if this had all been unknown and had left the situation less settled.

"Oh, yes," said Holmes, "I too found this fact most curious, or perhaps I should say, *most telling.*"

"You murdered me!" shouted the voice, returning now to its apparent rages.

"The woman was so much for sale that despite the promises of confidence she made to the party who bribed her for her knowledge, she gladly spilled all to me when I offered her a mere one-pound note. Included in this service was her deft description of this individual who had come to her for information."

Here my eyes went to Hilltower, though I saw the man was listening every bit as rapt and slightly puzzled as was I.

Holmes said pressing his attack: "Really, did you hope to dazzle me today with some panoply of seemingly unknowable facts regarding Slade's life, which you planned to sit there and unfurl toward me, one by one, til I was battered down with belief in your claims to host that murderer's spirit?"

Oddly, I saw it was not toward Miss Markham that Holmes spoke, but outwardly across the room itself.

"You cheated me of life!" the voice raged, and now Miss Markham's entire body shook with agitation, rocking back and forth in her seat in a most violent display of sheer emotion that had begun to remind me of a temper tantrum. "Thus I will destroy you!"

"Oh, your benefactor will certainly try," answered Holmes, "for his efforts began with that leaked newspaper story, a thing which caught even Hilltower by surprise, after he, ever-eager for publicity for his movement, accepted the reporter's request to come here, where it was soon leaked to him by 'someone' the story of the prodigy Miss Markham, beset by the tormenting spirit of a man brought falsely to justice by the great Sherlock Holmes, calculating that a story mired in the supernatural would reach a wider audience than one set in any other foundation. It was the opening salvo of what I have scant doubt was my foe's planned campaign of ruination against me. But he made a mistake, for via a description from the woman he sought to use to undermine me, I immediately identified him. He is here with us now."

There was an electricity of surprise in the room, and not because of the medium and her demonstrations.

"*You will die!*" thundered Miss Markham, as she continued to contort her body within its shackles.

"Oh, do give that up, child," said Holmes evenly, speaking now as if to a misbehaving infant, "it has grown tiresome."

Incredibly, the girl fell still and her eyes opened and went to Holmes, her face looking far more natural now, no longer the frowning mask of ire she had previously shown. The change was remarkable, and her expression was almost one of insult, as if she'd been slapped.

She has been spoiled for too long, I noted.

"Enough, really," continued Holmes, "enough."

He rose and I felt a jolt go through the air, from Hilltower most of all, who stated, "Please, sir, you must stay seated during the session, lest you cause deep harm to the medium, and the spirit as well!"

Ignoring him Holmes crossed the room til he was standing before the man with the long, wild beard, to whom Holmes said avidly, "Did you truly think I would not recognize you, Archer?"

In reply, the man leapt brutally at Holmes and there was suddenly a violent contest between the two, with he whom Holmes had called Archer producing a dagger from his belt, eliciting screams from the women, and in a pathetic side show, the girl, Miss Markham, still affixed theatrically to her chair by cuffs of apparently genuine construction, screamed, "Mother! Mother! Let me go! I am caught here!"

As the mother worked to free her child, I ran to Holmes' side, passing Hilltower, who gaped as if at a complete loss, his authority dashed on the rocks of the unforeseen, but I was not required, for with his skill in those Japanese fighting arts he often spoke of having acquired through some mysterious means, Holmes knocked away the blade from his enemy's hand, and soon had him pinned to the ground, though his foes was a strong man and a formidable opponent.

Reaching down and grabbing the man's beard, Holmes ripped it loose, revealing it to be a stage accoutrement fixed on with paste.

"Ah," he cried triumphantly, amusement in his voice, as he breathed hard at his exertion, "I perceive you still sport the scar across your lips I gave you when last you sought to attack me with a blade, Archer! Some fools will never learn not to challenge with their betters!"

On my own initiative, I hurried over to the chair and took the handcuffs from Mrs. Markham's hold, then passed back to Holmes and fitted them onto the wrists of this man, Archer, then helped Holmes convey him to a seat.

When next I glanced up, I noted Miss Markham and her mother were no longer in the room.

"I do not understand any of this!" Hilltower cried.

"It is simple," said Holmes, "you have been used. Your movement I may have dubbed a fallacy based on misguided hopes, but you are an honest fool for all that, as are many here with you, though not all, and Mrs. Markham and her daughter are cons, sir, out to rise through the undeniable talents for theatricality the daughter shows. You were easily taken in, and they have risen high by their cunning ways."

"But they have been proven in our trials and tests!" Hilltower whined.

"We shall perhaps speak more of this later," Holmes replied, almost with gentleness, "but first..."

He looked at the man shackled before him and said, "You shouldn't have returned to England, Archer, as now it's the rope for you."

"I think otherwise," the man, Archer said, a sneer on his features above the small but savage-looking scar which divided his lips.

"A telegram which Watson shall no doubt be good enough to go into town and send for me will see the first stages of achieving that end put into gear," Holmes said. "You'll spend tonight in a cell in London, and tomorrow I've no doubt both my brother Mycroft and some representatives of the government will wish to be present as Scotland Yard questions you about your past acts of treason."

The man Archer boasted. "I have friends in higher places than you know."

"Oh, yes, Mycroft has mentioned those, and also told me that your usefulness to them ended long ago, and they may now find it more convenient if you were to be disposed of by British justice. Relations between Her Majesty's government and that of the Kaiser are rather warmer than they were earlier in the decade when you were betraying your country on a routine basis and selling German agents the secrets that passed through your hands at the Foreign Office."

And now Archer shifted uncomfortably, and beneath his

efforts to leave his expression blank, I saw worry when he claimed: "I shall be looked-out for."

"I don't think Berlin will wish to jeopardize current cordiality by having reminders of a more contentious past from the early '80s resurface. I think I may confidently state that you'll be convicted of a plethora of past and current crimes against the Empire, and hanged at Reading before the end of summer. Perhaps in time some misguided fraud of a medium will likewise decry your own innocence as you have the artist Slade's, though I greatly doubt anyone will bother to think of you when you are gone."

Holmes stepped away, and leaning down across the fine old table, wrote out a note in pencil, which he handed to me and said, "I am not certain whom I can trust among the staff or membership here, for I am not sure how many have fallen into Archer's pay, so Watson, may I trouble you to go into town and see this sent off to my brother, at Whitehall?"

Somehow it felt refreshing, almost cleansing, to leave behind the house and all the subterfuge there, and find myself in the clear air of the starry night. In town I saw the message sent away at the train station, and returned close to midnight, where Holmes had moved his prisoner into the parlour, where he sat alone with him, Archer looking decidedly less belligerent than he had when I left.

"Watson!" Holmes called, "I thank you for your troubles. I have just been having the *most* enlightening conversation with this traitor to his Queen and country."

"I have said nothing!" Archer growled back.

"And yet you have revealed much even so," Holmes said smiling, pleased.

"Holmes," I said, "who is he? I gather he is a traitor but..."

"This specimen of villainy passed through my professional life before I knew you, Watson," Holmes explained. "It was 1880, a year before you returned from Afghanistan, and came to Baker Street, and took involvement with me in the case you would alliteratively dub 'A Study In Scarlet.' Mycroft and his colleagues had become aware of an informant within the Foreign Office, and enlisted my aid in identifying this person. My investigation revealed this faithless minion of Berlin to be none other than the man who sits shackled before you, a soul willing to sell out his nation for irregular sums paid him through the network of secret agents the Germans had scattered throughout London."

I fixed this Archer with a disapproving stare, feeling a condition of loathing swell inside me. "Of all men, those who betray others are the worst," I stated.

"Indeed!" said Holmes, before telling me all the rest.

It seemed that while Holmes identified Archer as the culprit behind the leak of sensitive information, the man retained enough friends in the German spy network to see him secreted out of the country and into hiding abroad, but so bent on revenge against Holmes was this vindictive man that he bided his time and had apparently reappeared the previous autumn with the workings of a plan in his mind. In the papers he had read of the case of Slade, the child-killer, and of the fiendish murderer's maintenance of his innocence to the end, and exploited this in a plot to undermine Holmes' reputation, and destroy him before the public by painting him as an overly-confident amateur who sent an innocent man to die so that he might further his own reputation.

To this end, knowing that general fascination with mediums and spiritualism had arisen again after lying fallow for a generation, Archer concocted a plan involving the use of "psychics" and set out to learn all he could of the private life of the condemned man, Slade, bribing his former mistress, and plunging into whatever he could himself find out, so that seemingly personal details which only Slade might know could be leaked, lending weight to the medium's claim that it was Slade speaking from the void, intent on clearing his name from beyond the grave.

He quietly sought out the best medium to use for his ends, and settled on young Miss Markham, whose mother was as greedy a woman as ever lived. She had come from humble origins in Yorkshire, and birthed her daughter out of wedlock at a young age, and had pulled herself upward by ruthless schemes, finally coaching her child around age fourteen in the theatrical arts of the supposed trance medium. Against Mrs. Markham's charms and her daughter's skill at the con, poor Hilltower, "an honest fool" Holmes termed him, was completely taken in, as he had doubtless been by a number of others before her.

And so as Holmes revealed, Archer had met with the Markham woman and her daughter, and coached them in stories concerning Slade, and then secured for himself a place in Rising Dawn, posing as a true believer of means. The work begun, the story of the marauding spirit of Slade was proliferated til Hilltower reached out to Baker Street, and the story soon found itself printed by a bribed reporter who drew Holmes forth to the Society's headquarters, to solve matters once and for all.

"The rest, Watson," he finished, "you know."

"No, actually," I said, "I don't. How did Miss Markham know of your visit to your sister Anna's grave? And however did she know of the clandestine code you shared with Mycroft, incomplete though you tell me it was?"

"Would you care to explain these matters, Archer?" Holmes inquired of his prisoner, bringing him into the discussion at last.

His brow curled in a look of brooding hatred reminiscent of a summer thunderstorm, Archer said, "You think yourself omniscient, so you tell me how that was done."

The taunting challenge in his tone was unmistakable.

"Certainly," cried Holmes, pleased, "nothing simpler! You held these dabblings your greatest tricks, things meant to confuse me and lower my confidence by implanting doubt, yet in both aims, you failed! The matter of my soliloquy at my sister's grave—and soliloquy it was, for one cannot speak to the dead—well, I am a man who does his best to keep irregular habits, finding it safer that way, though one ritual has come into place in my life, that of visiting Anna's plot at Highgate on the anniversary of her passing. I do it for my parents' sake, for the practice was their own, and I continue it out of a sense of filial duty. Archer simply waited in some place of concealment nearby, Watson, unnoticed by my normally well-attuned senses, both because Highgate is rarely an empty place, with mourners and groundsmen passing about, and because...."

"Because of the nature of your visit you were focused on other matters," I finished for him, sensing it would not be an easy thing to confess that even a duty to family would distract his keen sense of awareness of his surroundings.

"Indeed. And so in short, this verminous man listened in and relayed my words to the medium in his employ, Miss Markham, or rather more likely, to her mother, who was the girl's overseer, manager, and mentor, as well as her sole parent. Her sense of control over the girl being total, Watson....for now, though I think Mrs. Markham might soon find herself cast aside by her ambitious daughter, whose beauty outshines even her own."

"The cemetery is simple enough, but what about the code?" I reminded him. "That was the real puzzler in all this."

"Equally simple, but more disturbing. As he boasted, Archer retains his 'friends' in the German secret service, and clearly one—as I shall be sure to make Mycroft aware—is well-placed enough to be able to access certain sensitive internal files, including those which held the record of Mycroft's feverish ravings, among which were the bits of the code he babbled, though incompletely, as we saw. There is nothing anywhere in this case which stands inexplicable, and requires no forays into the preternatural to explain it."

I felt a deep sense of ease at this assurance, and a pleasant feeling of comfort was restored to me. The world was still a place of rationality, after all.

Before morning several coaches pulled up front, and Mycroft and a number of men with ill-defined positions within the government emerged in the company of Inspector Arthur Sanders of Scotland Yard, who, with several stern-faced constables from special branch, took custody of Archer, who cried out predictable invectives against Holmes before being taken off.

Mycroft stayed long enough to speak privately with his brother, a meeting I was not privileged to attend, but which doubtless saw Holmes passing along news of Archer's actions and his source within the Foreign Office. Mycroft and all who came with him were away again within an hour of their arrival.

As for Holmes, he asked me to accompany him as he sought out Hilltower in his office, where the so-called Chief Minister of the British Séance Society bore a look of utter dejection.

"They are gone," he said simply, "Mrs. Markham and her remarkably talented daughter have fled, seemingly as soon as things fell apart at the séance."

"I think you will find that throughout their time here among you, they were always prepared to depart at a moment's notice," revealed Holmes. "It is their custom in the sordid life they have chosen."

"Good riddance to them," I opined, causing Hilltower to glance up at me hurt in his eyes. "Surely you don't still consider the girl's powers genuine?" I demanded.

"She may have fallen to the allure of a bad man's wiles, Doctor," said Hilltower, with a pained tremble in his tone, "but I will forgive her her indiscretions there, for she is, to answer your question, beyond any doubt the most skilled trance medium of her generation."

I looked to Holmes, who shrugged with a lack of interest. Some men were never to be convinced of the obvious, I thought.

But Hilltower was not done, for he said, "You doubt me, I see, but what if I told you the girl, for her entrance examination here revealed to me, the location in my childhood home of a ring my mother dropped, and which she, while in this physical dimension thought lost? It was for all these years within a flower vase in her room, where it must have spilled off her finger while Mother was unaware."

"Did you examine the ring and satisfy yourself it was the same one, and genuine?" Holmes asked. "For it could have been planted there more recently by Mrs. Markham, you must admit."

"Absolutely am I certain it was genuine. It even bore the same inscription within the band. The girl could not have known of this private inscription, or guessed it was there, as it had been for three decades."

Holmes refused to be impressed, though I thought back to his admission that there were oddities in the world that defied easy explanation.

"There were many more wondrous things the girl did," Hilltower claimed. "Things she knew, and many departed spoke through her to their loved ones' complete satisfaction. She was taken in by a bad man, yes, but she herself is no fraud."

"I speak as one who is not partisan, sir," Holmes began, "though I offer you this advice in parting. If you wish to be the girl's benefactor, assuming you ever again find her, you should separate her from her mother, who is the serpent in the garden where her daughter is concerned, and who has already done much harm to young Miss Markham, and has, I fear, bent the course of her life in a dangerous direction. I doubt, however, that you shall ever encounter either of them again."

Here Hilltower emitted a sigh of sadness, and it was in that state that we left the poor fellow.

As we sat on the train back to London, each tired after the long night, I found myself thinking back over all which had transpired over the preceding days, and was left wondering at the future of the British Séance Society, filled as it was with some who were genuine in their convictions about the arcane, and outwardly evangelical in their dogmatic views.

Then I recalled the odd sincerity with which the mediums who had greeted us upon our arrival, Madame Bajusz, and especially Miss Curlew, had spoken of my own future. It had seemed as if the latter woman had been much affected when she told me my future would be marked by "twin tragedies."

I pondered this the rest of the distance to London, and

write this account today as one who has, for a year now, been a widower, and who was for a single hour the father of a son who should have been called James. I know not even now if the prediction of double tragedy made concerning my future was coincidental or otherwise, but in hindsight there is a keen temptation to fit those prophecies to these later events, and marvel at their cruel accuracy.

But what good can come from that?

Sherlock Holmes

And The

Case

Of The

Snowdonia

Werewolf

C. Thorne

THE CASE OF THE SNOWDONIA WEREWOLF

The first snows of the season had fallen that evening in north Wales, dusting the cold earth with crystalline whiteness, slick underfoot. Strong as the backs of giants, the rugged Cambrian Mountains, which rose above the village of Cwm Ystwyth, bringing a false twilight an hour early each night, blocked the salt-scented winds from the Irish Sea, so that dense mists often arose with sunset, mixed with peat-smoke from low-slung chimneys, to lie in eerie profusion, clinging in every hollow of a valley removed by a league's travel from the county road.

All was silent in this village where outside eyes rarely witnessed that which transpired within, and thus many of the "old ways" remained, carried over from pre-Christian days, and the worship of the heavens themselves.

Inside an ancient public house, warmed by a low peat fire and lit by the glow of lanterns locals had brought with them, their only defense against the darkness on their uneasy walks home to farmhouses scattered across miles thereabout, whispers had passed among those gathered under the uneasy calm, though panic threatened to grip them all, for far from the gas lights of cities, suspicious as a rule, they had begun to look to those tales from their history, and around the ever-moving shadows of the village's single public house, The Gray Man---*Y Dyn Llwyda* in the old tongue---a name had begun to find its way into thoughts of recent troubles, and grew more common with every tumbler of whisky or pint of ale which was poured.

The matter of a recent outbreak of livestock killings that had plagued the community during each of the last two moons had no peer as a worry in every heart there that night, though it was not til the memory, nearly a month-old, of an inhuman howl he'd heard echoing through the isolated valley had sent shivers down the venerable spine of one of those there, that anyone spoke of the thing dominating all their thoughts.

"I'll say what we all know," the iron-haired farmer spoke in a carrying tone of voice, a pint of bitter clutched in his knotted hand, his face grim with the stoicism that lay below its surface, for toughness was a thing much valued in a valley where even babies were taught early not to cry.

There was an increase of tension in the air as all waited, wondering if at last someone was to say it in the open.

"From the heathen days of witches and druids," the old man called, "'tis that curse of elder times which our forefathers warned us of. Gone these eighty years, the beast, with its blood-hunger, has returned from its sleep high up on Snowdon.... *Yr*

Wyddfa as the mountain is called in the old tongue."

A dead silence followed his words, and then first one, then several voices raised in agreement.

"*Oes*, oh *oes*, tis true…"

"The *werewolf* has come again!" the old man proclaimed, and a discernible shudder passed through the little pub.

After a moment it was clear that all believed the man's grim words, and to the very core of their souls there was fear. Sheep were the livelihood of nearly every family, and by the dozen each of the last two months sheep had been found ripped apart, showing no cut-marks of a blade, merely the result of frightful strength, and of teeth. The marks found upon the remains were those of a man, yet seemingly a man with the curving fangs of a beast.

For two months now this had happened as the night skies stood alight with an ivory glow, and the next, much dreaded, full moon was but five days out.…

"What can we do against this cursed thing?" cried one woman, thin, red-faced, her lean body solid from years labouring for life itself against the stony soil of the valley below the mountains. "What help is there when all our prayers haven't driven this demon away?"

Agreement, nervous and strong, broke the air, for souls with little to cling to in existence save pride itself stood frightened, and by admitting so together at last, their numbers alleviated their collective shame.

"The stories say we can't kill it," one man called out. "Only wait for it to get its fill, then return to its long sleep in a cave hidden somewhere under the mountains."

"*Oes!*" came cries of agreement.

"T'was said by my grand-nain when I was a little girl," a woman with red hair all but shouted, her fear extreme, "it must run its course, appearing for no reason save that which is known to its devil-heart, departing when its dark covenant is fulfilled, leaving misery and hardship and death behind."

"It will ruin us all!" cried a man.

"Tis God's punishment for our sins," said another woman.

There were thoughtful murmurs at this, each questioning his own spirit, wondering if it was some un-expiated transgression he had personally committed.

"Maybe it's the work of some secret witch, who has summoned it!" offered a timid young woman, her brown eyes darting about as she wondered if one who stood around her might be the agent of the dark foe of all goodness in the world.

"Are we helpless then?" a young father asked, his thoughts thinking of the modest flock in his fields, the sale of whose wool fed his two small children, a flock he could ill afford to lose when the beast came back, as he knew it would.

From the back of the pub a man moved to the center of the floor. He was of not quite middle-years, no more remarkable than any there save for the fact a half-decade ago he had gone to Cardiff to study for two years, before summoned back to take over his father's farm, and care for his mother and sisters. He was known locally as one endowed with a degree of outside education, a copious reader in a community of illiterates whose dawn-to-dusk subsistence-farming left them little time for such undertakings.

With a steady and strong tone that spoke of resolution amid indecision, this man, one William Rhys-Davies, by name, said firmly:

"When in Cardiff five years ago, I enjoyed going to the university's library and reading the periodicals there, especially one called *The Strand*. It contained the most wondrous accounts, written by a Scottish doctor living in London, who told of the remarkable deeds of his friend, a detective who took on the problems of others, and solved seemingly impossible mysteries, never failing. I think if I should write him and tell earnestly of what has befallen here, and which we fear is to occur again next week, he may come, and see things put right."

"How?" asked a one-eyed farmer to his left. "How can even a famous man from London stand before the devil's very offspring?"

"I do not know," Rhys-Davies admitted, "yet if any man can dispel this evil, it is he, as he finds truth amid all matters."

"Who is this man you speak of?" asked a farm-wife, her tawny hair having escaped its lank woolen ribbon so that errant strands were falling low over her pale neck.

It was a question others had wondered as well, and all leaned forward together in eagerness to hear.

"His name," said Rhys-Davies, "is Mr. Sherlock Holmes, of 221B Baker Street, London, and I will write him this very night."

Thus it was that some two days later my friend Sherlock Holmes and I found ourselves urgently invited to the hamlet of Cwm Ystwyth, of which I had never heard, where its people clung to a hard life, as they somehow had for millennia, under the craggy Cambrian Mountains, to investigate one of the most peculiar claims ever to reach us at Baker Street.

"A werewolf, Holmes?" I said with furrowed brow as I finished reading Mr. William Rhys-Davies' letter.

"Wolf-man or man-wolf," said Holmes, "I do not think the word order truly conveys any change in meaning, or menace."

"Imagine someone in 1887 believing in either thing," I said, my feelings uncertain. "Whatever do you make of it?"

Sitting with his long legs stretched out before him, his usual irreproachable posture not in evidence as he slumped that morning in his favourite among the chairs in the parlour of Baker Street.

"I think," he said carefully, "that whatever the case should be, our Welsh correspondent most certainly believes there is some deep and terrible force at work in his community, and his pleas are less ardently expressed than they should have been had he spoken more openly of the fears I believe lay in his heart."

"So it is no prank?"

"None whatsoever."

"How can you be certain of this?"

Here Holmes uncoiled and pulled himself up straight in

the chair, the lethargy of his late-rising dismissed in an instant.

"You see here, Watson," he said, taking the letter back from me and indicating a place with his fingertip, "the broadening strokes in the paragraph in which he lays out the matter after his rather slow build-up to it? That speaks of frankness and worry, even as the long introduction of himself tells me he did not relish arriving at the point of his missive. That likewise indicates the man feels a certain embarrassment to confess the truth of things to me, but knowing that he must all the same."

"I see. Is that all"

"Hardly. I find we are dealing with a man of intelligence, and some education, though an incomplete one."

"Incomplete?"

"I speculate that he once left his native environs and gained some exposure to the offerings of the greater world, but that some tragedy, perhaps, brought him home."

"And why do you say this?"

"Watson," Holmes chided my skepticism, "should you choose to dwell within a rural village in the middle of nowhere had you finished your studies and secured employment options elsewhere?"

I had to concede there. "Oh, yes, well."

"The writing shows he received to some extent a university education, though if you note, the longer he writes, the less in evidence the stylistic penmanship of a college man falls to the loops and cross-hatched punctuations of the rural schoolhouse, a place at the center of his soul no matter how far from it he might have moved at one point in life. This shows he was concentrating less on his letter as he penned that section---the description of the preternatural horror he believes is his people's foe---and that his mind is lodged more firmly in his thoughts on this werewolf of which he must finally bring himself to speak. No, Watson, there is no deceit here, no 'prank,' but rather a frightened man convinced of the truth of every word he writes."

"But a werewolf, Holmes? Who has ever heard of such a thing?"

"On the contrary, my dear Watson," my friend stated as he rose and passed to a nearby bookshelf, where a moment's perusal saw him select a maroon-bound volume and hand it to me.

"*Professor G. W. Ardmore's Bestiary of the Grim and Fantastical*?" I read aloud.

"The definitive classic on the topic of folklore of the mysterious," Holmes replied, "the 1791 edition. Most rare, and a book I have had occasion to consult in a professional capacity more than once over the years, as the Professor was neither a gossip nor a teller of fairy-tales, but a serious scholar whose lifelong medium happened to be the analysis of the odd and arcane from all across Europe, and this stands as his meticulous collection of accounts thereof. His research was impeccable in every particular."

I see," I replied, having rarely heard Holmes offer such un-tempered praise for a writer.

"My point, Watson, is that if you refer to the table of contents you will find an entire chapter devoted to the phenomenon of the lycanthrope, or *verrervulf*, as the Anglo-Saxons dubbed it, and see it is not at all an uncommon feature of rural folklore either in Britain or anywhere in the world."

"But campfire stories of long ago, surely?" I demanded, my face taking on hints of the incredulity I felt within.

"Oh, really, Watson? I refer you then to page 178, and the infamous Beast of Gévaudan, a giant wolf-human hybrid which undeniably terrorized the French countryside as recently as the 1760s, claiming in all some 240 victims in an area of fifty square miles. The creature's killing spree was well attested-to, and undeniable. But perhaps more daunting still is the Wolf-witch of Argyll, in your native land, which in the year 1500 killed twenty-nine Scots of Clan McDuggall, including the chieftain, and shows us our own island is not immune to such visitations."

"You are the most rational of men," I cried, "surely you do

not hold with there being any truth in these stories?"

"It matters little what I believe, Watson," my friend said, replacing the book on the shelf before tamping his pipe with broadleaf from a red-leather pouch, "the fact is these tales show such claims are hardly new, nor are they even particularly uncommon. Four years ago I read an article in *The Bristol Standard* about an attack there near Chester Road, along the waterside, in which a large shaggy mastiff-like creature which walked on two legs mauled a woman, who barely survived. The press had a three-day festival reporting on that. As for what lies at the heart of these accounts, *well.*"

He lit the pipe and inhaled with great relish.

As a doctor I tried to reach some connection between a rational explanation for a phenomenon I had never heard of til that instant, and the apparent reality of such events. "Is it explainable by some...affliction of the mind, perhaps?" I began. "A murderously insane perpetrator's *idee-fixe* centered upon the species *canis lupis*?"

"Perhaps," my friend admitted, "though in the case of the Beast of Gévaudan, a large wolf was eventually tracked and killed, and the attacks abruptly stopped. But was the wolf truly the culprit, or a victim of heated vengeance on his kind by a folk pushed past terror? Should rational thought truly assign such viciousness to one creature, acting alone, absent a pack, setting out into an area many times the natural range of most wolves? Could a single animal truly overwhelm so many human beings, Watson, including armed soldiers?"

"It somehow seems unlikely one wolf could do that," I admitted, "and yet if the attacks ceased, Occam's razor suggests it was so."

"Well said, Watson, for as I oft remark, when the impossible has been eliminated from conjecture, whatever remains must be the truth. Certainly there was nothing preternatural in the creature's taxonomy, but if we allow the possibility that insanity is not merely a human affliction but one which might befall members of the animal kingdom as well, I think the ferocity of this quite natural wolf's predations could well give rise to the mythology of which you so casually read in Professor Ardmore's *Bestiary*, with those the tales of a wolf-man striking pre-Revolutionary France. Likewise, I suggest the stories of such creatures bespeak of those dark imaginings which lie imbedded in the human brain, and rarely more strongly than in rural places, such as Mr. Rhys-Davies' native village of Cwm Ystwyth."

Taking another volume down from the shelf, this time a concise atlas of Britain, a beautifully-illustrated 1885 masterpiece so detailed it neglected nary a hamlet on the island, Holmes flipped to north Wales and peered down a moment before calling out with a chuckle:

"My, my, Watson, Cwm Ystwyth is barely a speck on the map, a collection of a dozen buildings amid outlying farms in the wildest district in all Wales!"

"And you intend to go to this place in pursuit of a creature which surely cannot be real?"

"This matter interests me, Watson," he said, unoffended by my tone, "as such, do you truly need to ask? Of course I do."

"You will go and hunt a *werewolf*?"

I did not know whether to laugh, or worry that some flicker of brain-fever had overtaken my friend.

"I will travel to the ends of the planet to peer into the heart of any mystery which catches my interest," he replied.

"But a wolf-man…?"

"Watson, come now, listen to yourself. It is easy to stand on a bright morning in the heart of the greatest city on the face of the Earth and mock our correspondent's sincere words, but imagine yourself in the dark of night, in the shadow of inaccessible mountains, isolated, the rest of the world a far-away place you shall never visit, and twice with the coming of the full moon, some terror has struck and left behind mutilated and half-consumed animals in its wake. Do you tell me you should be immune from all thoughts of an explanation placed readily into your hands by your trusted ancestors?"

"Perhaps not," I admitted.

"As I have said many times, Watson, there is no supernatural, we may all rest assured of that, but clearly something is afoot in that superstition-cloaked corner of Wales, and I hold it to be a fine use of my energies to learn what it is. As an added bonus I may do a community of farmers some good by my undertaking. Is that truly something for a man of the modern world to mock?"

"Of course not," I said chastened. "My apologies, Holmes, for I was callous in my speaking. But do you mean to leave today?"

"At once," he answered, as he penned a note and sealed it inside an envelope. "In fact I have written my apologies to the warden, Sir Jeddiah Baines-Robinson, of Lancing Prison, who had requested an interview with me on the morrow, and which I shall now have to postpone to some indefinite future time, as this 'Snowdonia Werewolf' sparks my curiosity much more than the warden's claims of an improbable escape artist among his inmates, who slips from his cell to work mischief by night, only to return before dawn. You, are of, course, welcome to come along to mystical Cymru with me...if you do not hold this confrontation of superstition beneath the investment of your time, that is."

"*Holmes*," I chided, "I have said I was sorry for my disdain, and of course I should very much love to go."

"Capital!" my friend the consulting detective exclaimed, as he set in to grab the bag he kept ever-at hand, packed and ready for a moment's hasty departure. "For as *The Plowman's Almanack* shows, the next full moon rises tomorrow. Thus time is of the essence!"

He headed for the door before halting and turning back to me to add:

"Oh, and Watson?"

"Yes?"

"Pray, do bring along your army revolver, and arm yourself as I have...."

I can report that though we left at once, it took Holmes and myself less time to get from London to Wales, than did the remainder of our journey from north Wales to the village of Cwm Ystwyth itself, the former being a simple matter of boarding a train from Victoria Station to Liverpool's Lime Street Station, and a second south to a Welsh town called Bangor, but the rental of a gig and a decent horse so that we might transport ourselves into the Cambrian Mountains was a more protracted and costly affair, and took us til nearly sundown to reach our destination, and only Holmes' keen memorization of the map from the atlas in Baker Street saved us from becoming completely lost amid the unmarked country trails that passed as roadways in that part of the Kingdom.

As we traveled and the sun dipped lower in the sky, finally falling entirely behind towering Snowdon itself, the air grew colder and our surroundings quieter, as we departed an area that was merely rural, and entered a place of absolute isolation. We passed the final distance of about a league from the last road, and set down the final path to Cwm Ystwyth, and rarely in my life had I ever been more grateful to see a collection of buildings as I was that evening when we at last, after many hours, came to the village and pulled up outside a public house there.

Holmes stepped directly inside the pub, and as he entered, all talk ceased and absolute silence rose, as every face on the premises turned toward the two of us, framed as we were in the doorway. I knew visitors were rare in this lonely place, and were more likely to be dubbed "strangers" than anything else, but Holmes seemed unfazed by the stares and cold reception, and simply announced:

"My name is Sherlock Holmes, and I come from London in search of a man named William Rhys-Davies, who has written to me concerning the peculiar problem your village is facing.

Would one among you be this person?"

The change in the house was remarkable, and I could veritably feel the suspicious tension drain from the air, replaced by a sense of hopeful gratitude, as the publican behind the bar, thin-figured but sinewy with muscle---as all within seemed to be---called over, "Welcome, sir! Come in and shut the door, will you not?"

I complied, closing the thick wooden door behind me, as the publican said soberly and with the sternness I have often noticed in the Welsh:

"Glad we are to see you, gentlemen! My name is Owen ab Owen, and this is my place. The man you asked for, Rhys-Davies, is not among us this evening, being home on his farm with his wife, and children, his mother, and his old maid sisters, also in-dwelling there."

"I see!" Holmes replied rather heartily as he stepped forward to receive the pint of ale hospitably gifted to us, as I did my own, though in truth I found it a rather bitter libation.

After taking a long pull off his pint and evincing no objection to its flavour, Holmes turned from the bar toward the large room itself with its stone walls and time-darkened beams overhead, peering for an instant at interior windows, so old the glass had thickened near the bottom, reminding me that all glass was in fact, as a professor of mine had informed me long ago, flowing liquid in a state of constant, albeit inconceivably slow, movement.

"My good people," Holmes began somewhat dramatically, "I see you know something of me, doubtless courtesy of my correspondent, Mr. Rhys-Davies, himself, and what you have likely been told is in fact quite true, I do put an end to mysteries when I encounter them, and bring truth to the fore, where til then only shadows of the unknown had lain. And so shall I do so here in the matter of this supposed werewolf who so troubles your community."

There was a murmur of voices, and through them all I heard one woman say, "Thank Jesus!"

Holmes smiled and said, "The best remedy now, beyond, of course your already having requested my aid, is calm, my dear people, as I find panic does far more harm than the object which inspires it."

His aura of commanding authority rising brilliant as sunshine above the backward trepidations of the locals gathered around us, pints in hand, Holmes stated:

"Who among you might direct my friend, Dr. Watson, here, and myself, to the farm of this aforementioned Mr. Rhys-Davies?"

A plethora of lilting Celtic voices were lifted at once, creating a din in the air that served no purpose save to assault the eardrums, so that Holmes turned back to the publican, Mr. Owen ab Owen, and asked:

"Perhaps, sir, it might be best if I received this vital instruction courtesy of yourself?"

"*Oes*, indeed," said the publican, "glad to assist, sir."

Armed with directions to the Rhys-Davies farmstead, an additional two miles beyond the village, a distance we would be required to travel through a country darkness impenetrable many nights, though illuminated around us by the belly of a chalk-white moon, we set off, and did not need to spark a Lucifer for the lantern. Even when we reached the shadows of the mountains themselves we proceeded through our surroundings, all quite visible as we went down the twisting path which took us from the humble village to the outlying farm.

Within an hour we found ourselves at the gate of what was clearly a well-managed if not especially prosperous holding, with a stone house larger than most we'd passed, and rock fences marking paddocks where sheep and cattle had been brought in for the night. I judged that whatever else may have been said of the writer of the letter which had called us here, Mr. Rhys-Davies was an industrious labourer who valued his holding, and was making the most of what the harsh surroundings offered him.

However, before either Holmes or I could step down from

the gig and make our way to the farmhouse, an irregular undertaking to be sure at so late an hour, we were set upon by a tremendous fit of barking, as two small but fierce sheepdogs came barreling out from the barnyard toward our conveyance, spooking the horse, who rose up a little and flung her front hooves about, showing the whites of her eyes and flattening her ears.

"Calm yourself, old girl!" Holmes called to the beast, who, oddly enough, did seem to be somewhat pacified by his words, and stilled herself.

The dogs meanwhile, black and white with shaggy but sleek fur, the sort of intelligent and hard-working specimens common on farms throughout Britain, circled us, hackles raised, teeth bared, meaning business.

I was wondering what we should do next and was on the verge of raising my voice to cry out for aid from the house, when the door to the same structure opened, and out strode a man armed with a double-barreled shotgun, his face, from what I could see in the moonlight, cloaked in a state of determined agitation, as I could hardly criticize, for I felt certain we were the only visitors to his home who had ever arrived in the dead of night.

"Who are you, and what do you want here?" the man called, not quite aggressively, though with nervousness.

"Reprieve from your watchdogs for a start," Holmes replied with a touch of sardonic amusement.

"Ginger! Mick! Heel, beasts!" the man called, and instantly the well-trained duo obeyed and backed away from us, still suspicious but complying with their master's words.

"Now," said the man, "would you care to answer my question?"

"You are, I perceive, "Mr. William Rhys-Davies," began Holmes, "the most educated man hereabouts, a farmer of some modest prosperity, a thing to merit praise considering the difficulties presented by this infertile region, and while there is much else I deduce from my initial glance at you, I should note that I am here because you sent a letter to me, my good, sir. I am---"

"Mr. Sherlock Holmes?" Rhys-Davies exclaimed with something like utter delight.

My friend proclaimed himself: "None other."

Instantly Rhys-Davies lowered the shotgun, which he'd not quite pointed at us, though had certainly held ready should he have decided to. He exclaimed, "My relief at seeing you is absolute, sir! And beside you then must be the good Dr. John Watson, by whose noble efforts I know of you, having been captivated by his accounts of your work when I was able to access them at the library at my college, in Cardiff."

"Where you studied mathematics and engineering, I believe?" Holmes asked.

"Y-yes," Rhys-Davies replied, taken aback. "How did you guess?"

"I did not guess, I perceived, which is something entirely different."

Seeing the man's puzzlement only grew by the second, Holmes, in high spirits, said:

"The outbuildings in your paddocks, while well-constructed, are all venerable, save one, which I perceive has been erected in the last three years, for I note in it a deviation, and I must say an improvement beyond the others, by the inclusion of a chimney, which shows a fireplace has been added so that lambs born early in the season may be kept warm, and increase their chances of survival, a thing which would add, of course, to your income. I note this because I see signs that the builder of this not remedial structure, and its novel inclusion, was left-handed, as I noted at once upon your approach, you are. I then decided the odds made it far more likely that you were the agent of this building's construction rather than anyone else in the village, and seeing a quite impressive spirit of innovation therein, I gathered you had some background in engineering and mathematics...hence it was those subjects I stated as being your course of study at university."

There, in the cold night under the glowing moon, the farmer was sufficiently dazzled by Holmes' soliloquy to stand agape a moment before noting approvingly:

"It's all as you said, sir, all exactly! I thought up the innovation of the fireplace and how it could be incorporated into the building itself without increasing the chances of structural damage, and raised the place by hand---by my dominant left-hand, I'll confirm, noting you are correct there as well!"

Holmes lit his pipe and barely covering his delight that his suppositions had been confirmed as correct, he asked:

"As the hounds are quelled, may my friend and I step down now, and trouble you to see our rented horse duly stabled for the night, while we speak a moment about this troubling spree of violence which besets your community?"

"Oh," Rhys-Davies said hurriedly, "my apologies, of course, of course."

The Welshman set the shotgun across his shoulder and approached to give us each a vigorous handshake as we stepped down from the gig. In a trice he had the horse we'd rented in Bangor expertly unhitched and led her into the stone barn. As he worked he asked:

"So are we to set out tonight into the valley and to the mountain?"

I noted the "we" and approved of his spirit.

However:

"Tonight?" asked Holmes. "No, my good fellow, I see no reason to head out into the darkness tonight when I have the morrow to conduct my investigation, though if you'd be so kind as to have Watson and me come into your home for a while, I should like to hear more than your letter told about this apparent fiend which stalks the moonlit hours."

Rhys-Davies took us into his house, where two children and four women were waiting in the simple parlour, then made introductions to his wife, Alys, his sisters Eilonwy and Rhedyn, and to his mother, a woman less advanced in years than I may have expected, until I put my mind to the fact that marriages were often conducted at a relatively young age in rural places such as this. After the curtseys and bows, lastly, Rhys-Davies pointed out his small sons, Dylan and Cymber.

That done, Mrs. Rhys-Davies asked us if we'd supped, with the truthful answer being that we'd had nothing since leaving London, a fact which brought her to quick action, and Holmes and I were soon presented with bowls of hearty mutton stew, and thick slices of a delicious soda bread, spread with rich honeyed-butter the delightful hue of a pale daffodil. It was all utterly delicious.

Thus warmed by the blazing peat fire, and filled with a wonderful meal, our hostess' next question was where we meant to spend the night.

"Madam, I had thought that after your husband and I had a talk tonight about..." Holmes' eyes turned to the boys, and unsure what they knew of matters, said with circumspection, "*the events* which drew us from London, that perhaps we might return to town and find a room at the public house where we first alighted, the Gray Man, I mark it is called."

"Oh, that will never do," Mrs. Rhys-Davies said, the lilt in her voice turning her words to nearly a chirp. "All the way back to town, just to come here again tomorrow? Nay, nay, we have a room upstairs, and I'll insist you stay for the night. I'd not send the devil himself back out on a cold night like this."

As I was unsure of what Holmes might say, I was quick to accept the kind invitation, and Mrs. Rhys-Davies hurried upstairs to prepare the room, while her mother in law and her husband's sisters went up after her a few moments later, leaving Holmes and I to discuss things with his client, while keeping little ears safe from hearing of the horror that it was claimed preyed on the living under a full moon.

Our host showed us politely to chairs beside the low, warm fire, where the peat smoke was quite pleasant in a rustic fashion, and took his seat only after we had ours. The Welsh, I thought, may have been the sort who kept to themselves, but once their favour was won, their hospitality was indeed total.

"Mr. Rhys-Davies," Holmes began, sitting back in the wooden chair to which he'd been shown, "I pray you will now tell me of the events of the last two months, as they pertain to the matter I am to investigate."

The client lit his pipe, long-stemmed hand-carved, with a taper which he held to the fire, and after a few puffs he offered:

"One cannot but grow up in these parts, gentlemen, and not hear of a multitude of legends of the things which reside hereabouts, mostly unseen but ever-present. Knockers in the mines, the dwarfs which dwell under the mountains, the bog witches which haunt the lakes and take unwary children, and of course the fairy-folk, who leave rings in the grass to show they'd danced there in the darkness, but perhaps the one most dreaded of all has always been the werewolf said to sleep in a cave up on *Yr Wyddfa*----Snowdon, as you say---who wakes after his hibernation, which can last longer than a man's life, and comes forth to feed his great and terrible hunger."

"I dare say a folklorist could fill an entire career here," Holmes remarked.

"Easily," Rhys-Davies agreed.

"And growing up and hearing of these things, "I asked, "did you believe in them?"

The man hesitated a moment and said, "No....but having been raised on such stories, they tend to be bolted into the mind. *Something*, I tell you, is assailing this valley, and causing much destruction as it does."

"When the attacks first came two months ago, it was perhaps something of a surprise to you, if not an absolute shock, let us say?" Holmes inquired.

"Accurate, I suppose, sir, though I sought for a reasonable explanation, and even wondered if a bear had defied the claim that its kind had been hunted to extirpation, and had found its way into the valley. Even that seemed a more likely explanation, but then the second month....when we experienced those attacks as well, once again on the night of the full moon...."

"Yes, I can imagine," I said softly.

"Tell me of the attacks," said Holmes without further preamble, his eyes looking into the fire with a hardness that told of deep concentration.

"The first incidents," said Rhys-Davies, "came on the second of September, a night when rain had given way to clear skies, and the moonlight had a strange quality as a result, which I remember well. I had seen the livestock in and was still awake, though my wife and all the others here, my mother and sisters and my sons, had gone up, when the dogs barked most furiously, rather as they had tonight, which is one reason I came out from the house armed as I did…"

"Quite understandable," Holmes allowed with a small gesture of his hand. "And what did you find upon venturing outside under the vivid moonlight?"

"Absolutely nothing, really," Rhys-Davies admitted, a touch of shame in the admission. "Though the dogs were staring off toward the mountain, their hackles raised, seeming as afraid as they were boldly protective, but though I walked to the edge of the paddock and looked hard, I saw nothing at all."

Holmes leaned forward and demanded:

"And yet?"

Rhys-Davies nodded, "I *smelled* something odd in the air, sir, like a great wet beast, though I saw nothing whatsoever."

"And what did you do?" I inquired.

"I stayed out another moment in the chilliness, smoked a cigarette, and told the dogs they'd done well, figuring whatever it had been they'd sent it scurrying off and no harm done. I had finished my smoke and was on the verge of turning around and going back into the house, when from the farthest edge of my hearing I detected a noise, so quiet, truthfully, I was not sure then and still am not sure now that I heard anything at all."

"And what was this noise?" I asked, beating Holmes to the question.

Rhys-Davies looked away, as if embarrassed, yet answered, "It was a deep and dreadful howling, some miles away, enfolded in the cold darkness."

This admission caused Holmes to raise an eyebrow, and I felt my heartbeat pick up a pace.

"After another few moments, I went back inside, but felt uneasy, and I confess, I sat by the window for probably another three-quarters of an hour before I finally grew too tired to continue my lookout, and went on to sleep. In the morning all was well here, as, thank God, it has remained, yet an odd feeling stayed with me, so much so that I told my boys I'd drive them into town, for school, rather than have them make the walk as they usually did."

I thought of the quaint single-room school-house we'd passed coming into the village of Cwm Ystwyth, and knew my own dear mother had once gone to just such a place a half-century before, up in Scotland.

"I got to town and dropped them off," Rhys-Davies went on, "and figured since I was there I'd see to a few matters before heading home, thus I was in Cwm Ystwyth til the forenoon, and was on the verge of taking my leave when Mr. Jones, who farms a goodly stretch on the far side of the valley, came into town boiling with anger, and telling the story to any who'd listen, of some beast which had come in the night and taken a dozen of his best merinos, fine wool-producers, including his great ram, a famous beast, unafraid of anything, its horns curving a yard long. All had been torn apart, and in the case of the ram, its head he found lying, as if flung, a dozen yards from its body, and all the others, his best ewes, especially, were slaughtered on the ground, some of their bodies partly eaten, others simply killed for no apparent purpose, torn and dashed about, and in many instances strewn. An entire flock he kept out in his north pasture was gone, along with both the dogs who herded them, good animals, protective and true-hearted with the loyalty of the breed."

It was a description of a fearsome scene indeed, and I was by no means unmoved.

"Well no sooner had we heard Jones out that morning, than a second farmer, David Lloyd-Owing, by name, who farmed farther out still, near the break in the valley below the lower mountain, he came to town whipped into a froth telling of five of his sheep killed as well, some gnawed on, by the looks of it, others chased down and beaten into a pulp, most with their heads twisted off their very bodies."

"Twisted?" asked Holmes. "That is a specific word. Why do you say their heads were 'twisted' from the bodies?"

"Because it is the only term I can give to this."

"I see," Holmes replied.

"I went out with many of the village men and we saw what he spoke of, and I can tell you, this was not a case of some animal biting through the sinews and cordage of the sheeps' necks, it was as if the heads had been pulled off by some almost unimaginable brute force. It was a thing most horrific to see, I assure you."

"From what you say, I do not doubt that," Holmes said thoughtfully. "And beyond the obvious sentiments toward horror, what was the general reaction? What was being stated even then?"

"No one that morning said what I know we all thought of, not even I. Not yet, we didn't."

"The werewolf?" I asked.

The word seemed to cause the man's spine to stiffen.

"Yes, Doctor," he confirmed, "none other, though I grew angry at myself for such a thought, and commiserated with those who had their losses, and went back to town with the group, I alone among those not personally affected had an especial reason to feel a chill next to my heart, for I thought back to the night before, and my dogs reacting as they did, and the wet beast odour I detected in the air, and the..."

Here he paused, distraught.

"By the howl you heard in the distance," Holmes finished when his client hesitated.

"Yes," he admitted, "that sound, not quite baying, not quite roaring, a bizarre sort of cry...I can hear it still ringing in my mind, a disturbing sound, carrying over the hollows and through the air itself."

"Were the farmers compensated for their losses through insurance?" I asked him.

"In one case yes, in the other no, and while most of us were cautious with our animals for the next few nights, my neighbor a mile down the road, Davis---you passed his holdings as you came from town---he sat out with his sons the next night, all armed, but all was quiet and there was no repeat of the violent attacks, not then, and all returned to the usual stillness of the nights we typically have here so far from all else in the world, for any predators, save the occasional wild mongrel cur, have been killed off. Honestly it is among the safest places on the island to raise livestock."

"Statistically that is very much so," agreed Holmes. "Wales is on the whole an almost ideal place if one seeks a secure life, untroubled by misfortune."

"So you can imagine how for the next three weeks we almost let ourselves forget the animal deaths, but as we approached the full moon, which came on the night of October the 2nd, a tension returned, which shows that whether we dared whisper it yet or not, the old stories were to be found in our thoughts."

"The expectation was that the werewolf would strike again?" I asked.

"It was," Rhys-Davies confessed, "and I was no more immune to it, despite my time away in Cardiff, where I studied engineering, as you know. I tried to tell myself the idea was ludicrous the stories fanciful, only myths from less enlightened times, yet when the 4th came, I sat out atop the slate roof of my newest barn, the one I constructed out there as you saw, and waited til dawn. There was nothing, not so much as a whisper on the breeze, a protesting bark from my dogs, no smell upon the wind, no dreadful sounds from the distance. It was as placid a night under the bright moon as one could ever hope to see."

"But in the morning," Holmes stated, "the reports came in."

"I drove my boys to school once again, having made an excuse to go into Cwm Ystwyth, though truthfully I, like all farmers hereabouts, was anxious to know if the predations happened again."

"Which they had," I said for him.

"Even worse this time," our host confirmed. "Four farms struck, four herds wiped out, or left so decimated as to amount to the same thing. Wilson, of Hill Brook Farm, he had to slaughter the only three sheep who'd survived at his place, as the beasts were driven mad by the terror of the night, their fellows lying in heaps around them, blood everywhere upon the grass. As I saw with my own eyes, the sheep trembled and convulsed and quivered madly, so that putting a blade to their throats had been a mercy."

"And the effects of the strike on the second full moon?" Holmes inquired.

"Many of the remains showed the bites of some great maul, no wider, perhaps than a man's, yet the fangs the creature evidently possessed did terrible damage. And once again the strength of the fiend was shown by the fact some of its victims were simply pulled apart and flung like bits of rags. A defiant ram was found in three pieces in the meadow, fifty feet away from where a pond of blood showed he'd been killed. But this time, well, there'd been a steady rain late in the night, and the ground had been left wet, so that..."

"Tracks," Holmes surmised, then pressed: "Describe them."

"Yes, there were tracks abundantly present this time, and they were not those of a wolf, or no wolf I had ever seen, or a bear or anything else that nature might provide. There upon the pasture earth were the clawed prints of a foot very like a large man's, though at the ends of the toes were signs of claws long and curved, which had pressed into the soil. There was also to be seen evidence that while the creature ran on four legs, as might be expected, at other times it had walked on two."

The claim struck the air like silent thunder, and even

Holmes frowned.

"These tracks," Holmes pressed, "were any captured in plaster, by any chance?"

"Alas they were not," said Rhys-Davies, "though the idea did occur to me, but in bad luck a great autumn storm hit that afternoon and washed away everything, even the blood upon the meadow."

"Tomorrow," said Holmes, "I should like to be taken to one of these locations."

"Of course," said our host, his client.

"The beast preyed only on sheep?" I asked.

"There were also two cows killed at a neighbouring farm," Rhys-Davies replied, "and a horse, and of course the dogs I mentioned. I feel lucky not to have lost my own sheep dogs that first night in September. They are not only workers which earn their keep, but like friends to us, of course."

"Oh, yes," I agreed, "I have always found the dogs I owned quickly became as part of the family."

"The remains of these unfortunate creatures out amid the pastures," Holmes asked, "what became of them?"

"Well, most were too destroyed in the literal sense, to be useful for anything, nor would, I think, anyone have wanted to have tried to butcher the meat after it had been touched by... such an assault, not when the assailant's foul slobber was so coated about. In some cases the animals were left to lie on the ground, though a few were buried. Mostly I think it was one or the other, leave them where they fell, or throw them together in a hole."

"A field where they were left to lie," said Holmes, "that is the place where I should like to be taken in the morning."

Rhys-Davies nodded, "Certainly."

Holmes was thoughtful for a moment and then finally asked:

"Frankly now, Mr. Rhys-Davies....what do you believe is behind these localized atrocities?"

The man sat motionless for a quarter of a minute as if

under a great struggle, then he finally said:

"I think, frankly now, that whatever it is which has acted around us under the full moon, it is not explainable by science alone."

"You think it a werewolf, then, as in the legends," I pressed him.

As if the admission caused him something like actual pain, our host, who had once studied amid the gaslights and modern minds of Cardiff, said at last:

"I do."

Silence held lease for a long stretch of limping seconds before Holmes said:

"Thank you. I think, sir, that is all that might be gleaned for tonight, but I should like to affect an early start on the morning, so if you would be so good as to show Watson and me up to the room your wife so excellently prepared for us, I should be grateful indeed!"

A moment later, with nothing more said of the werewolf of Snowdon, Mr. William Rhys-Davies made it so.

Up in the plain, small, but well-kept room in a farmhouse I judged to be perhaps three centuries in age, Holmes lit a single candle, and fell almost at once onto half of the bed we would be sharing for the night's duration, a tiredness seeming to hang on him even moreso than it did on me, for the day had started long ago and some distance off in London, and many miles had passed since.

As I knew my friend could fall asleep almost at will, I was quick to press him for answers, by asking:

"Holmes, what did you make of all we were told of downstairs?"

He replied:

"We were not mislead by the letter, for our courteous host

did not dissemble, he told the tale as he recalled it and invented nothing. In all particulars I think it is a precise account of events as they have transpired since the second of September."

"Surely you disagree with his conviction that a werewolf from myths is behind these atrocities," I said, "so what explanation comes to you in rebuttal?"

"I have none, Watson," he said bluntly, surprising me.

"None at all?"

"At present I do not. I trust the men of these parts to know the work of a pack of wild dogs, or a wolf, or indeed, likely a bear, though they'd never seen one, as there have been none here for many generations. If they tell of a thing which defies their grasp, I cannot as yet contradict them, or impugn their intellect or judgment."

I thought on this before saying:

"I think there was altogether too rapid a leap to conclude the killer was a creature from legend. There must be a ready explanation."

"I agree," Holmes answered, his hands folded across his chest, his eyes already shut, and sleep fast approaching. "Yet unless you can supply one, my friend, I shall proceed with a glaring blank at the center of my thoughts, and let the evidence provide what it may. That is ever my method, Watson, you know this."

"And if tomorrow's investigation seems to confirm the most unlikely of explanations?" I demanded.

But to my frustration, Holmes was already fast asleep.

If the evening before, I'd noted that dusk came early in these parts due to the towering mountains blocking the sun in its final hour, morning likewise came equally rapidly in the country, well before dawn, and the sounds of the rising household broke slumber's hold even as I opened my eyes and saw that beyond the window all remained held fast by the darkness which came after moon-set, but before sun-rise.

"Yes," Watson," said my friend, already up and in the midst of dressing across the room, his form barely visible until I'd lit a candle, "we are guests of particularly punctual risers."

"Quite...so," I said, as a yawn bisected my words. "As one must be in a hard country like this."

I, too, climbed from the warmth of the bed into the teeth-chattering cold of the Welsh autumn, the unheated room utterly motivating one to pull on chilly clothing and head downstairs, where the warmth of the fireplace made life more endurable.

It was into a scene of industry that Holmes and I descended, coming upon a family in motion, each of them with a task and each undertaking that task with well-practiced alacrity. The boys, young as they were, were outside bringing in kindling to replace that which had been used that morning; Mr. Rhys-Davies was in the barn, seeing to his animals; and the women were getting together a breakfast, which I saw was to consist of porridge and rashers of thick bacon, which I thought smelled absolutely wonderful mixing with the peat-smoke, and the tea in the kettle seeping over the fire.

After returning the calls of "good morning" tendered to us by the family, Holmes and I went outdoors into the brisk dawn, where the sun was showing the merest hint of rising in the east, and the grass, in its armor of frost, crunched under our feet.

"Care for a hand?" I called to our host, as he fed livestock, and prepared to turn his flocks out into the slopes of the mountain foothills, where his fields lay.

"Oh, I can always use that!" Rhys-Davies replied. "I hope you gentlemen slept well?"

"Quite well, thank you," I replied, as I took a bucket and tossed its contents on the ground where several shoats waited, porcine snouts upturned in ready anticipation.

Holmes, however, lit his pipe and looked toward a cow which stood beside a gate, waiting her turn at milking, and declared:

"It might interest you to know I perceive that beast is by far the most intelligent animal in your yard, Mr. Rhys-Davies."

Both our host and I paused and looked toward the cow Holmes indicated, each somewhat taken by surprise to hear the great detective make such a statement.

"She is?" Rhys-Davies questioned.

"Oh, yes," said Holmes, "for in addition to possessing, I think you might agree, a most learned light in her eyes, she has, as you may notice, created for herself a padding of mounded straw to stand upon, thus keeping her delicate feet out of the mud."

It was true, now I saw it, though it was a detail I doubted I should ever have noticed on my own, but the cow was indeed the only one whose hooves did not rest in the dampness, but rather under each of her legs lay a small pile of straw just large enough for her to step onto.

"Well I never!" said the Welshman.

"Ha!" exclaimed Holmes. "I hazard to say if you check on her each morning hereafter you will find it is her usual practice, and quite a leap in understanding on a cow's part it is to grasp that with a little industry she may create for herself a more comfortable existence."

"I say there, Gemma," Rhys-Davies called to the cow while smiling, "it seems you are the brightest of the lot, my girl!"

It was remarkable, I thought, that Holmes' abilities even extended to evaluating members of the animal kingdom!

As we worked together, with even Holmes rolling up his sleeves and not sparing himself from the mucking out and tending to the place, while Rhys-Davies saw to the milking, our host and I were treated to my friend's unveiling of his plans for the day ahead.

"Mr. Rhys-Davies," he began, "it is of primary importance this morning that as soon as practicable, we travel to where the remains of the victims of these attacks may be found. I shall need to make as thorough an examination of the evidence there as I am able, all things considered."

"Then I think Mr. Abernathy's holding would be best," Rhys-Davies answered as he sat on a three-legged milking stool, "he lost more than most, and left the sheep lying where they fell."

"Splendid, that would be ideal," offered Holmes, as he tossed fragrant straw into the environs of a clean stall, performing those duties of farm life with a strange aspect of almost appreciative zeal. After a moment he added:

"Do you know, one day, when all of this life is behind me and I have nothing more I wish to contribute to the art of the detective, I think I shall find great appeal in returning to a place in the country, where perhaps I shall keep bees, and make a study of their fascinating matriarchal social structure."

While I could not possibly imagine Holmes giving up London and trading it all in for a little home in some rural spot, I did not challenge his comment, knowing that day, if ever it came at all, would surely be long in coming.

After the chores were seen to and the plain if delightful breakfast enjoyed, our host hitched up his wagon, and transported us across the winding dirt trails that constituted the roadways in these parts, taking us across the shadowy valley, and toward the Abernathy farm he'd spoken of. The place came into view across a long vista, as we rounded a hill, and I saw lying before us another of the well-kept holdings of the Welsh countryside, making up in pride and evidence of hard labour what it lacked in the degree of overall prosperity one might have seen in a farm in the Home Counties of Kent, or Surrey.

We arrived at the gate, a strong but much-weathered wooden barrier at the end of a dirt drive that led from the path to the house itself, stone, as were all the houses thereabouts, and waited until a man emerged from the place with a nearly-grown boy trailing him.

"Rhys-Davies!" he called.

"Mr. Abernathy!" our host returned the greeting.

"I believe, sir, you have heard of my houseguest, Mr. Sherlock Holmes, who has come down from London to see what help he might offer in our time of torment and trouble."

"Oh, *oes*," said the farmer, using the Welsh word for the affirmative, very alike and yet markedly different from our English version. "Heard of you, sir, and pray God you can lend us some comfort in this hour."

"I plan to do more than that," Holmes told him as he stepped down from the wagon. "It is my intention to get to the heart of the matter, and see you troubled by it no more."

He waved a hand carelessly, as if wiping chalk from a blackboard.

Cheered by these tidings, Abernathy asked:

"And how might I help you in that this morning?"

So it was we were soon shown across his property and up into the grazing land that marked the farthest boundary of the eighty-three acres he laid claim to, taking us across the rising swell of his holding, a strenuous walk after my many years of easy living in London, though my friend and Rhys-Davies seemed to take it all in stride, so I had to hide my exertions---or try to---and follow along.

The mountain range which straddled just beyond us, containing as it did the tallest peak in all of Wales, or Cymru, as natives proudly called it, Mount Snowdon---*Yr Wyddfa*---rose over all else, the heights wreathed in clouds and mist. It was, despite the difficulties of trying to make a living here, a beautiful place, this Welsh countryside, both like and unalike the highlands of Scotland, and a thought came to me that someday this entire landscape might make a fine preserve for others to come by train from the cities and visit in a condition of awe.

I saw our destination before we arrived, and the tragedy of the scene there was readily discernible, and more than a little disturbing, for cast about in an area of perhaps half an acre lay the now skeletonized remains of ten sheep, their bones resting exposed amid shreds of wool, and bits of flesh which clung tenuously onto the spears of ribs and femurs, many of those visibly broken, even shattered, telling of a great force necessary to inflict such violence upon the poor beasts in their final moments.

"Dear me," I said aloud, though neither Holmes in his concentration, nor the more stoical Welsh farmers, joined me in making any comment.

I watched as Holmes went from skeleton to skeleton, reaching down and lifting a leg here, or prodding at a ribcage there, looking at nearly all through his Swiss magnifying lens, before settling onto the ram who lay farthest from the group, its head missing, and its body lying in a strange angle, its hindquarters slightly higher than the fore-part of it, as if....

Holmes spoke aloud what I had nearly grasped as testified-to by the evidence of position.

"This animal fell to earth," he said, "after being flung a great distance, and landing as we thusly see. Its flight was no less than twenty feet, and served to shatter whatever bones had til then remained unbroken."

"Oh, the strength required to throw a full-grown ram so far!" I exclaimed. "The beast had surely weighed no less than thirteen stone!"

"Yes..." Holmes agreed, slowly, his mind taking all this in and churning through facts in pursuit of explanation.

He leaned low and studied the wool-covered skeleton, largely desiccated now by the elements after two months of lying exposed on the hillside, and said:

"This beast suffered terribly. I see its right front leg was snapped in two, and done in a single sharp motion, as deftly and easily as I myself might break a match stick in twain."

Even the farmers winced at the thought, and, doctor though I was, I felt uneasy at the idea. To snap a bone so readily...?

"The ram attempted to engage its assailant, giving its life, if you will, in one last and decidedly valiant effort to defend its flock. For its bravery it received no reward, but was---"

He rose and demonstrated what had transpired.

"---snatched in mid-charge, bitten savagely on the side of its face, then its head was torn free from its body and cast---"

He turned and looked about til his eagle-eyes spotted a skull barely visible in a patch of weeds higher still up the hillside, and noted it for our benefit, finger outstretched.

"---there. It was then that the bestial attacker, in a heated fit of utter and absolutely frenzied rage, broke the ram's leg and crushed his sides as if deflating an accordion, and threw the carcass the distance we see here, some ten paces, meaning the assault would have happened...just over there."

He indicated an otherwise non-descript section of ground.

"But the one feature in this that most calls my eye to it....would be the impressions left behind by the creature's teeth."

Here all straightened from where we had beheld the indicated piece of ground, and were, if possible, even more keenly focused on his narrative.

Rather than continuing directly, Holmes rose from the crouch he'd assumed, and undertook a second, longer exercise in examining the dead ram under his lens, and as he did so, a look of something close to troubled contemplation came over him.

"What is it, Holmes?" I demanded.

"The teeth marks..." he said, "I confess these do...*puzzle me.*"

His face was marred by what I took to be a definite sign of frustration, so I asked:

"Holmes...?"

Looking then at the four of us, myself, Rhys-Davies, Abernathy, and his silent son, the detective said:

"The impressions both *are* and *are not* those of a man."

The farmer Abernathy became agitated at this puzzling and distressing statement. "What do you mean, sir?" he said in a rush. "How can it be but one or the other, not each?"

"That, my good man," said Holmes, "is the source of my dismay, for I see here the signs that a man has inflicted these bites, and bitten so deeply as to scar the leg bone itself to leave such markings, and *yet...*"

He traced an area of deep scratching, almost a shattering, and said:

"This aspect of the same bite reveals that the maul which inflicted the damage also possessed fangs of an overdeveloped sort, and the teeth were sharp, and much more pointed than those of any natural man."

The news was chilling, even to me, a man versed in medical science, dweller in a great and modern city, yet to the farmers native to this backwoods place, it seems to confirm their worst nightmares concerning the last two months, and justified their fright of the night which lay ahead of them, for the boy, who had said nothing thus far, keened:

"God help us, it is the werewolf!"

Heading back to the Abernathy farm, Holmes remained utterly calm, even as the locals were agitated by his revelations up on the hill-pasture, and as we walked silently down the steep hillside, the three Welshmen spoke rapidly to one another, sounding to my ears almost to have given in to a condition of restive panic.

I little blamed them, for after hearing what my friend had told us, I was left in a state of confusion, and did not know what to think. Holmes had always counseled me to follow only the threads of evidence, and to bring no prejudices about any matter into the equation, yet try as I might to tell myself such a creature as a werewolf did not and could not exist, I had seen the condition of the sheep-remains on the hill, and had studied the infliction of violence that had been the poor beasts' final lot, and had heard Holmes, certainly as coldly logical a man as ever drew breath, declare the facts concerning the teeth which had bitten into the bones of the fatally-courageous ram, marking them neither those of a man, nor those of a beast. What else was there for me, then, but thoughts similar to those which the locals seemed to find confirmed their oldest legends?

When back on the grounds surrounding the stone farmhouse, Holmes broke his relative silence and charged the owner and our host with an important duty.

"I must bid you, gentlemen, to undertake a most important mission, if you are willing to aid our cause today."

"*Oes*," said Abernathy.

"Of course," agreed Rhys-Davies, "anything. We can only consent, having seen the horror of which our foe is capable."

"Then," said Sherlock Holmes, "my direction is thus. I need the pair of you, and anyone else you can muster, to go into the village and throughout the countryside, asking any whom you can find, farmers and all, to gather at the Gray Man public house at mid-day. Save the church, I believe that to be the largest building in town, and one likely to be known to all. Tell them it is vitally important, and that I shall have news for them, and instructions for the coming night."

"I had somehow hoped something might be achieved, some miracle, I suppose," confessed Rhys-Davies, "that might spare us another night with that fiend active among us, out in the valley."

Holmes nodded. "I am truly sorry, Mr. Rhys-Davies, but an immediate remedy does lie beyond me at the moment, though I have a plan, and within that plan I have hopes. I fear, however, we must allow our adversary free-range tonight, if we are to bring things to a satisfactory conclusion."

"You have hopes as high as that?" Abernathy demanded.

"I have some," Holmes said simply.

"Then share them, I bid you!" the farmer cried.

Holmes stood in thought and finally allowed cryptically:

"I have a theory, although I admit it may be flawed. It is the best I can come up with in the face of evidence, but I will tell you, frankly, now, that we are dealing with a very real and entirely dangerous creature which runs loose across the valley at each full moon. That is reality, terrible and unwelcome though it is. And I tell you further, it is little short of a miracle that no human life has been lost to this foe, for I assure you it would not hesitate for the slightest moment to inflict the same injuries upon any man it did upon those hapless sheep. It is a most deadly and horrifying enemy, indeed."

His words had the effect of widening Abernathy's eyes, and making his son's mouth drop open, and even I felt myself want to flinch at the thought of his description.

"So it *is* a werewolf?" Rhys-Davies asked, his voice tremulous as he surrendered at last to the forces of superstition which lay in his native blood.

"It is what it is," Holmes allowed with a dismissive gesture. "And I shall meet it tonight if all goes well with the plan I will reveal to those who gather at mid-day, as I have instructed. Now, if you please, gentlemen, you can be most usefully occupied by seeing yourselves off and about the mission with which I have charged you."

We accepted Rhys-Davies ride back to the village of Cwm Ystwyth, while he went on, as did Abernathy in his own wagon in the other direction, to spread word of the meeting Holmes had called, and send others forth to spread word as well.

"I think you certainly daunted them, Holmes," I said grimly when we were alone on the dirt street underfoot in the heart of the village's scattered handful of buildings, all stone and all quite old.

"It is well I should," he said, "for what lies ahead tonight is most perilous, and our chaotic foe shall be ruled by naked bloodlust alone. It is a force beyond reason which shall run wild tonight, and woe unto any who should stand in its path."

With that, he strode away with a gesture indicating he sought some time alone, which I had little choice but to grant, and watched from afar as about a hundred yards away he found a stone settled into the ground, sat rather sagely upon it, and began to smoke amid his exercises in deepest contemplation.

I, myself, leaned against a rock wall in the environs of the village and began to write out notes on that which had transpired since we left Lime Street Station, in Liverpool, but as it would happen, I would have less time for this undertaking than expected, for a young copper-haired girl, surely no older than six, came wandering over to me from one of the houses in Cwm Ystwyth.

"You're the gentleman from London?" she asked in an accent which was so markedly Welsh I almost marveled that her young lips could form words that liltingly lyrical.

"I am one of them," I answered, leaning low to better reach her height, "and my name is Dr. John Watson. And who might you be, my fair lass?"

"Tegan Deryn Evans," she said, "of the Mullins House Evans."

The last identifier, I thought, related to there being so many Evans throughout Wales, and even I'd heard of three separate families of that name living around this tiny place.

She added: "We're the most thought-of branch of Evans, our lot."

She's an opinionated little miss, I reflected, amused.

"Well Miss Tegan Evans," I allowed, "I am most pleased to make your acquaintance today. And how old are you, if I may inquire?"

"Eleven," she replied, surprising me with that news, for I'd believed her far younger, and this made me look at her with a medical eye, and decide her growth had been severely stunted by some episode of illness, or perhaps by the hard life of the valley. If she'd said she was half the age she'd given, I'd sooner have believed it.

"So you've come to catch the werewolf, have you?" she asked straight away with a peculiar look in her eyes, dispelling my thoughts at her small stature.

"I have come with my friend," I said, "that gentleman in the black Ulster overcoat whom you see sitting on that stone yonder."

Her eyes did not seem to travel to the place I'd indicated, yet she said: "He ought not to sit there,"

"Whyever not?" I asked.

"That stone is very old and quite special," she informed me in her unsmiling manner, "and its name is *traed y cawr*, which means 'the giant's toe' because a hero once cut it off a giant's foot, and it turned hard."

"Is that so?" I replied, thinking of how in Wales it seemed everything had a legend attached to it.

"*Oes*," she answered, "a thousand-thousand generations ago."

"Well," I said, "my friend, Mr. Sherlock Holmes is his name, is among the most clever and determined men in all of Britain, and he has done many amazing things in his day. If anyone can catch this beast some call a werewolf, whatever it is, it will be he."

"Oh, it is quite surely a werewolf," she said, serious and almost affronted to be so doubted. "I can tell you so."

I chuckled. "I shall take your word for it, my dear."

She caught my note of humour and replied:

"Does your clever friend, Mr. Sherlock Holmes, imagine that if he goes seeking it, the werewolf won't take his life as easily as a cat takes a bird?"

I was inwardly more worried about the night ahead than I would ever have admitted to this proud and serious soul, yet with loyalty to our cause I answered:

"My friend is a brave man, and has many skills. As for myself, I was a soldier in the Northumberland Fusiliers, and after going to places called India, and Afghanistan, I know something about self-protection. I think this werewolf would flee back up Snowdon if it knew who was on its trail."

Instead of laughing, as I'd hoped, the girl told me:

"I'm going to be a poet when I am older."

"As a writer, myself, I can say I believe you'll be a good one," I told her, politely.

"I shall be a bard, and write a song about tonight," she continued, no trace of whim or humour in her words. "You'll be in it."

"Well, I thank you," I said, taken aback at the idea.

"*Oes*," she said, "a song of the men from London who came, and were torn to pieces by the werewolf of *Yr Wyddfa*."

At that the smile drained from my face.

"Well," she said, turning from me, her next words sounding both sincere and yet taunting, "do try to die bravely tonight, Dr. Watson, so I can say you did in my song."

She walked away, passing the village houses to go toward the countryside, her coppery hair catching in the sunlight with the brightness of burnished metal, the black cloak about her shoulders blowing behind her in the wind, like a cape, and I felt that I had grown rather cold inside.

◆ ◆ ◆

Holmes approached me at 11:30, as some farmers were beginning to arrive in town for the mid-day conference, and suggested I join him in the pub for food.

"If I know the Welsh," he said, "they shall be too courteous to interrupt a fellow about his meal, whereas if we stay outdoors, we shall all-but drown in an ocean of questions I'd soonest answer but once."

Inside under the low ceiling of the Gray Man, with its smoky environment and dim interior, we were served the all-purpose local dish, mutton, in the form of chops, well-seasoned and nicely grilled, along with another Welsh staple, leeks, likewise grilled, and mushrooms, accompanied by more of the fluffy soda bread such as Mrs. Rhys-Davies had presented us with back at her house. I had two pints of ale, being thirsty, though for his part, Holmes asked only for tea, preserving, I guessed, his mental acuity in a state unhindered by even a modest quantity of alcohol.

"Holmes," I began offhandedly as we ate, "I was confronted earlier this morning by a most peculiar girl."

"You were 'confronted'?" he said showing only a modest interest in my news. "That is rather a strongly defining word."

"Approached, then. Spoken to."

"Ah, there you have it, Watson, you were 'spoken to' and that is quite a different matter."

"It was all quite odd, as was she, herself."

"Then she is in keeping with her native surroundings, the Welsh being a breed apart, I have found. Is this not your own experience of them?"

"I...I suppose," I said.

"If you have found them so then you are not wholly unobservant."

"You are being deliberately difficult, Holmes, as I believe you know."

"The Scots, now, as an Englishman I find your race almost ideal as conversational companions, yet the Welsh, well." He cut a slice of mutton. "I think it is the difference in their peculiar stock of the Celtic bloodline, differing markedly from your own, and wholly apart from those of us of Anglo-Saxon heritage."

I stared at him a moment, til having finished with his bite, he said:

"Put the conversation from your thoughts, Watson, and let us instead attend to our meal, for it may be some time before we have another."

If ever, I thought, grimly, then asked:

"Holmes, you have no interest at all in anything I could tell you concerning my encounter with this child?"

"What is of no use to my cause is of no interest whatsoever to me, so, no."

This left me shaking my head, not having expected him to dismiss my news so lightly out of hand, and I wasn't certain I should not feel insulted.

Yet I did let the matter drop, and we lingered until just after the clock struck twelve, then made our way out the door, the publican following us, and shutting the Gray Man behind him, not wanting to miss out on anything said.

Outside on the dirt road, gathered in a great semi-circle were perhaps a hundred men and a few women as well, and behind them a scattered handful of children, too young for school, the parents not wishing to leave them behind during a time of crisis.

Rhys-Davies approached and said, "Word was spread, as you see, and I think near to everyone in the valley is here. What have you to tell us, Mr. Holmes?"

He, along with everyone in the crowd, stared at Holmes most seriously as the detective stood before them, tall and impressive, his features sharp, his black hair blowing slightly in the wind. He seemed a general among soldiers, or a professor among a class.

"I thank you, Mr. Rhys-Davies," he stated, "as I thank you all for being present. I think I shall make your attendance worth your while."

Several heads nodded in hope, and all eyes were fixed upon him. I, however, noted that the child, Tegan Evans, was not among those gathered.

"As I have told Misters Rhys-Davies and Abernathy, there is indeed, as you feared, a dangerous creature loose in your valley, one which has shown itself more than capable of defeating with ease the stoutest rams in your pastures, as well as a horse, which is itself no simple foe, and cattle. I have said this beast would not hesitate to kill a man were he within its reach during its blood-furies, and so I believe it to be."

A woman cried out, then swung a hand to cover her own mouth.

"Therefore," continued Holmes, "I will give you instructions, which I urge you to follow to the smallest degree. Any deviation, and loss of human life may ensue."

The seriousness of these words was lost on no one, and all stood still as stones, listening.

"I have marked upon my map the locations of the attacks of the previous two months, and have somewhat triangulated an area in the mountains which I theorize may be the home to this creature, whatever it shall prove itself to be—"

"A werewolf!" someone muttered and several voices

agreed, though mostly all listened quietly.

Ignoring this, Holmes went on.

"I have made an educated guess this morning of an approximate area where the next attack is likely to fall."

Now many voices spoke out, consternation acute, fears on display.

"I may be wrong there," Holmes admitted, "for I have but little to go on, and this creature has shown itself to be fleet of foot. It may well strike miles from where I expect it, and against that too I must plan."

"But will it attack at all?" asked a woman from the back of the crowd.

"I see little reason to hope that it shall cease," Holmes answered. "Should it do so, then that is splendid, yet we must prepare for the worst, and make every effort to end our foe's bloodthirsty predations, or I fear it is but a matter of time til one of you standing here today falls beneath its fangs and claws, and its overpowering physical strength."

Sobering, indeed, I reflected, as from behind Holmes I looked on at the crowd, simple, hard-working folk of ancient Celtic stock, none of them deserving this unnatural torment.

"What must we do, Mr. Holmes?" It was Rhys-Davies himself who asked the question.

Holmes nodded. "Exactly as I instruct you all, and nothing else. No more, no less. Follow my directions exactly, and I think we shall all live to see tomorrow. Deviate, and..."

He did not need to finish.

"Now listen carefully, one and all..."

His instructions were not complicated, and held much of simplest common sense. All would bring their livestock into their stoutest barns tonight, and seal them in. Families themselves would take to their houses, lock all doors, and not venture out til morning, no matter what the enticement or provocation.

"The creature has perhaps shown itself reluctant to enter houses," Holmes said, "and I do not think that a coincidence. I hope we might rely on that tonight, to some degree."

He stressed that while all may arm themselves as they saw fit within their houses, none should for any reason take firearms outdoors, telling them that the firing of guns in the night was of much greater danger to all than any other immediate threat. The temptation to hunt down the creature must be resisted, or all might be lost.

"Do I have your word on this?" he demanded of the villagers.

Speaking as one, the local people gave it.

"Now," said Holmes, with great relish, eyes shining," here is how I will confront the creature, and bring its marauding to a sudden and final end…"

He revealed the name of the farm whose fields were most likely to see a visitation by the beast that moonlit night, one belonging to a tired-looking and unfortunate fellow called Awbrey, who held sixty-five acres on the deserted outskirts of the valley.

"I am sorry to say that unlike all others hereabouts," Holmes told him, "I must ask you, Mr. Awbrey, to leave your animals out tonight. I know you shall incur losses, but it shall be for a higher cause, and if it is within my power to make it so, I tell you this shall be the last time you will be so troubled."

Awbrey did not look happy at Holmes' news, but wordlessly nodded his agreement, showing the stolid stoicism of the valley.

"It shall be at your house, Mr. Awbrey, by your leave, that my friend Watson and I shall wait, with Mr. Rhys-Davies as well. If I am right, that is where our adversary shall come, and where blood shall be spilled under the pale moonlight."

People stared at Awbrey, few envying him his impending losses, yet it was in a steady voice replete with fortitude that the farmer answered:

"*Oes*, I shall do it."

"You are a splendid fellow!" Holmes told him. "And I shall be with you, don't forget, an advantage of no small value. Now," he called, "should I be in error and the attacks befall another farm instead, I bid you each to keep your shepherd's horns near to hand, and if trouble comes, sound them as loudly and for as long as you are able."

For as long as they are *able*, I thought reflectively.

Holmes told them:

"I have noted that under ideal conditions, such as we shall have on this dry cool night, the sound from these instruments can carry for a league, and upon hearing it, my friend and I shall come as swiftly as our means allow. But I tell you, frankly, I think you are all safe tonight. All save the admirably noble Mr. Awbrey, whose sacrifice will be done for all of you, as I hope you will now take a moment to consider."

The people did exactly that, and cries of, "Thank you Awbrey!" cut through the bright, chilly air.

"Now," said Holmes, with a discernible eagerness that seemed to contain no trace of trepidation, "I think there is little more to be said, for though I know you all wonder at much, and naturally have many questions, I must tell you, I fear I have few answers for you."

This was met by disappointed murmurs.

"However," Holmes added, "I hold hopes that the morrow may bring answers to all which at present so torments your curiosity. For now, I thank you, and bid you do precisely as I have recommended, so that we might see this matter through."

With that, my friend turned from the crowd and re-entered the Gray Man public house, where I followed and told him:

"Holmes, I think you managed that well. There was fear among them, and fear creates tension and problems, yet under your guidance that was held to a minimum."

"I thank you, Watson. Now we shall see."

Yes, I thought, *now we shall see.*

◆ ◆ ◆

I noticed that as we sat inside the pub, Holmes kept referring to his watch, and while at first I assumed this was his natural state of anticipating the evening which lay ahead, I was soon to discover his frequent reference to the timepiece contained a practical purpose, as just after two a coach was heard to pull up out front, sending my friend launching from his chair like a coiled spring.

"A-ha, Watson, he has come!"

I hurried after Holmes as he trotted across the floor, his face caught in a glow of triumph.

He threw open the outer door and I spied a coach there, and in the back of the coach lay a cage, and within that, a small bright-eyed dog.

"Watson," said the detective, "I dare say you recall our friend Toby, whose nose assisted us in several matters, particularly the case you dubbed 'The Sign of the Four'?"

"Toby has been brought?" I exclaimed, pleased.

"No, Watson, Toby is enjoying his dotage these days, but may I introduce his son and heir, Coney, whose nose is rated the equal of his illustrious sire."

The dog before my eyes was so much like Toby of old that I had trouble accepting it was not him, the brown and white markings being the same along with the general size and shape as he gave us a bright-eyed look.

"Well hello, Coney," I said as Holmes opened the cage and allowed our leashed comrade to leap down.

The dog waggled his tail in reply, and sniffed at my thrower leg before waddling—again much like his father---toward a convenient stand of bushes, it having been, I reflected, a long trip, after all.

"Before we left Liverpool you might remember I sent off several telegrams," Holmes told me.

"I do," I confirmed.

"One was to Mr. Hacker," his master, in Lambeth, who was

delighted to send Coney here out to us by train---at my own expense, of course."

"Of course," I agreed. "Your purpose, is obviously is to track the creature?"

I gazed up into the mountains towering all around us to the west, and reflected on the thousand hiding places to be found there amid so any miles of ruggedly unreachable terrain. A tracking dog simply made good sense.

"One might well think so, Watson," Holmes said, "and yet...." He flashed the quickest smile which told of inner satisfaction. "In truth that is not my exact intent, no."

"A subterfuge, then?" I guessed. "Is the dog merely for show to create some false appearance?"

Holmes merely smiled again, less to me than at my words, and kept his own confidence.

"You are ever so nebulous, Holmes," I said in frustration, shaking my head.

"And yet, in the end, do I not ever reveal all to you, my dear Watson?"

"Yes, you do at that," I admitted.

"Then continue to have faith, my good man. Now, I think we will all benefit from a little rest, you, me, and the devoted Coney here, before evening shadows come spilling down the mountains, hopefully finding us primed and in waiting on the farm of the admirable Mr. Awbrey."

"An excellent idea," I admitted.

We did manage to find rest inside a room upstairs at the Gray Man, where the publican, Owen ab Owen, kept a chamber to let on those rare occasions when some visitor to the valley should require lodgings. He was good enough to charge us nothing, telling us:

"More than thanks, t'will be if you stop the werewolf who stalks us all."

"I believe it shall be done," Holmes said in confident reply, a miniscule, swift smile appearing and then vanishing from his lips, quick as a blink.

It was late afternoon and the shadows were long, yet the sun was still a good hand's distance from reaching the crest of the Cambrian Mountains when we set out from the Gray Man, and headed toward the place on the road where we'd arranged to meet Mr. Rhys-Davies, and from there travel on to the Awbrey farm. I was armed with my service revolver, and I'd seen Holmes check his own firearm and place it upon his person before we left the pub.

The road outside was largely deserted, I think in no small measure owing to Holmes' speaking to the villagers that afternoon, cautioning them to be securely indoors before sunset. It seemed all had heeded his advice, and as we left, even behind us we heard the lock snap shut on the door to the Gray Man, where it seemed Owen ab Owens was locking himself and his family away.

It was a place under siege, this community known as Cwm Ystwyth.

We retrieved young Coney, a serious sort of dog for his age, being I judged, no more than two and half years on the outside, and at the end of his lead the little animal eagerly pressed forward, all-but straining at his leash, wishing ardently to push on toward what he clearly regarded as some great adventure.

We three progressed in the lowering autumn sun, its light warm but the air colder than I liked, the wind off the mountains making things even more brisk, and after a time heard the clopping of horse's hooves as Rhys-Davies came in a dogcart, as fitting a means of transport as a wagon, and perhaps moreso with Coney added to our company.

"So it begins, eh?" the Welshman called with resignation, as he stopped for us to hop aboard.

"And soon to end," Holmes told him, "either for the predator who will be descending from the darkness of the mountains, or for us."

For myself, I much preferred Rhys-Davies' optimism to my friend's foray into baldly stating the reality of our mission, a sentiment which put me in mind of the strange Evans girl from that morning, and her gloomy prognostication.

...do try to die bravely tonight, Dr. Watson, so I can say you did in my song...

I shivered, and told myself it was from the clammy cold.

We made it to the Awbrey farm as the sun was just touching the tips of Snowdon, and the farmers saw the horse properly secured in the barn, though I lacked faith that its aging wooden door, painted a bright green against the uniform gray of its stone walls, could truly deny the mountain-beast entry, having witnessed the results of its phenomenal strength.

"Gentlemen," Holmes announced, stepping a little ahead of the rest of us, Coney's rope in my own hand, "we now move to one of the more difficult phases of our little arrangement tonight: *simple waiting.*"

He indicated a little hilltop just beyond a pasture where ten sheep were still placidly grazing, despite the hour, enough to entice our adversary yet not so great a flock as to constitute an unmanageable loss to the farmer.

"That," said Holmes, "is where we shall go."

Gathering to conceal ourselves behind four large stones which jutted from the earth, a not infrequent feature of the landscape around us, Wales veritably being a nation of stones--- some apparently the severed toes of giants, I reflected---Holmes bid us find a comfortable posture and remain as hidden as possible.

"Our wait is likely to be a lengthy one, gentlemen, as the moon will not rise for at least two hours, but that cannot be helped, for it is neither prudent to our cause, nor safe for our persons, to be seen."

"What if the creature detects us through other means?"

Rhys-Davies inquired.

"If you notice, I have selected a spot which conceals us downwind from the peaks," Holmes replied, "minimizing somewhat, the chances of that. If we stay low and keep still, we may be unseen and unheard, yet I tell you earnestly, gentlemen, our undertaking is an exceedingly hazardous one, and I do not approach it with the confidence I do so many other snares which I have set in my career."

"There's a legend that only silver may harm a werewolf," Awbrey said uneasily.

"Such talk is exactly that, my dear fellow," Holmes told him, "a legend."

"For my part, from Afghanistan to Britain, I've never seen anything which was immune to a bullet," I answered, hoping to quell the farmer's fears, while desperately hoping we had not found the one limit to the capabilities of lead.

Our canine companion was the calmest of us all, for after sitting beside us a moment, he turned about several times, then plopped down and curled nose to tail, and promptly fell asleep.

"Ha!" Holmes said with a snort. "You see therein, gentlemen, the wisdom of the animal kingdom. We would all do well to shed our tensions and likewise be at peace while we keep our vigil."

Saying this, he leaned back against the surface of one of the massive stones, and seemed to enter a meditative state, fully awake, yet somewhat removed from his present surroundings.

The remaining three of us stayed nervously focused, our eyes taking in our surroundings while I took up my army field glasses and gazed at the mountains, almost shivering to see the wild landscape drawn so close it was as if I could stretch out my gloved hand, and touch it. Amid the rocks of the slopes---so many places for a predator to conceal itself, I thought---nothing moved save stray patches of weeds caressed by the growing winds. Below us the sadly doomed sheep had drawn together for warmth, growing heavy with sleep, as pre-moonrise darkness fell over them.

An hour passed in this manner, then a second, and half of another, seconds dragging as we sat under the light of a moon swollen near to bursting, it seemed, rising by the minute past the eastern landscape, not a thing of beauty under the circumstances, but a frightening portent of what our tense bodies knew was coming.

Then in the space of one sparse moment, all changed.

I had happened to be training my field glasses at a particular expanse upon the mountainside, when a movement caught my eye. Upon a modest pathway a shadow darker than the shadows around it was steadily coming down the mountain. I stared, unsure I was truly seeing something of significance, but then I spied it move again, and I knew.

"Holmes," I said in a tense whisper, "it is coming."

With an economy of movement, stealthy yet sudden, Holmes threw off his meditation and slid past the farmers til he was beside me. He snatched the glasses from my hand, and I saw his face alter, his jaw clenching tighter, as he said:

"The foe at last, and precisely where I predicted he'd come!"

The Welshmen were no cowards, but I saw their courage set sorely to the test as they stared into the darkness, seeing nothing until in an instant I shall never forget, the creature bounded down the mountain and into the pasture with a gait that was peculiar, being neither the graceful gallop of an animal, nor the purposeful stride of a man, but a hybrid of the two, disturbing to behold.

"The werewolf!" breathed Awbrey, awe-struck, horrified, paralyzed with terror.

For my part I could not take my eyes from it as with great speed this man-beast burst onto the green grass of the pasture, black fur waving around it in the wind, perhaps no taller than any of us, but much broader and stronger, the ears atop its bristling head wolf-like and pointed, and visible even from so far, long terrible claws hooked out from its fore-paws, its onrushing movement sending the terrified, bleating sheep scattering in all directions as it bore down on one ewe, racing with terrible speed toward her, emitting grunts and growls horrible to hear.

My hair stood on end and in something like shock, all I could think was: *Dear God, it is real after all!*

Holmes cried out:

"Watson, hand Coney's leash to Rhys-Davies. Rhys-Davies, hold the hound securely. It must not engage the creature! Come with me, Watson! Hurry now!"

With that he climbed over the rock which had concealed him, and dove beyond. In an act of what I must confess was considerable courage, I followed.

The creature had by this time snatched up the hapless ewe and bitten into her neck, silencing her terrified cries amid an outrushing of blood, ruby in the moonlight, then after seeming to slake his thirst, the werewolf rose onto its hind legs, assuming the posture of a man, and threw her lifeless form behind it, where the dead sheep, a creature of no less than ten stone, sailed fifteen feet before rolling across the ground in a tangle of limbs.

The beast lifted its head and seemed to cry out to the heavens above in savage delight, then returned to four legs and ran toward another sheep, which tried vainly to elude it.

"Ho!" shouted Holmes, waving his arms and doing all he could to draw the notice of the beast. "Over here! Come to me!"

The werewolf reached the fleeing sheep and with a single motion broke its back, sending its lower legs dragging below it as with its front legs the pitiful animal continued its feeble efforts to run, only to have the vast black beast snatch it up and tear into its stomach. Thus it was a moment before it seemed to hear Holmes' cries, then casting the dead sheep away, it turned its gore-smeared face toward my friend and me, and from forty yards off, it dropped back to all fours and charged straight at us.

As I have found it so often does in moments of mortal peril, time seemed to slow around me. To my rear I was aware of the baying of Coney, the hound, and the horrified shouts of the Welsh farmers, warning us of our peril, but most keenly of all I was conscious of Holmes running *toward* the onrushing monster, which charged toward him in a mass of black fur, its blood-crazed eyes seeing only my friend three or four paces ahead of me, and under the radiant moonlight all my brain could think was:

This is to be a disaster!

Holmes halted so abruptly I nearly collided with him, and something in his halt seemed to trigger a change of behavior in the beast, for it, too, slowed and leapt up onto two legs, and advanced on us, no less murderous in intent and scarcely less rapidly, but almost as if in response to a challenge it intended to face hand-to-hand, closing now to within a score of feet.

Holmes' arm moved in a flash, mirroring my own action, as we pulled our revolvers, yet even as I drew I shouted:

"Wait, Holmes, do not fire, for look, that is no animal, it is a man!"

And so some facet of my own humanity tricked me into believing as the towering black menace plunged straight at us, its eyes intelligent but frenzied, great hooked fangs visible in a mouth parted with a growl of savage rage, its furred hands and muscular arms reaching for us in anticipation of tearing into our very flesh, some new species for it to hunt and destroy.

And as I hesitated, my uncertainty destined to be fatal to myself, Holmes fired three well-placed shots in rapid succession, and so close were we to the tyrant that I saw its fur lash sideways as each round found its mark above the heart.

For an instant I thought Holmes' marksmanship was to have no effect---

only silver can kill a werewolf!

---for the momentum of the creature pushed it forward, its broad strides coming within a man's length from where we stood, then it faltered and fell all at once, a look of incomprehension mingling with the sheer bloodlust of its rage as it struck the pasture ground and rolled to a stop veritably at our feet, the great bulges of muscles along its back twitching and jerking spasmodically.

My panting breath coming in jagged gulps of air, a tremendous sensation of nervous excitement driving through me, I cried:

"Holmes, have you truly killed it?"

The detective crouched low over the furry mass sprawled below him, the stink of it redolent even in the open air, a mixture of a stark beast smell and a profusion of visceral gore and blood.

"I believe I have, Watson," he replied, superhumanly calm even in this instant of expended nervous energy. "It seems silver was unnecessary after all."

The steadiness in his tone shocked me more than the sight before my feet, for how any man could remain so collected at such a moment defied my medical understanding.

From behind us Awbrey and William Rhys-Davies came running, Coney proceeding them, though still held by the long leash gripped tightly in Rhys-Davies clenched fist.

"My God," Awbrey exclaimed. "Look at the thing!"

I did just that, focusing myself at last, as all at once I perceived what Holmes had already discerned by this point.

"That is no werewolf," I cried, "or even a wolf-man! It is---"

"A great ape, Watson, yes," said Holmes.

He shoved the beast onto its back, so that it seemed to stare up at us with huge dead eyes above its face sticky with redness.

"Though this is no ordinary ape..." he revealed. "Normally, despite lurid tales, the gorillas of equatorial Africa are a relatively gentle lot. This beast, though...it has known a life of utter and unnatural torment."

With the barrel of his revolver he tapped at the fangs in the animal's mouth.

"Obscene," he uttered. "These are the teeth of a species of bear, and have been surgically grafted into the animal's mouth."

Grabbing its paws in his hands, he proclaimed with a frown:

"The claws as well, are surgically implanted into the very bones that lie beneath."

"It is grotesque!" I cried. "The poor animal, no wonder it felt only such fury."

But Holmes was not done. Rolling the ape onto its side, he felt at its hip and said:

"Ah, yes, as I suspected. Watson, place your hand here, and let your thoughts be those of a physician."

Even now, though the form below us was clearly dead--- mercifully dead, I thought---I had to compel myself to touch it, and as I pressed down through its matted, thick fur to the warm flesh below, I felt several knots in a series and half-healed protuberances jutting from the great mass of muscles there.

"It has been subjected to a long series of injections!" I cried.

"Indeed," Holmes agreed. "Someone has been using a hypodermic needle to fill this much-abused creature with a formula to drive it quite literally insane, and destroy its natural passivity in order to replace it with an uncontrollable bloodlust."

"It is no werewolf," Awbrey, slower of mind asked, causing Rhys-Davies to look back at him and simply say:

"No."

Holmes took Coney's leash from his client's hand, and announced:

"Which brings me to the second stage of my work tonight. Awbrey, Rhys-Davies, stay with the creature's body, or go to town and spread the word, but do not follow me. Come, Watson, if we hurry he will not be far ahead of us, for the mountain paths slow human progress."

"Who?" I called as Holmes hurried on, trailing Coney, who, having stuck his snout against the fallen ape's remains, now rushed eagerly in pursuit of its scent-trail.

"The true monster of this case, the man who engineered all which has befallen this Welsh valley these last two months!"

"The ape had a master?" I cried.

"Assuredly," replied Holmes, "and we shall find him on the mountainside."

I ran after him, though I found my progress up the

trail was less rapid than that Holmes or Coney, whose tandem journey seemed almost effortless. We ran nearly a mile from the green valley to a pathway which wound deeper into the elevated wilds, Coney baying, nose to the ground.

Finally, Holmes shouted back to me:

"Nearly there, Watson, hold fast!"

And so his words proved prophetic, for as we passed a final curve in the path, marked by a large boulder which had fallen down the mountainside at some moment in the long-ago past, Holmes emerged, pistol in hand, to a flat, clear area, and I saw his eyes brighten and his face set with both triumph and disgust, as he said:

"Ah, as I scarcely dared hope, I see you made no further effort to retreat."

The mystery of whom he addressed came clear a moment later as I reached the spot where Holmes stood, Coney sitting calmly beside him, quarry found, job done.

We had come to a small encampment, where a large canopy stretched above a tent, and beside it a steel cage, which I saw had been assembled on the spot rather than toted intact up to this height. There were stores of food in cans, a number of notebooks, and a glass-fronted metal case filled with vials of some formula, above several tin syringes, and hypodermic needles to fit into them.

The man Holmes addressed had steel-gray hair, black clothing of an odd, almost military fashion, though devoid of insignia, and far from shrinking before my friend's presence, he stood in calm defiance with a rigid pose of great confidence, staring back at the detective, neither aggressively nor with any trepidation.

"You are Mr. Holmes, of Baker Street, I gather," the man said arrogantly, his tone possessing the clipped syllables of one who'd known the highest reaches of formal education our Empire offered.

"None other," answered my friend, his confidence matching the other man's tone. "And as you know my name, I take it you know that of my friend as well."

"Dr. John H. Watson," the man said gazing toward me, a cocky grin breaking his face. "The people I work with make a custom of keeping tabs on all who are worth knowing."

"A practice you and my friend share," I spoke up to tell the haughty fellow.

Holmes gave me a quick sidewise glance of approval, then said:

"I do not know your name, sir, for that knowledge is denied my immediate abilities, though I can tell much about you."

The man gave him a slight nod, as if telling him to go on, before saying:

"I have heard much of the little parlour tricks you do to please the gullible, so let's have a sample, then."

I began to see there was some odd dance at play here, and the battlefield, if indeed there was to be one at all, was verbal, and intellectual, and I sensed there was much here I did not yet have sufficient facts to grasp. I did not quite sense immediate and potent danger from this man, but something like latent menace, for even before Holmes he showed no trace of fear whatsoever.

"I can see," Holmes began, rising to the challenge, even at such a moment as this, "that though I perceive you have spent over two months camped out here, when in London you live on the upper floor of a tall building which sits in the general vicinity of Pimlico. And that as a schoolboy you were present in Regent's Park in 1867, to witness the ice skating disaster there---"

I saw the normally expressionless man start at this improbable and far-reaching assertion.

"---that you are unmarried and retain no manservant, therefore dress and shave yourself, rather badly, to put it earnestly, that you are not a smoker..." Looking to me he added, "And men who do not smoke are seldom to be trusted, Watson."

His cocky aside at such a tense moment further puzzled

me.

"I note you attended both Harrow and Oxford. You have served in the army, as an officer of artillery, in Egypt, and...."

Here Holmes frowned deeply and it was almost in anger that he charged, "....that you are well-placed in the employ of none other than Her Majesty's government, in what is semi-accurately termed, the secret services."

The man assumed a cold grin on his otherwise stoical face, and said:

"Correct in all particulars, Mr. Sherlock Holmes, though how you know this, I am unsure."

"Are you now?" The challenge stirred Holmes, who proudly stated, "Then permit me to reveal more. I say that you dwell on an upper floor, for that is made evident due to heightened muscular development on your left side, though I perceive you are a right-handed man. In a nation where travel on the left side of a lane, or even a stairwell, predominates, as it does in our own, I grasp this enhancement indicates you have frequently ascended many flights of stairs on a daily basis, exercising that hemisphere in the process."

Interesting, I thought....

"Pimlico I discerned as your residence when for an instant as you moved, I spied the label on your coat was that of a tailor shoppe there, and as men take less care as a rule than women in purchasing their attire, I hazarded you attained it near your residence, also in Pimlico."

The man nodded almost imperceptively.

"Harrow and Oxford, well, unless concealed, which you did not trouble to do, those institutions leave indelible 'tells' in the speech, almost in the manner of battle scars. The Harrovian 'h' for example, was prominent in your words. As for the army, it is hardly uncommon among mid-level government agents, now is it? The artillery was revealed by a certain tilt to your head when you listened to my replies, a custom I have come to associate with a degree of hearing loss so many artillerymen acquire during their service."

"And Egypt?" the man demanded.

"You have a little scar on your hand of a shape which suggests it was inflicted by a *nimcha* blade, common among the bedouin of the Nubian desert, against which Her Majesty's forces so successfully took action back in '79, about the right age for you to have been present."

The man's mocking amusement faded somewhat, replaced by a begrudging look of frank surprise. He said:

"While I could pretend to be unimpressed, and accurately claim I have met more remarkable sorts than you in my time, in truth I would give a month's wages to know how you guessed that I was a witness to the Regent's Park ice-skating disaster."

"That," Holmes said with arrogant disdain, "was no guess, nor will I ever tell you how I knew this of you."

"You know my history and identity?" the man challenged him.

"Hardly. You are a stranger to me, known but these five minutes."

"You are a mind-reader then," said the man, sounding serious, "and not the first I've known, as there was a fellow I once had to deal with in Cairo, a French agent, who could read the minds of others, and so could not be left to work against us."

Holmes challenged:

"Ah, you speak of the French provocateur, Barbier, missing these eight years? He was no mind-reader either."

"I tell you, he was."

"Sir, you do not hold the perspicacity your over-confidence lets you believe you do, if you subscribe to the validity of clairvoyants among the French foreign services. I can, as it happens, read your thoughts even as I stand here, and yet I hold no supernatural gift. I see it is disdain which fills your mind. Disdain for me, and for all the people who dwell hereabouts in Wales, whom you have so violated in the name of science run amok. It is in fact not remorse or guilt which occupies your thoughts, but resentment of me for having brought an end to your long and cruel experimentation this night."

The man chuckled coldly and offensively, and said:

"As all that is true, then you must, having discerned something of who I am and for whom I work, grasp why I undertook this series of tests of what is, I assure you, a long and completely sanctioned project, authorized by my superiors in London."

"I do not know all," Holmes answered, "though I can fit the facts together and form a hypothesis, and see why it is you evince so little fear of me, for you feel yourself protected, just as you felt yourself entitled these past two months to come to this faraway place, and use the cover of an old legend, to release your 'soldier' loose on the hapless animals who dwell here."

"You are again correct," the man said, his words cruel and devoid of conscience, "and also correct in choosing that word, 'soldier.'"

"'Soldier?'" I demanded, unable to hold my silence any longer. "Holmes...what *is* this?"

"Watson," he said, "it is the workings of our government at its most inhumane. Over the past two months this valley has borne witness to a test of how a gentle creature could, with the administration of immoral drugs, be turned into nothing less than a savage killing machine."

"To what end?" I asked.

"It was but the first stage, a sort of early run, but when the formula was perfected, the next step would be to administer it to a human, in order to destroy all that is noble and decent in him, and transform him instead into a limitless killer, a new form of, yes, *soldier*."

I grasped the concept at last, and recoiled in utter horror at the thought that there were men in my very own government, their identities and function concealed from society, who sought to corrupt human beings into mindless agents of the most violent and fearless forms of warfare. It was unimaginable.

"And what," I demanded of the man, "if your experiment had resulted in the loss of human life here-abouts?"

The man stared expressionlessly at me until he replied, "Acceptable."

"His goals were worse than you have allowed yourself to think, Watson," Holmes told me, "for the exact intent of the heartless husk which stands before us, was the wanton and chaotic murder of residents of the village. It was a source of frustration to him that it had thus far failed to take place."

The man nodded. "Since you know I stand above the reach of the law and need never fear arrest for anything I do in my work, I shall grant you the courtesy of confirming that all you have said is true, and what you witnessed tonight was the latest iteration of some three year's work, beginning with mice and rats, progressing up to dogs, and finally to this ape, the most man-like of nature's beasts. We have been quite happy with our results here, but the time was fast approaching when we should have needed to progress to the final stage of things."

"On human subjects," I said with disgust.

"Of course," replied the man. "On prisoners next, back in the capital. It is all for a higher good."

"You were *hoping* a person should be killed this month?" I asked, anger vivid inside me.

"It was necessary for it to be so," he told me, no shame whatsoever in his voice, "for we had to know the formula would drive Tongo there to kill. Based on what I observed as he charged toward the two of you, and his almost certain death, given your arsenal, I would say the question of the drug making a soldier fearless and bloodthirsty has been answered, and happily no doubt to your thinking, without the loss of life being utterly necessary."

"How did you quell the beast after his episodes of violence?" I asked. "How was it he did not turn on you?"

"He feared me in his normal state," the man said, "though in his aroused condition, after the injection of the drug, he feared no one, and it was I who took to the cage, for my own safety. The effect was only good for about an hour, after which, as its effects rapidly fell off, hence he did not during any episode run wild through the village itself. Tongo was trained to come back to me here, having been so... conditioned."

The man laughed and I knew he spoke of torture inflicted on the ape.

"You are despicable," I charged him.

"Well said, Watson," Holmes agreed, though I saw he no longer held his revolver. "However, I fear he is, as he told us, beyond the reach of law, as well as past the reproach of human conscience."

"I hold that the ends of our experiments more than justify the means, Mr. Holmes," he said. "You know the state of affairs on the continent these days, both from the papers, and from your brother Mycroft---oh, yes, I know of him, don't imagine I do not---and must grasp that it is imperative for our very survival that we remain ahead of the newly-risen power of Germany, as well as more traditional enemies, the French, the Russians, even the untrustworthy Americans across the ocean, always seeking to rise above their rightful station, mongrel nation that theirs is. So we must be smart, Mr. Holmes, we must be more innovative than our would-be foes, and if we can arrive at a drug which increases the fighting ability of our forces, well, the killing of a few score sheep and even a man or two from this worthless little hamlet is clearly justified when compared to the good of the entire empire."

"It is all terrible," I reflected.

"Yes, Watson," Holmes agreed, "but for now, at least, we have brought this man's experimentation to an end, and prevented the loss of human life in these parts. I would say that is an achievement of which you are entitled to feel some pride. Beyond this, however..."

What he thought of his next sentiment revealed itself on his face.

"I fear even I have little more to offer against such forces as this man represents."

"A wise outlook, Mr. Holmes," the man, doubtless powerful in his own fashion, replied. "Though I should advise you to keep your silence on this program, ultimately it matters little whether you do or not, as we are beyond outside hindrance."

"I believe the locals of Cwm Ystwyth may have something to say about this!" I said heatedly.

The man shook his head.

"They have a superstitious fear of these mountains, Doctor, especially great Snowdon, beyond, and rarely set foot here. I don't think they shall discover this site, as you only did by the use of that cur there. I have little minded living in this cold and wild place, for in my years of service I have assuredly dwelled amid far worse, but now that matters have ended, I do look forward to a well-deserved return to London after ten weeks away, for unlike the townspeople, I know my way down the other side, where I will be met tomorrow by the men who'd expected to come and resupply me, as they do each month, but I'll leave with them, and take anything of value from here with me. The rest the elements can claim, for I doubt anyone else will trod here for a century, if ever."

"I believe I shall see what Mycroft has to say about the existence of such a program," Holmes said to the man. "It may be he has more influence than you think, as well as greater ethics."

"Do as you wish," the man told him. "But your company tonight grows tedious."

With that, he turned his back on us, and prepared to break camp, even there in the nighttime, setting a small fire, and feeding papers into it, and shattering vials of formula against the mountain itself.

"It is time Coney took us back down the mountain, Watson," said my friend, his tone lacking the usual note of triumph I had come to expect at a case's end.

An hour's less frantic travel set us into the valley once more, and across the pasture a crowd was in place, most holding candles, lanterns, even blazing torches, gathered around the body of the ape on the ground, that miserable and much-abused creature they'd mistaken for a werewolf.

"Mr. Holmes! Doctor!" Rhys-Davies cried as he came running toward us. "It's good to see you again. You've been gone these nearly two hours, and I'd begun to fear the worst!"

"We are unharmed," I told him.

"We are all astonished to see what it has been which has set upon our flocks and fields," Rhys-Davies told us. "A great African ape! Who would have suspected it? Why just look upon that brute, like something out of a lurid magazine story!"

"*Oes*, and the fiend is rightfully dead now!" a farm-wife called triumphantly.

I did not disillusion any of them in their moment of relief by pointing out how the tortured beast had been surgically augmented with fangs and talons, or explain why it had been drugged to brutal madness, merely let them gawk and enjoy their moment of spectacle, happy in their certainty that their months-long nightmare had been brought to an end.

Holmes likewise held his silence, and said little at all, even to me, but moved out past the group and took a place atop the jutting stones which had previously concealed us. I knew he longed to be away, back to London, on to the next case, a predator among his criminal prey. His spirit, if it was at all like my own, felt more shame than satisfaction.

As soon as I could, I got away from the press of locals and joined my friend by the stones, where he sat smoking his pipe, eyes distant, face serious and unhappy.

"You are thinking of the forces which lie hidden among our government, marring the nobility of our great nation, the Mother of Parliaments?" I asked.

"Watson, just when I believe I have experienced the limits of depravity to which mankind may stoop, the floor descends a little farther," Holmes replied. "It is a thing to sicken even *my* heart to think of soldiers stripped of their very souls, and turned into a beast such as we saw this night. Yet I fear the genie cannot be returned to the bottle, and such a thing is coming."

As a former military doctor, I shared his horror, perhaps even exceeded it with my own, but as a man, I found myself grasping at satisfaction in the fact that we had also done some good in our visit here, saving lives, and releasing others from the grip of fear, and this I told him.

"Yes," my friend said simply. "There is indeed that, and you should be proud, Watson, at the courage you showed on behalf of your fellow man."

After we were together a moment in silence, I said:

"Holmes, you had the dog, Coney, sent out from London. You...suspected, then, something like what we ultimately found to be the truth here?"

"Oh, yes," he answered, "my suppositions were almost precisely correct, for I knew there were but two possibilities, the first, that indeed it was a werewolf, a species unproven by medical science, undiscovered in the world despite a thousand years of stories, or the second that someone, for whatever reasons, wished us to believe so. If it was the first possibility, well, there was little I could do and very likely stood to die in that pasture, but if it was the second, then only a dog could lead us back the way the beast had come, and therein reveal the creature's master."

"Ingenious," I answered.

"Merely a following of the facts, as ever, Watson."

"There is something that puzzles me," I said, "as it did the fellow himself when you brought it up."

"Oh?"

"The ice-skating disaster in Regent's Park. However did you know of that from clues upon his clothing?"

Holmes laughed despite the conditions of the night, and said, "I did not."

"What? Yet you were correct!"

"Yes, though not from my perceptions of him out there. Well, save for one, perhaps."

"Then how was it done?"

"Through an improbable coincidence too remarkable to be plausible for all that it was true. I recognized him from a photograph that I saw some years ago, taken on-scene during the ongoing rescues by the pond."

"What?" I exclaimed. "Truly?"

"Odd how little he had changed in the ensuing twenty years."

"Holmes, do you mean you recall every face you have ever seen in a photograph?"

"Oh, yes."

I had to halt for a moment and process this fact, which in its own way exceeded even his remarkable feats of deduction.

"And what do you think your brother shall say when you tell him of this atrocity going on within the government?"

Here Holmes looked more serious than ever, and his silence lingered before he answered, admitting at last:

"I spoke that name, and made my threat for a purpose, Watson, as a test. I was not sure my suspicion was correct until the moment I espied the agent's reaction to my words, then I knew."

For an instant I was no more enlightened by his explanation, then I breathed out the word *no*, my nerves alive with realization, dreading its confirmation.

"Mycroft, Watson, is the man at the head of this hideous program."

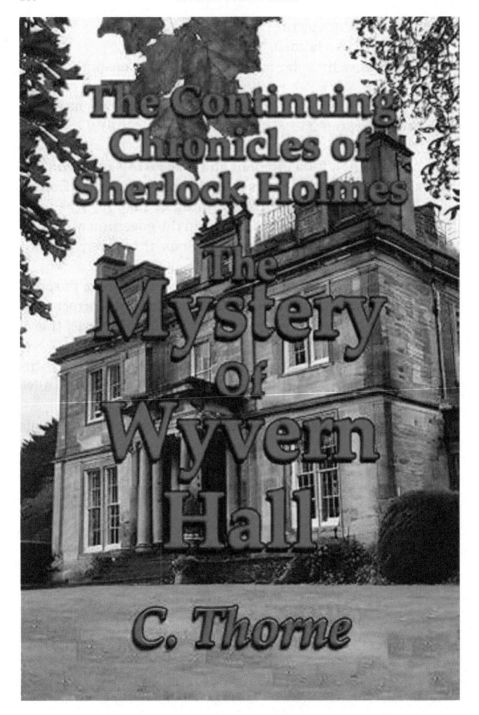

THE MYSTERY OF WYVERN HALL

I remember them as such happy times, undoubtedly tinged now with the omniscience of hindsight, those days spent with my first wife, Mary, for however much a widower may love a later bride, as I love my second spouse, Norah, there will always remain a place in his heart where joyous recollections lie next to the pain of loss, and so it is with every occasion I think back on those brief years of my first union.

Thus as I bring to mind the mystery that took us to an old manor house in Kent known as Wyvern Hall, it is with a smile of both fondness and wistful sorrow that I remember Mary placing Holmes' note in my hands, a moment after it had been delivered to the door, and her saying to me:

"It seems Sherlock wishes you to be with him, John."

I read the note, which said little more than had Mary's summation of my friend's invitation to meet him at Baker Street if I were free to travel to the country, but despite the tug such an offer made in me, I held that as a married man my duties lay with my wife and home. Thus I was about to pen a note expressing my regrets, when Mary spoke up, chiding me in her lovely, light-handed way, urging:

"Come, John, you have been a busy man this last fortnight, seeing to your cases, and then being ever at my side with every stray moment you've caught around your patients' demands, and it seems to me you might well benefit from a little excursion to the country with your dearest friend. The excitement might do you good, and as a doctor I don't have to tell you the salubrious effects of fresh air on the constitution."

This was all true, and I *had* been kept busy the last few weeks tending to my ever-expanding medical practice, but while I veritably longed to give Holmes an affirmative reply and hurry over to Baker Street, I also felt no small wish to remain with my wife, whom I loved with all the devotion a wedded state could bring to a man's heart.

Mary was quite familiar with Holmes, not only from our friendship, and her and my not infrequent connections with him in the course of our lives, but because she had herself hired the great detective in the recent past, being at the heart of the case I dubbed *The Sign of the Four*, when my friend's inimitable powers had brought the mystery to a successful close, and in so doing, placed the two of us in one another's lives, soon to become man and wife. In many ways I think Mary was nearly as fond of Holmes as I was, with the added sentiment of her deep gratitude to him for relieving her of burdens placed upon her delicate shoulders by the matter itself: a service for which he had charged absolutely no fee, claiming the delight he received from aiding a woman in need, combined with the mental stimulation of the exercise, was more than sufficient.

I considered Mary's words of urging and the temptation increased to the point I asked:

"You're really quite sure you wouldn't mind if I did slip away with Holmes for a day or two?"

"I will count every moment you are gone, John, and let my missing you add to the great joy that will come at our reunion." She said this with that charming combination of whimsy and earnestness I always so loved in her.

"Well then," I announced, "I had better pack a bag and be on my way!"

Which I did with a happy urgency, adding a kiss to my wife's lips as I slipped outside into the windy blue skies of a late November morning that managed to at once combine merry sunshine with an invigorating chill.

I caught a cab to take me across town to my former (and unbeknownst to me then, future) home at 221B Baker, where my summons at the bell brought the kind face of the landlady, Mrs. Hudson, to bid me welcome.

"I do believe Mr. Holmes was hoping to see you this morning, Doctor," she said as she led me upstairs.

"How has Mr. Holmes continued to fare since I moved out?" I inquired.

"Oh," she answered, "you know how he is, coming and going at all hours, sometimes looking nothing like himself, either, mind you, in those disguises of his, but in the end he's always back again soon after, cheerful as a bee to me, and I could ask for no kinder tenant to occupy my lodgings, fuming chemistry projects, and experiments with pistols shot into the mantle in the dead of night notwithstanding."

"I am glad to hear it!" I said, pleased that matters were proceeding quite normally by Holmes' unusual standards.

She knocked on the door to the parlour upstairs, and a voice called:

"Do come in, Mrs. Hudson, and bring Dr. Watson with you,

if you please!"

"Ah, you knew it was him, of course," Mrs. Hudson called laughing.

"Why of course," Holmes agreed, "for I have long committed the sound of each of your footfalls to memory, and would know either, anywhere, and could offer an accurate hypothesis concerning what sort of person might make any other footfall I should happen to hear. Yours and Watson's I would recognize in a crowd of a hundred in the depths of Siberia, if it came to it."

"Somehow I doubt that not, Mr. Holmes," the landlady said, a twinkle of merry amusement in her eye.

She left us, and Holmes all but shouted:

"Watson! I was hoping you would find release from employment and matrimony in order to join an old friend in his adventures. Have a look at what came by special express courier about an hour ago. I sent for you at once upon reading it."

I was handed a sheet of cream-coloured writing paper, J&W watermark within, and jotted in a strong, surely masculine hand was a report which put a frown on my face, and left me to utter:

"Oh, dear me."

"Yes," Holmes agreed, "you see why I must leave at once."

The letter had come from a place called Wyvern Hall, near the heart of Kent.

"I looked up the place of the letter's origin," Holmes said, "and if one were to draw a triangle between Canterbury, Dover, and Folkestone, Wyvern Hall should sit in very nearly the center of those lines. It is shown in *Bradford's Records of the Gentry*, as being occupied most recently by one Reginald Drew, Esq. a landed gentlemen, and the hall itself dates to 1266, with the last wing added in the 1670s. From the illustration, it stands an impressive place."

I listened, but re-read the letter, which stated:

Mr. Sherlock Holmes:

Word of your reputation as a solver of the darkest of mysteries has reached my ears even in so far-off a place, and I ask you to come to Wyvern Hall, and lend us all aid that your abilities render possible, as my daughter, Liza, some fourteen years of age, has gone missing, and has not been seen now for nearly forty-eight hours. A most thorough search undertaken by many participants has not availed us of her whereabouts, or led to her return. She is a good and dutiful girl, if somewhat ethereal at heart, and I know she would not have undertaken to depart on her own, nor can any explanation, such a suitor, or grievance against her mother and me, be brought to mind, for all is happy in our lives.

Please come, sir, and name what fee you shall, for I am a man of means, and you are our last hope in this desperate hour.

We await you at Wyvern Hall, Kent.

I am, til then,
Your servant,

Reginald Howard Drew, Esq.

"It is a letter which tells of pain and woe, and much paternal worry," I commented. "I know you lack details, but have you any thoughts?"

Holmes lifted up the carpetbag he kept ever-ready should he be called upon to depart at any hour, and said to me:

"I can only speak in the most common of generalities, Watson, yet I can tell you, when a person with no reason to depart turns up missing, and no demand for ransom or logical explanation presents itself, the result is too often that a tragic conclusion lies ahead."

"As in some accident?"

"Perhaps."

This was a dreary summation, though I did not doubt an accurate one, and as I followed my friend back down the stairs and toward the street, my own red leather valise in hand, I considered that it was likely a grim situation we set off to approach.

We grabbed the first available hansom off Baker Street, and were within Saint Pancras Station in time to catch the next train to Canterbury, the South Coast Flyer, known for reaching speeds of fifty miles an hour, placing us in that ancient holy city just after eleven o' clock: excellent time.

We then hired a driver with a good team to take us to Wyvern Hall, some nine miles farther out into a lush green country filled with empty hop-fields six weeks past harvest, and marked with trees poking up above every hedgerow, their leaves aflame with a late-autumn majesty of so a striking a vividness that I effortlessly recall them in my mind's eye even now.

Having sent Mr. Reginald Drew a telegram from Canterbury, our arrival was anticipated, and that gentleman, tall and red-faced, and the very image of a country squire down even to his fox-hunting boots, came hurrying out the double-doors at the old stone house's front, to greet us.

"Mr. Holmes, Doctor Watson!" he cried in a strong, reverberating voice of command that hinted at origins in a northern county. "You cannot know what a welcome sight you are to me, nor how eternally grateful I am that you have come after my desperate summons! What is it I might do to aid you, and set you to commencing your investigation?"

Before Holmes could answer, a voice, female and high, strained with emotion and what sounded to my doctor's senses as near-exhaustion called out:

"Find our Liza, sirs! Do find her, I beg you!"

Mr. Drew turned from us toward the person who was making this beseechment, a handsome woman of middle years, a wave of white in her otherwise honey-chestnut hair, which was somewhat less than perfectly dressed at present, excusable of course under the trying and terrible circumstances.

"Mathilde, please, you must wait inside," Mr. Drew instructed, though with gentleness. "Hysteria will not aid Mr. Holmes in locating Liza and restoring her to us. Now please, difficult as it is, retire to the drawing room, my dear."

Holmes, looking toward the woman, said in a placating

and decidedly kind tone:

"It may be I shall soon be in to speak with you, Mrs. Drew. You may yet be of great help to me, but for the moment, your husband is correct, and it is to him that I need speak at present."

Holmes' words seemed to reach past the woman's nervous desperation when her own husband's had not, and after another instant she nodded and turned and let herself be led back into the great stone expanses of Wyvern Hall at the arm of her lady's maid, a charcoal-haired woman of primarily French appearance.

Drew seemed embarrassed and said:

"My apologies."

"Understandable, sir," I told him, "no explanation required."

"If you'll both come with me into the hall, I will tell you what is known to this point, scant and inadequate though it is."

We followed the client through the great wooden double doors at Wyvern Hall's entrance, into a foyer of some stark Medieval grandeur, great darkened beams overhead, and heavy gray floor-stones under foot, and were led into what had doubtless served as some lord's great hall in earlier centuries, a long, rectangular room with a high hammer-beam ceiling, and thin narrow windows that ran from the mid-point of the walls to nearly the ceiling, admitting sufficient light, though the hall maintained a shadowy dimness that required the presence of several sconces of candles to brighten its reaches.

Drew indicated chairs for us near the head of a long table, and only after we were seated did he take his own place, before sending the butler at his elbow off to gather refreshments for us.

"A tray, if you please, Jones," he instructed the man, who was of middling height and years, with receding dark hair and a clean-shaven, expression-less face, and who bowed before stepping off to carry out his master's command. Drew then opened a folder and removed an item from within.

"This, gentlemen, is my daughter, as of last month, when she sat for this at a studio during a day-trip to Canterbury. We were there for the hop-harvest festival put on by the brewers of

Kent."

Drew handed Holmes a photograph in a silver-gilt frame that showed a plump and merry-looking girl with rosy cheeks, the generously-aligned features of her face more those of her father than her mother.

Holmes stared at the image a moment, then commented:

"I see nothing of melancholy in her eyes."

"No," Drew stated, "she has never had an unhappy day in her life, I feel. It is beyond thinking that any action associated with her disappearance could have any sort of upset at its heart."

Holmes placed the photograph flat against the tabletop by me, then asked:

"It is now Thursday, the twelfth, and your note mentioned your daughter had been missing for forty-eight hours. Is this a generality, or as precise as you can be in this matter?"

Drew told him:

"It may have been longer, sir, and likely was, as on Monday night Liza was seen to her room by her maid, who, after inquiring if she required anything else from her, left her seated in a chair by her bedside, near a single candle glowing in the darkness. This was the usual custom."

"And when was this?" Holmes asked.

"Nine-thirty or so on Monday night."

"So in truth Liza may have gone missing at any hour between that moment and dawn, extending the frame of reference to closer to sixty hours on the outside. I suppose the moment her maid returned to the room in the morning and found her not within was when you counted the beginning of her disappearance?"

"Precisely the scenario," Drew agreed, "the maid, a girl called Ernestina, well-liked by my daughter and striking me as not the sort to draw any suspicion to herself, knocked on Liza's door just after seven, bearing the tea tray and preparing to assist her mistress as she did each morning, only to find Liza was not in her room, nor she soon learned, was she to be found in any of the places one might rationally expect her to be."

"Was her bed slept in?" Holmes asked.

"It was not," Drew admitted. "The sheet was still perfectly made, no warmth on the mattress, no indications Liza had gotten into it at all."

Holmes nodded, pondering this. "Tell me," he said, "all which transpired after this disturbing development became known to you."

"Of course true worry was not in me that first hour, though news was brought down to my wife and myself as we took breakfast in the east dining room. Her mother, however, grabbed her heart and said that she had a most dreadful feeling, and in fact had been troubled by frightening dreams of Liza crying out to her from a place of darkness and fear. I did not quite assign merit on this claim, as frankly my wife is an excitable woman, much given to placing stock in her slumbering visions, and ever seeing doom in matters which ultimately prove of but small import. I did, however, set the servants to look throughout the house, and sent the youngest boy here, Sulkes, he is called, his Christian name, incidentally, running to the barn, where I had the groundskeepers, and horsemen, and our driver, Hayes, brought up, and I bade them look across the grounds of the estate. They did so, and neither the inside search nor the one outdoors resulted in Liza being brought home."

"How long did this continue?" Holmes demanded.

"Past noon, at which time I sent for the constable in town, Mr. Harris---a good man, though hard of hearing and a bit on in years---and he told me he regretted that duty bound him to bring his men onto the property and drag both the decorative pond out on the lawn, and the larger lake down by the mill. At which point my wife covered her face and ran screaming into the house, where I went in after her, judging I could do more by calming her down than by standing idly, gaping like a landed eel while police threw hooks into the waters to drag for my daughter's remains. It was a horrid hour, that, I tell you."

"Yet fortunately they did not thusly find her," I supplied.

"Yes, quite," Drew was quick to agree. "That would have

been the fulfillment of a nightmare."

"I think you are holding up well, sir, if I may say so as a doctor," I told him.

"I take heart that I have done what I could, and that is all," he answered me, his tone that of weariness past concern for all save the most necessary of courtesies.

At that moment the butler, Jones, returned bearing a tea tray, and I saw Holmes' eyes pass across him without any sign of real interest as Jones poured us each a cup, along with setting down a platter of crust-less potted meat sandwiches. He then stepped back toward the wall and assumed the expressionless, on-hand pose of well-trained butlers everywhere, arms at his sides, his gaze a thousand yards off.

I took a sip of tea, as much from politeness as the fact I was actually growing thirsty, but Holmes declined with a gesture of his hand.

"How long were the waters you mentioned searched?" he asked instead.

"Across the entire day, and quite thoroughly, with every foot of the pond plumbed by the terrible hooks. Some other oddities, surely unrelated to us or our brief tenancy here, were withdrawn from the waters, however, including a white dress of some apparent antiquity, appearing Georgian by the look, but no sign of Liza or anything connected with her. Toward dusk the search of the waters was called off."

"That was on Tuesday, the first day," said Holmes. "What were the developments of yesterday, the second day of Liza's vanishing?"

"I brought out Lady Mercy, my best hound. At nine she's too old to run with us on our fox hunts, but in her day she had the finest nose of any dog I ever knew. I could have used a younger, fitter animal, but my faith in old Mercy was undimmed. I let her get a good scent off clothing from my daughter's closet, then walked with her all around the perimeter of the house, and then far out onto the lawn and grounds."

"And the result?" I asked.

Drew shook his head. "Disappointing. Mercy picked up signs of Liza's passing at every moment, but none led off the lawn itself."

"That in itself is somewhat peculiar," Holmes said. "Liza has never been inclined to go beyond the immediate environs of Wyvern Hall?"

Drew shook his head. "She is not a walker, but quite a sedentary girl, I'm afraid, more inclined to always have her face in a book than to be out in the healthful sunshine, such is my own inclination, as my squirely ruddiness no doubt betrays. I've long since given up trying to encourage the habit of exercise in her, though in her youngest days she would go out with me as I strolled our environs. She has gone into town by carriage, certainly, but I cannot think of an occasion in which I have ever seen her simply take off walking across the property."

Holmes sat with absolute stillness a long moment, and both Drew and I waited. I could tell some significant thought was taking form within the cloisters of his mighty brain, but when he spoke it was only to ask Drew:

"You mentioned your tenancy at Wyvern Hall has been brief. When did it start?"

"We moved here after signing a twenty-year lease in April of this past spring, so seven months almost exactly."

"Were there others who sought the lease on this property as well as yourself?" Holmes asked.

"Several, one doggedly so, though I outbid him. I understand he withdrew from his attempts with some unfortunate degree of bad blood regarding the matter."

"What was the name of this party?" inquired Holmes.

"A Mr. Kinkaid Mattingly, of Hastings, Sussex. An elderly gentleman of some wasp-like, tyrannical temperament, and a desire to own an historic property."

"Have you had contact with him since assuming the lease on this house?"

"I have had none," said Drew. "In fact I received word that the gentlemen passed on in June. He was nearly seventy, and I am not sure why, given his advanced age and the state of his health, he had been so determined to sign a long-term lease on Wyvern Hall."

Was there some clue in this? I wondered.

"And before that you were in the north?"

"Outside Leeds."

"Has Liza been happy here?" I asked.

"Extraordinarily so," Drew replied. "She was never what I would describe as unhappy in Leeds, where we resided since she was eight, but since our coming here she has...I do not know how to describe it, save to say she has formed a kinship with this place, and its grounds. She has explored every nook and cranny of the house, and read everything she could find on its history. She has even gone down to the kitchens to listen to old Mrs. Hubbards, a semi-retired cook, who has been here for decades, telling her about other times. I half-think Liza might have planned... that is to say that she might *plan---*"

The changed in tenses did not escape Holmes' notice, or my own.

"---to write a history of the place, for all the attention she has given it. The effect this place has had on her sensibilities, and in kindling her curiosity, is unprecedented and remarkable. It is as if she has found the one place in all the world where she was always meant to be."

I found that an odd remark, but made no comment.

"I see," Holmes stated, for his part. He then leaned in closer toward his client, though several feet of tabletop still separated them. "Mr. Drew," he began, "I have it in mind to ask you a difficult question. It is one I should have made eventually in any case, yet in light of the change in tenses you used a moment ago when describing Liza, I will ask now."

"Yes?" the man said rigidly. "You may ask me any question you feel you need to."

"Do you, sir," said Holmes, "believe your daughter remains yet alive?"

The man went quite still and his face was set into a state of stoical fortification when at last he said:

"While hope is a strong thing in a father's heart, and hope yet lives, I have felt more and more that some tragedy, which I cannot explain or understand, has befallen Liza, and that she is..."

He drew a deep, sharp breath, then uttered words I saw were supremely difficult for him to speak:

"That she is no longer among us."

This was, I thought, a terrible admission, and I felt pity for him.

Holmes, though, thought a moment and asked:

"And what is the opinion of your wife?"

"Mathilde is unshakably certain Liza is alive, though equally sure she is in some terrible peril. She clings to this idea, and cites her dream of that first night, and when excitement overcomes her she runs through the house crying out for Liza, calling her name in pitiable and desperate tones. I fear the effect this disappearance will have on her may permanently mar her sanity, and I cannot say which eventuality might prove worse, that Liza be found deceased by some misadventure, or that we never find her at all, and are stuck living with that terrible unknown scarring our lives."

"Both terrible fates," I supplied.

Holmes then asked what I found to be a strange question, bordering almost on the cruel:

"If your daughter should be found to have perished here, Mr. Drew, would your tenancy at Wyvern Hall remain?"

"I do not see how it would be either my own wish, or more particularly that of my wife, to stay here under those dreadful conditions," Drew answered. "Not with so many reminders of our daughter's happiness here, and the tragedy it would then have led to."

"I should find that an understandable sentiment," I said.

"Oddly, sir," said Holmes, "in your overview on the situation, you leave out one strong possibility. It is one that seems past your ability to fully consider."

"What is that?" Mr. Drew asked.

"That Liza has been taken by force."

Drew shook his head. "The idea has come to me, as has the possibility she has for reasons I cannot understand, voluntarily left with someone, but I say to you even as devoid of prejudice against these possibilities as I may be, that I do not believe either scenario is the explanation. I should almost be glad if she had gone on her own, and even if she were taken by an abductor who had somehow made his way into Wyvern Hall and secreted my girl off into the night, for I should face that as the action of a knowable enemy, but my innermost sense is that this has not happened, leaving me only able to say....I do not know what the answer to this miserable torment is."

"Of course not, nor should you" said Holmes, "for it is my task to learn that answer on your behalf, as you may only be expected to go so far, and are wise in now leaving the rest to me."

"I thank you," Drew said. Then as if not sure what else to add, he asked:

"Would you like to speak to Constable Harris? I can have him summoned here to Wyvern Hall within the hour, and he may be able to tell you things which go beyond my own impressions of the search."

"I thank you," said Holmes, "but that will not be necessary, as I find my own investigations quickly supersede those of the police. However, I made a certain quasi-promise to Mrs. Drew outside before my entry here, and should ask to be admitted to the drawing room, where I believe she waits. I would seek to both offer her some comfort in the reassurance that I have rarely failed to find the missing I have sought-after, and also, by your leave, there are certain questions I should like to put to the lady."

Drew said:

"Yes, that will of course be permissible, even welcome, though I bid you recall my descriptions of Mathilde, who is a woman easily excited by nervous anticipation, and by events of a negative character. I ask you, therefore, be as gentle with her as you may, Mr. Holmes. These past two days have tried her soul nearly to its limits."

"I give you my word I shall, and Dr. Watson will be with me, a medical man of sterling reputation and with the capability to render all necessary aid to Mrs. Drew, should she react with distress."

"Then let us go to her now," Drew said, rising.

"I ask a favour, sir, if you will humour me..." Holmes began, his voice rising.

"You wish to see Mathilde without my being present?" Drew guessed mildly.

"Would this be an indulgence you would grant me?" Holmes asked.

"Of course," Drew replied. "I will deny you nothing, as I have promised. I shall have Jones, our butler, show you the way and will remain here, awaiting you whenever you wish to see me. I am present to aid in any way I may, however inadequate that may be."

Jones released himself from his unmoving pose by the wall, showing how attentive he was despite giving an impression of that almost catatonic state proper butlers took on, and led us from the great hall toward the withdrawing room, where Mrs. Drew was likely expecting us.

As we progressed I thought of what Holmes and I had thus far been told, and had to conclude I felt little save a blank sense of puzzlement. One theory which came to me following Holmes' earlier remark, and which I wanted to mention to him soon, was of an abductor carrying young Liza from the manor, perhaps drugged in some fashion, and setting her straight onto a horse, which then galloped off into the night. It would explain the lack of any traces of her for the dog to find outside on the earth, and if Holmes agreed it was a theory worth pursuing, I thought we could have Mr. Drew summon this Lady Mercy once again from her kennel, and seeing if she showed signs of following any strange trails off the grounds.

Still, I said nothing as we were brought before Mrs. Drew, who rose straight up from the sofa upon which she had been reclining, in a folded pose. She advanced toward us, her sheer desperation putting aside the niceties of ladylike courtesy, and simply demanded:

"Any news?"

"I fear not, Madam, as I have only just come from speaking with your husband."

"Oh," she said, "yes...I quite understand, it's just...one hopes, and time seems so distorted when trapped in worry. You've been here less than an hour, haven't you? I have not slept, you see, since that last night my daughter was among us."

Feeling my medical impulses take over, I said to her:

"Oh, but you must sleep, for it is during times of distress when the body most needs to be sustained. I could give you something to take at a later hour which would help you fall asleep, if you'd like, and if your husband is agreeable to the idea."

"No," she said at once. "I thank you, sir, but, no, I must be awake and know at once of my daughter's return."

Poor woman, I thought.

Perhaps there was something in my face which gave away my pessimism, despite the theory of the type of abduction I'd just been pondering, for she looked to me and said:

"Please, sir, do not think you need shield me, for I know my daughter is alive. It is a connection to her I have always felt, and I feel it still, though I sense about her a tremendous sense of terror and difficulty...not injury, but... Oh, I cannot place it into words, all is futility, but I know she is alive, for, you see, I lost two of my children in their youths, and I *felt* their passing, Doctor, and knew the precise instant when the light of their souls was extinguished in this world. I tell you, believe this if you believe nothing else I might ever utter: my Liza is alive!"

It was an ardent entreaty, to say the least, and I looked to Holmes, who did not look back at me, merely fastened his gaze onto the woman, and I read no small sense of evaluation there.

"Mrs. Drew," he began some seconds after she had finished her claim, "I will tell you, I have no reason to believe Miss Liza has perished, so your fervent hopes are not a thing I would discourage, nor would I lightly dismiss a mother's instinctive sense of her offspring's condition. It is a thing I have witnessed on other occasions, and hold it in some respect, despite my capacity to explain such phenomena through the power of reasoning alone."

Mrs. Drew placed both hands above her heart and uttered: "Thank you."

"If you would be so kind as to allow yourself to take your seat, Madam," Holmes told her, "I do wish your comfort during the questions I have come to ask you."

These words resulted in Mrs. Drew obliging him and sinking back to the emerald-green fabric of the sofa, where she seemed to recover some portion of her social graces, for she urged:

"And won't you gentlemen please do likewise and take a seat?"

Thus invited by the lady, I selected a padded chair at the distant right of the sofa, and Holmes one just opposite me. When we were in place, Holmes began.

"Mrs. Drew," he said, "your husband has told me of the efforts to locate Liza, including the searches within the bodies of water on the estate, and of the employment of a skilled bloodhound in his attempt to track her. None of this has yielded either your daughter's rescue from some difficulty she might be facing, nor rendered a single clue. Have you any insights beyond these methods of search which could aid me in my own undertaking?"

Mrs. Drew thought quietly, though her left foot swung in a slow circle, so profound was the agitation she barely contained. Finally she said:

"It is a mystery of an utter and absolute nature, Mr. Holmes, and I can think of no one who would wish to harm my daughter or secret her away, nor can I come upon any motive for her to leave us without word. She is not quite a reclusive young woman, but certainly what one might term a 'homebody,' and has no friends in town, or any neighbouring estates, either, and no interests in the outer world."

"Is it at all possible the young lady had acquired a paramour of whom you and Mr. Drew remained unaware?" Holmes asked, delicately.

"I will," the lady told him, "state now with complete candor and finality, that there is no romantic assignation anywhere at the heart of this. My Liza has never been courted, nor is she yet of an age to be. She is also particularly young for her years. I can't think of any time she was ever off the grounds by herself. There cannot have been more than two or three occasions since our relocation here that she was ever in town at all, and then with me and her father. I would rate this the most impossible among any explanations one might put forward concerning her disappearance."

"Then what *do* you hold to be the explanation?" Holmes inquired of her, though his words were spoken softly and with a gentleness rare to him.

A burst of deep frustration flowed from Mrs. Drew, resulting in her throwing out her hands in an almost violent gesture, as she declared:

"I have none! If I had I should have gone to her, wherever she is right now, afraid and alone and in terrible distress, which is what I feel in my soul is her state, Mr. Holmes! Please, sir, help her return to us!"

I saw she was a woman on the brink of hysteria itself, for every soul had a limit, and I noted she was perilously close to her own. Without good news, or the ease of a night's sleep, I feared the client, Mr. Drew, might soon find his concerns focused upon the well-being of an additional member of his household.

"Holmes," I said quietly, "I think it best we leave Mrs. Drew alone, and not pose any more questions to her."

I expect Holmes was about to demonstrate his agreement with my advice, when Mrs. Drew abruptly became composed, and said:

"I am sorry, Doctor, I let myself become lost in feeling for that instant, but I assure you, I should never forgive myself if I failed to offer whatever assistance I could, so please, feel free to ask me anything, and I will answer."

It was almost exactly the same words her husband had put to us in his own offer of unlimited aid.

This declaration seemed to satisfy Holmes, for he thought for a few seconds before he asked with great delicacy and tact:

"I was told a moment ago in the great hall that Liza is something of a scholar."

"She is," Mrs. Drew said, and a smile actually penetrated her look of worry. "In fact she is a well-read girl, and I am glad our era permits young ladies the undertaking, which was more restricted back in mid-century, when I was her age and it was said scholarship was detrimental to a girl's physical and spiritual health."

A terrible misunderstanding among doctors and the clergy of those days, I thought, disapprovingly, for I was all in favour of a woman being educated.

"I understand," prodded Holmes, "the history of Wyvern Hall itself was a particular subject of interest to her?"

"Indeed, it had become something of a preoccupation in the weeks leading up to...to these last few days. Of us all it was she who immediately found the greatest charm resident in Wyvern Hall, and she took to it here far better than I ever imagined."

"And what did she relate to you and her father concerning her discoveries?"

"She knew the history of its earliest structure, a fortified manor dating to the reign of Henry III, which today lies incorporated into the design of the hall. She told me this, as well as informing me that the wing in which we now sit was put up not long after the Stuart Restoration. Great improvements were made in the last years before we took the house's lease, the former owners having gone bankrupt, I understand, before selling it off to an agency in London, but it is still an expensive place in which to live, or so Reggie, er, that is my husband, Reginald, tells me."

"And had Liza learned something of the history enacted within this house?" Holmes pressed.

"Yes, random things she gleaned from books. There was a Roundhead officer once held captive here, she claimed, apparently for ransom, which when paid saw him set free once again. There was a tournament held out on the lawn in the time of Henry VII. Also a trio of nuns was once given a room in the highest tower, and lived for two decades in a retreat from the world, while praying for blessings on the family, here, who housed them. I believe she said this was in the 1450s or thereabouts. She thrived on acquiring all this knowledge of the Hall, which she said soon after we came here felt more like her 'true home' than anywhere she had ever been. Truthfully she seemed at once to become a part of this place."

There was, I decided something almost sinister in the woman's words, and I sensed Holmes agreed, for he asked:

"Was Liza's sentiment toward the manor...a healthy one in your eyes?"

"It was not quite an obsession," the missing girl's mother answered, "nor a *mania*, as I understand that affliction, but I would call it a deep fascination. Aside from speaking to a retired cook here and others with long-standing on the estate, she had discovered a number of tomes in the library, which detailed the goings-on here I have mentioned. Some of these were old stories compiled by one of the ladies of the manor, who dwelled here in the 1720s or...something like that, but who wrote much of older times."

"And where are these books at present?" Holmes demanded.

"I confess I do not know. As she removed them from the library, then I suppose they are in Liza's room."

"May we be permitted to search for them in each location?" Holmes asked.

"Of course. Please, you have my leave to feel at liberty to go anywhere on these grounds, and see whatever you feel may be of help. If you need a servant to assist, merely ask."

Holmes stood, so I did the same, and he bowed to the lady and said:

"I may require the assistance of a servant, but til then, Madam, I thank you. I know this is time of unparalleled difficulty, but I share your optimism concerning your daughter's condition, not the least of which because of your testimony to the fact that she still lives. You have given me much to think on, and I will go now to do my utmost to bring this horrid matter to the best possible conclusion."

The lady spoke her thanks, and we went back into the outer hallway, where from the corner of my eye I saw she fell back against the green sofa, as if spent.

"To the library now?" I asked, once we were back in the long gallery that lay between the withdrawing room and several other places within Wyvern Hall.

"I think not," said Holmes, "for I believe I can learn more by what lies within Miss Liza's bedchamber. Let us proceed there."

After informing the dutiful Jones of where we wished to go, we were taken up to the second floor, where a few moments later the butler pushed open the oaken door to the young woman's private domain.

To my surprise, Holmes reached out and took hold of the door, causing Jones to hastily withdraw his hand, though I felt sure Holmes had not meant this as an offense against the man, but had merely lost himself in a thought, as he often did. This was confirmed when in the next instant he opened and shut the door several times, both rapidly and also slowly, as one might if one wished to be stealthy.

"The door makes no sound," he said. "Note that, Watson."

"No, sir," said Jones, with full propriety yet also a slight touch of impugned dignity, "I see that there are no squeaky doors here at Wyvern Hall. It simply would not do to allow a place so venerable and grand to slide so much as an inch into anything but its finest condition."

Holmes turned to him with a quick spin and said:

"Ah, I salute your attention to detail, Jones. It is a fine thing to see a servant so dedicated to his employment."

Jones bowed solemnly and stated with pride:

"My deepest thanks for your considerate compliment, sir, I am sure you are correct."

"I see you share a reverence for this place not unlike that of your young mistress."

"I do, sir."

"If I might ask, my good fellow..." Holmes added, "have you any insights to offer, or even theories of your own to add, concerning Miss Liza Drew's sudden vanishing?"

An expression of deepest sympathy came upon Jones. "I regret I know nothing, sir, nor do I have anything of substance to add by way of assistance."

"Nothing whatsoever?" Holmes pressed, and it seemed to me he was looking at the man with a particular intensity. "I find in my work it is often the servants who know more about the goings-on of a home than the masters."

"I'm afraid I do not, sir," maintained the butler, the height of propriety, showing both sympathy and detachment in equal measure.

"Tell me then of this young Ernestina, Miss Liza's personal maid," demanded Holmes.

"A good girl, sir, or so my impressions have been, having known her but for a short time, she coming into Wyvern Hall with the family upon their taking of the lease last spring."

"She is diligent in her duties, and of sound character?" Holmes asked.

With utter calm, Jones replied:

"I would answer affirmatively to each question, sir."

"Her account of the events on Miss Liza's final night before her disappearance...you have heard this, and feel no reason to doubt her claims?"

"I have not formed a strong opinion there, sir," he answered Holmes, "though as my betters see no reason to doubt the young woman's account, I feel it is not my place to initiate such troubling sentiments."

"This Ernestina was the final witness to a young woman who is now missing," Holmes said, "so some might say a great focus *should* fall upon her. Was it in your presence that this Ernestina was spoken to by the constable from the town?"

"Not 'in my presence,' sir, but the girl was interviewed, as was I and several others on staff here. The constable was not, so far as my lack of expertise in such matters allows me say, troubled by anything the lady's maid Ernestina reported, or by the testimony of any of us. I should be surprised more than words can convey if it were ever shown that impropriety on behalf of any member of staff played any rôle in the matter of Miss Liza Drew's vanishing. I can, if it please you, have the girl Ernestina brought for you to interview."

"Unnecessary," Holmes answered him. "What were your own whereabouts on the night Miss Liza vanished?"

"I was abed, sir, being privileged to have completed my duties relatively early, and had retired for the night by Mr. Drew's leave. It is something of a luxury to be in bed before ten when one has the responsibilities of a butler in a large country house such as Wyvern Hall, and I was grateful to have a little extra sleep."

"How many years have you served here?"

"Six years, sir, all as butler. If I may volunteer the information in light of current events, my letters of reference prior to my time of service in this house, have been impeccable, and I am understandably proud of the high regard with which my employers have held me ever since my days as a footman at Howland House, on the north coast of the county, back in the early '60s."

If I had to guess I would say his statement was completely true, and little to no fault had ever been found in the man's performance of duty. Yet Holmes went on, asking:

"And what, Jones, were your impressions of the young lady?"

"My impressions of Miss Liza, sir? I'm sure I composed

none at all, nor would it have been my place to have done, as I serve at the pleasure of my employers, sir, I do not presume to judge any of my betters, from the Queen down to the children of those who employ me in my present capacity."

I could not decide if Jones were maintaining what he thought was a dutiful detachment from matters outside his station, or if he were taking Holmes through the steps of some stubborn dance, but my friend still did not allow things to drop so easily, for he then said:

"When you found Miss Liza about her solitary walk in the house, late at night when all others were abed, what were you left to think?"

Here Jones did bat his eyes and show a modicum of expression in the form of surprise.

"I was not aware those incidents were known to you, sir," he said, "and I do offer my apologies for not volunteering them of my own accord. A servant, if he is a good one, sir, must be highly selective in what he 'sees' and does 'not' see, you understand, and the activities of one of my betters in her own home was not my affair to make note of."

He had seen the girl wandering at night? I thought, hammer-struck. *What was this about?*

"Of course," said Holmes lightly, "and I am coming to gain the greatest of respect for your dedication to a higher model of conduct for a butler."

"Again, I thank you, sir, and in answer to your inquiry, I felt nothing whatsoever at discovering Miss Liza on that occasion alone in the eastern hallway after-hours, holding a candle and simply making her way along. The hour was odd, true, but there was nothing distressing or untoward in her behavior. She was, quite simply, walking, nothing more."

Somehow this felt like too much, for however determined Jones was to become an emotionless machine of absolute service, he was still a human being, and therefore some reaction must have taken residence in him when he encountered his employer's daughter out of bed and wandering...though how

Holmes had known of this incident I could not imagine, yet it was no more remarkable than any of scores of other unexpected facts I had known him to reveal.

"What precisely was young Miss Liza doing when you spotted her in this undertaking?" Holmes demanded.

"As I have said, sir," Jones said mildly, "the young lady appeared to simply be walking slowly, and nothing else."

"Was she looking about her?"

"Not that I noticed, sir."

"Besides the candle, was she holding anything at all?"

Here Jones hesitated, and however dutifully circumspect his replies had been thus far, I sensed he was reticent to reveal all of what he had beheld, leaving me to wonder why.

"As I think on it, sir," he said at last, "I do seem to recollect she had a small tan-jacketed book tucked under her right arm."

Holmes received this news without expression, but said:

Ah….a book, I see." This seemed to satisfy him, possibly even please him, and he stated:

"Jones, I thank you, for you have been most helpful. The Drew family is fortunate, indeed, to have an attentive and dutiful servant such as yourself in their employ…though I know your devotion is firstly to Wyvern Hall, whoever may occupy it."

What did this mean, I wondered.

Jones, likewise, appeared about to say something in reply to this, but declined and instead bowed and offered his thanks with humility, before asking if we needed anything else, to which Holmes stated we did not, so the man went on his way with a precise and orderly stride, disappearing into an adjoining hallway with all the silence of a drifting ghost.

He was, I decided, surely the epitome of what most gentleman wished for in a butler, his personality concealed to the point a person could not be certain he even possessed one. Yet, when the door was closed, Holmes opined:

"That man is an insufferable toadstool on a rotting log, Watson."

"Jones?" I inquired. "I was just thinking how I took him for a nearly perfect model of deferential courtesy."

Holmes scoffed. "Had that milquetoast but spoken up about the detail concerning his observation of the young lady out of bed in the recent past, walking about in the night, the information would have been of great use to all concerned. I would warrant he had no intentions of mentioning it save that I coaxed it from him."

"Holmes," I said, addressing my puzzlement at last on that subject, "no one downstairs mentioned Miss Liza walking about at night, so how did you, yourself, know?"

"It is part of a unifying theory, Watson, and I took a chance on one minute segment of it being correct. As it was, much else may be."

"A guess then?" I posited.

"An 'educated inquiry,' let us term it," he quibbled.

I then mentioned my theory of an abduction in the night, tying in my idea of a villain's flight on horseback with an unconscious Liza secured in his arms, thereby leaving no trace of her scent for the dog to pick up, but at my ardent words Holmes simply shook his head.

"Unlikely, Watson, as no hoof-marks were upon the lawn. Mr. Drew is not a foolish man, nor likely is the local constable, whatever his limitations in intellect, being a policeman, yet neither reported such a detail."

"Oh, I see," I said quietly, deflated at his dismissal.

"But," he said, "other trails of a more germane sort are at-hand. Come, do you espy that small stack of books by the girl's bedside? Those stand to tell us much. Help me scan through them."

So I went with Holmes across the floor of the rather large, if somewhat plain, bedchamber, where there was little to see save a wardrobe, a dressing table capped by a mirror, and a small trunk at the foot of a mid-sized bed with four posters, surrounded by a thick set of old-looking curtains of a jade hue which at present were drawn back, but which in the night might be loosened about the one lying in repose, protection against the cold winters that could roll in off the Channel.

These same curtains met with Holmes' disapproval, as he snorted and told me:

"I would never sleep under such an arrangement, Watson, with my sight of the outer room blocked by drapery which left me lying vulnerable in the night to the approach of an assassin."

"An assassin?"

"Oh, yes, I must always expect an act of retribution to be launched against me on behalf of some criminal element or other, as several such have already come to pass, none successful, as you see, though the incident with the razor-sharp knife thrown at my neck in Covent Gardens four summers ago by Riccardo Viscuso, the Sicilian cut-throat for hire, was a near thing. He tried to keep the code of *omerta* as to whom had hired him, but I pierced the veil of his dogged silence and brought truth into the light. I later had the pleasure of seeing Viscuso hanged at Reading, though for older crimes."

For I presumed different reasons, Mary shared something of my friend's distaste for bed-curtains, insisting there be no such installation around our own, back home, though as for me, I felt an indifference toward the arrangement.

I asked:

"Do you think such a scenario has come to pass here, then, someone entering the room unseen due to the curtains?"

"No, Watson, I tell you there is no evidence for any abduction. There has been no ransom demand, and frankly, you saw the girl in the photograph, she is both young in years and not of an appearance to inspire such heights of obsessive interest in a man. My thoughts here were more of a personal nature, as I am aware that I am rarely in more vulnerable a state to the retribution of the many enemies I have made, than when I lie in the depths of sleep, as, alas, much against my will, I must. In fact I have made arrangements for self-protection, and it would not do for one to come un-admitted into my room in the night."

I wondered what these "arrangements for self-defense" were, but did not ask. Some sort of snare-trap, perhaps? One did reel to consider what intricate traps the mind of Sherlock Holmes could devise.

He handed me the book on top of the stack, then took another for himself. The title of the volume I was given read:

A Gathering of Accounts and Musings Rendered Upon the Subject of Wyvern Hall, in the County of Kent, Compiled by Mistress Della Holderness, Summer 1745.

"Quite some title," I joked, but Holmes was poring too deeply into his own tome---*The Story of the Shameful Fall of Miss Katelyn Jethroe*---to grant a reply.

My own volume was as dry as the title, but I discovered that someone, presumably Miss Liza, had marked several passages with bits of ribbon, and I found each page thus separated from the others gave a description of some noteworthy event from Wyvern Hall's long history. In one instance there was an overnight stay in the progress of a queen consort and her retinue through the Home Counties. A great banquet had been thrown in royal honour, and had apparently been quite the occasion, drawing gentry and nobles to Wyvern Hall from far and wide.

Another page which was marked told of the family then in residence, shutting the gates and keeping the entire household inside for a month during an outbreak of plague in 1665, much like a scene out of Boccaccio....or, I thought, *The Masque of the Red Death*, by that American writer of the macabre, Edgar Allan Poe, who'd been popular when I was a boy.

In general, I found the long-dead Mistress Holderness had been as much a compiler of gossip as real history, though found she was, in her archaic prose, something of a deft storyteller, for I found my eye wanting to linger over individual pages rather than abandoning them to scan for some useful clue as to what may have been in Miss Liza's mind in recent days. It was simply too immense a volume for me to land at random on anything particularly telling, and I was on the verge of saying so when Holmes finally spoke.

"Watson, what I hold is a sort of Gothic romance from a

past era, the 1790s," he remarked, "yet is, I think, based on some ancestral memory of events which took place hereabouts in the area, though Wyvern Hall itself is disguised by the author and dubbed Drake Hall."

"Wyvern and Drake, each mythical dragons of a sort," I chuckled. "So Miss Liza was an aficionado of Gothic romances?"

I only caught after the words had already left my mouth that I'd referred to the girl in the past tense, and felt a little ripple of shame, for it was better to retain hope on her behalf.

"To an extent I suspect all girls of a certain age are vulnerable to such tales, Watson," Holmes answered. "Think on the perennial popularity of Miss Austen's *Northanger Abbey*."

"What is the plot of the book you hold?" I asked.

"Ah, that is not the question, for I think there may have been another aspect which drew our vanished Miss Liza to this account, as it concerns a bored young lady who falls romantically in love with a dashing suitor from below her station in life."

"That sounds like pretty standard fare for such stories," I offered, thinking that I'd never known a girl not to dream of some handsome stranger entering unexpectedly into her life.

"Indeed...." he agreed, though he was not facing me, as his eyes moved rapidly through the pages, reading at a much faster rate than ever I should ever have been capable of doing, five complete pages in a minute. "And while I will note that while the story is undeniably cast against a setting based on Wyvern Hall, it also contains...."

Here his voice trailed off, and I waited, unsure if I should turn my attention back to my own book of semi-factual events from local parts, or wait for him to finish his thoughts, only to see that he had suddenly frozen into place, alarm now radiating from him.

"Watson...." he finally uttered, his face troubled, his body tense. "Oh, Watson, this could be very bad indeed."

Holmes," I demanded, "what have you discovered?"

"I can," he said with a mingling of caution and something

close to horror, "discern that the pages of this chapter have recently been read on many occasions, marking it a favourite of Miss Liza, and I greatly fear what its mingling of legend and invention suggests in light of her disappearance."

"Well whatever does it say?" I demanded with agitation, as frightened by his reaction as I was curious at his deduction.

He read me the passage which had so jarred his mind, and I grasped the cause of his fear, and at once came to share it, for surely those words hinted at the dark explanation to everything, and a more perilous revelation could scarcely be imagined.

"Can that be the answer?" I cried, rising and wishing to set off into motion, but not knowing the direction to travel.

"I think we have happened across the answer," the detective stated, "and now, Watson, it has been two full days, and perhaps half of another, and as you are a doctor, tell me, what are her chances of still being alive under the circumstances we presently fear?"

Forcing the book's dreaded revelation from my mind, I said:

"She is young, in good health, and carries a bit of extra weight, all things that would be in her favour, but after two and one-half days we are approaching the margins of what the human body can be expected to endure."

"My thoughts as well!" cried Holmes, who was now pacing across the room, his mind whirling to pierce through a thousand locations, and deduce which one held the answer.

As another story by Poe, *The Premature Burial*, flashed through my thoughts, I said with feeling:

"Holmes, this is a fate which cries out with true horror."

For the pages upon which Holmes had paused were those which told of the young lovers from the tale discovering a secret room hidden within the walls of Drake Hall, the literary surrogate for Wyvern Hall, and hiding away from the disapproving world, leading first my friend, and now me to conclude Miss Liza had been captivated by the idea of such a hidden and forgotten room existing in the house, and after reading and re-reading the tale many times, had spent her nights secretly questing for this fanciful room, only to find it surely against her every expectation, and she was now trapped somewhere within the Hall itself, having discovered a concealed doorway she found easier to enter through than to open again when she wished to leave. The explanation seemed unlikely, but somehow I knew in my heart it was correct. There was, indeed, a hidden room in the house, and the girl was there, and after so long a time trapped inside....would she even still be alive?

"Where could this room be in so vast a place?" I called out, as my friend paced, his face pulled tight with concentration as thoughts rushed within him. "The story suggests a place at the foot of a tower."

"There are eight towers, Watson, and by what signs are we to recognize a room so cunningly hidden? By what mechanism should such a door be opened? It is a formidable task, even now that I fasten upon it."

"If a fourteen year old girl can penetrate such a contraption, I think you can, Holmes," I said, buoyed by the thought.

Without replying, he rushed past me and was out the door and into the hallway, leaving me to scuttle after as he hurried to the nearest tower, which rose above the outer walls to a height of sixty feet, ivy-covered on the exterior, but dark and damp there on the inside. He peered closely at the wall, then fit his fingers into the mortar, scraping at it and tracing the fit between the stones, but after a moment I could see such an endeavor was destined to yield no result. He turned from that first tower and veritably ran off in the direction of another, though that undertaking, too, resulted in uncharacteristic failure which left him sneering with anger.

After a lack of success at the third tower, he halted and said with more inner calm than his exterior expression displayed:

"No, this is wrong, I am relying on the elimination of possibility, when I should be employing deduction alone. Think on this matter, Watson...where are servants likely to be in the hours of early night?"

"Abed, I should think," I supplied.

"As a rule, though where would a butler be going at such an hour?"

"A butler?"

I thought of the dutiful Jones, and tried to match some aspect of his labours within the house with a purpose for his being up at the late hour at which he'd encountered Miss Liza in the hallway. The more I considered the scenario, the more puzzling it became, for I could think of no duties that would keep the man out in the hours of darkness when sleep was such a precious commodity to any busy man, so why *had* he been up and afoot?

"Holmes," I said at last, "you did not ask Jones *why* he was in position to see the young lady at that improbable hour!"

"I did not," he agreed, "for I intuited our ever-proper servant should have fabricated a lie."

"A lie, you say? So he had an *improper* reason for his being where he was?"

"Oh, yes, otherwise he should have reported the girl's behavior to her father. Why else did he keep his silence *save to protect himself*?"

"You knew this when you spoke to him," I cried. "Was he keeping an assignation with another on staff here?" I asked, slightly aghast at this reality intruding into matters, and proving the butler's refined propriety a mere façade.

Then there came a thought which all-but made me reel with its indecency.

"Unlikely," Holmes said in any case, quashing the idea before it could fully flourish in my mind and run off into directions best left unconsidered. "I did not detect subterfuge in the man's overall demeanor, for he was as he presented himself to be, a servant so long dedicated to the utmost performance of his function that it had replaced his original nature. Nor did he strike me as a man of burning passions. It was only when

I pressed him about the encounter in the hallways, which he wished not to mention at all, that he fabricated as he did, though I gathered at once that his reasons did not concern Miss Liza directly, but rather there was another motivation behind his actions, and his facile attempt to conceal his undertakings from me."

He scoffed to show his sentiments regarding Jones' amateurish attempt to deceive one such as he, but as for me, I pressed:

"Then what?"

"Watson, did you take notice of his shoes?" he asked.

"His shoes? No...?"

"They were noiseless, Watson, wherever he walked, for they had felt glued to the soles."

"I did notice the quiet with which he moved," I said, "and at the time he left us thought his silence was rather ghost-like. Also his stride...there was excess care in it, rendering his steps odd, somehow. It was so he would not slide, wasn't it? What is the significance of that?"

"It is not the usual practice of a butler to undertake such an action, which left me wondering at once why he made such a little-noticed alteration to his shoes. I concluded it was not because of any request of his employers, for who would ask such a thing of a servant, thus I knew it was but a personal decision, which went unnoticed. I decided the facts suggested he was satisfying his sense of curiosity concerning some event in which silence was required. And when is silence most necessary?"

"When one is sneaking!" I cried out. "He was regularly following Miss Liza through the darkness each night!"

"Indeed, Watson, for it was not merely on the single occasion that Jones saw the young lady slip from her room, it was often. He followed her from a distance, perhaps in the beginning suspecting she was pursuing an improper act of some sort, stealing sugar from the kitchens, let us say, for she is not a slender girl, and had this been so he would have been duty-bound to report her conduct to her father. However, upon finding that she was not doing what he might have expected, but obviously seeking out something hidden among the walls here, he grew perplexed, and made a regular practice of waiting for her in the dark hallway, to observe where she went. I imagine through those first nights his puzzlement was profound when he saw she had no apparent destination in mind, but sneaked through Wyvern Hall tapping at stones and peering at walls, going behind tapestries and studying her environs, in search of what, he knew not."

There was something here I could not understand, and asked:

"Then why *did* he not inform her father of her behavior as it was ongoing, and why did he not report it after her disappearance?"

"I noted something peculiar tonight, Watson. Each of the volumes showed signs that Miss Liza was not the only recent reader, and one book in particular revealed to me that certain pages were more commonly read than any others."

"Which book?"

"It was the least worthy of them all, a fanciful adventure story which told of the concealing of the lost treasure of the House of York within this very place, under the command of King Richard III in the days before Bosworth."

"What? There's treasure here?" I cried.

"Hardly, Watson, for there was no great York treasure horde save that which lay within the vaults of the Tower itself, the same which sits there today, the legacy of all British sovereigns. It was a tale told to stoke the fires of imagination alone, yet Jones read this and assumed if a young lady from among his betters believed in its existence, it was surely a truth. He observed her across many nights, Watson, having arrived at the conclusion it was this treasure Miss Liza sought, never dreaming it was but the place where lovers in a Gothic fiction so romantically concealed themselves that filled her thoughts. When Liza went missing, he kept what he knew silent, thinking if he told how he had seen her roaming in the night, it would come to light that she was questing for a forgotten room filled with treasure, and every opportunity for him to take the treasure for himself should vanish."

"So," I exclaimed with disgust, "Jones decided a girl's life was worth his acquiring a fortune that does not even exist!"

"Precisely. He is a butler of outward perfection, but in his heart roils the same low impulses of avarice one might find in the basest footpad."

"Holmes, his indirect actions are deplorable enough, but is there a chance he has directly harmed the lady himself?" I demanded.

"I think not, Watson, for if you remember, I kept Jones long occupied in conversation back at the girl's bedchamber an hour ago, and I read no signs I should expect to find in a man concealing an act of murder, but rather I detected a well-concealed frustration, for the events of the last two days have put a halt to his own searches for the treasure just when he had narrowed down the location, being close enough behind Liza in the darkness to know approximately where she disappeared....wherever that is. His crime lies in suspecting that his employer's daughter did indeed find the hoard, but for some reason cannot release herself from the room itself, which I feel is halfway accurate, for though the room confines her, it does not hold treasure...it likely holds nothing, including food or water to sustain her. Thus her life is ebbing by the hour."

My frustration was driving me almost to despair, and I all-but shouted:

"There are a hundred places the builder of such a room might conceal it, Holmes, so how are we to narrow it down?"

"As I now deduce that we have a witness to all but the final moment of that night," he said calmly, "we have no need to continue our search. Not when the man can be persuaded to tell us."

I had been so agitated I had not thought of this, though I am sure after a second's calm I would have, though even as the glee at this development rose in me, another thought intruded.

"But, Holmes," I said, "what if, thinking only of the treasure he believes is within his reach, he refuses to tell us what he knows, and continues to play the part of innocent ignorance?"

"Oh, Watson," my friend said, steadily, "you truly are so decent at heart that your thoughts cannot go in any other direction, can they?"

"Holmes?"

"Watson, do you seriously think I would allow an innocent young woman to perish in so a hideous manner, while a man held out the knowledge to release her from her torment?"

"But...how?"

"By whatever means is required, Watson," he said darkly. "By whatever effort it takes. Come, let us find this odious servant..."

As we walked, Holmes stated:

"There are two possibilities which diverge like a fork in a road. Either Jones knows the location of the room from having followed the girl there, in which case he is a villain of the first order for allowing a young girl to face such a terrible death as he waits to make his own attempt at opening the room, or he does not know *exactly* where the room lies, in which case his crime is more indirect, and rooted in silence."

"Which under the circumstances is nearly as egregious," I said.

"Precisely," said Holmes. "It is time we found out."

"You mean to pry the facts from him directly?" I asked, unsure how I felt about that prospect, but in my desperation not entirely appalled by the idea.

"The direct route is not the best one here, Watson," he said, dismissing my concerns, "so I will set a snare for the fellow, and see which rules him more, his greed or his prudence."

Here he paused and commanded me:

"Watson, do fetch a stoppered flask of water and bring it with you. I shall meet you downstairs in the Tudor library."

To what end could a flask be used, I wondered, even as I

hurried to do as he said and made my way to the kitchen, where an aged woman called Mrs. Hubbards aided me by finding what I sought and filling it with well water from a ceramic ewer. I then sealed the flask with a cork, and after thanking the woman, hurried on my way. I became turned around for the merest moment, Wyvern Hall being so vast, but it was not five minutes since I left Holmes that I entered the reaches of the library, a rectangular room on the ground floor, where many shelves rested against the high-ceilinged walls, each filled with displays of books, some of considerable age. Under other circumstances I may have found great interest in looking through this collection, but as it was, I arrived just as Holmes and Mr. Drew were stepping in before me, in conversation.

"Mr. Holmes," Drew was saying, barely containing himself from flying off into a huff, for he remained in the state of deep agitation that had ruled him for most of a week, "I have done as you said and followed you from the great hall into the library, asking every step of the way for news, yet you reveal nothing and but bid me be patient, as I have these last minutes of our journey, so I beg you, *tell me if you have news, sir!*"

"Ah, Watson," Holmes said, "come and join us. You have procured the item I asked you to retrieve."

"I have, it's here on my---"

"Splendid, so keep it til I ask for it!" Holmes interrupted, leaving me with the impression he did not want the item reveled. In any case Drew was scarcely paying attention to me, so riveted onto Holmes were all his attentions.

"Sir..." Drew began. "Tell me something, I do beg you, not even as a client to his consultant, but as one man to another!"

Holmes faced him and with sympathy in his bearing, said:

"I do thank you for your humouring of me, my good Drew, and for the selfsame patience on your part, which you have referenced. I do have news to impart. To begin, where is your butler, Jones, at this moment?"

Drew became flustered that talk should go into that direction, but faithfully answered in a great burst of exclamation:

"Seeing to his duties below-stairs!"

"Excellent," Holmes remarked, "then summon him, if you'd be so kind."

Staring for only an instant, Drew stepped to the corner of the library and gave the red velvet cord which dangled there a strong pull. Somewhere far off in Wyvern Hall, I knew a little bell would be ringing.

"Now what is the situation," Drew insisted. "You have not, I gather, found Liza, but there has been progress, yes?"

"There has been a development which gives me the best hopes I have had since arriving here this afternoon," Holmes told him. "and I require the presence of Jones to proceed further. Well, I confess, that is not quite accurate, for I could proceed absent the man, but as he stands to expedite matters by his presence, I would be foolish not to make use of him."

"Jones?" Drew said, befuddled. "How on earth can my servant---"

At that instant the expressionless and utterly calm butler silently entered the room through the outer door, concealed as it was behind a shelf of faux volumes designed by some long-ago architect to hide the exit to the casual eye, creating the illusion one was utterly surrounded by an island of books.

"You rang, sir?" Jones inquired, seemingly placid and poised to render whatever service might be asked of him, though I saw his eyes were quite bright with attention.

"Er, yes," said Drew, "I... Well blast it all, Holmes, why exactly did you have me call the man?"

"Jones, come and stand precisely here, before me if you would," Holmes instructed the servant, a look in his eye I had seen many times, for it was the half-concealed gaze of a hunter who at last circles his prey before the long-anticipated kill.

The butler showed the faintest trace of incomprehension, but did as instructed and moved across the floor about a yard off from his master, while Holmes stepped a few paces back from him, and I stood where I had been, off to the left of things.

"*Mr. Drew...*" Holmes began, "I regret to inform you that this man has acted against your house, and betrayed the trust you have so diligently placed in him."

"What," cried Drew, "Jones here? But he was interviewed by the constable, and has been the very epitome of duty, most particularly during these past days of crisis when we have relied on his steadfastness."

Jones remained devoid of emotion, and might as well have been hearing news of a delivery of tea-cups from London as listening to a detective speaking out against his good name, though finally he said:

"I am sure, sir, I do not know to what actions on my part you refer. Have I given unintended offense in some manner?"

"Yes, Holmes," said Drew, "do speak clearly and out with it. What is it you accuse this man of doing?"

"I accuse him at the very least of endangering your daughter's life with his negligent passivity, by leaving Miss Liza to die slowly and horridly within a place of concealment inside this house."

Still Jones did not flinch in any way, but said:

"Sir, I can assure you I know nothing of any such matter, nor do I comprehend why this gentleman, Mr. Holmes, would speak such unpleasantness of me."

"What do you know, Jones?" Drew demanded.

"On my honour, sir," the man said mildly, "I know nothing more about the disappearance of Miss Liza than I have already told."

"Shame!" Holmes barked. "You speak of honour? You have none, Jones! I name you vile, I name you reprehensible, I name you an assailant most foul."

Here Drew, confused but swept up in desperation, strode before the servant and demanded:

"What have you done with my child?"

Jones fell silent, and the impression he broadcast was that of such clear bewilderment that for an instant I felt myself wondering if just perhaps, on just this one singular occasion, my friend had fastened on to the wrong idea. With perfect self-control and an absolutely deferential tone, the butler said:

"I am unable to provide you with assistance there, sir, as I do not have the knowledge to help in this manner. I maintain that I have done no wrong in this regard, and regret that suspicion of any sort has fallen onto me. I will of course offer my resignation, if that is what you wish, Mr. Drew, with my departure occurring at a time of your convenience."

It was certainly the oddest interview I had ever seen Holmes undertake, and I feared whatever the truth of the matter, it seemed Holmes was getting nowhere, and the momentum gained by surprise appeared to be ebbing.

Drew fell into a chair, the impression that he was crushed under spent emotion, drained, predominating. He demanded:

"Mr. Holmes, what evidence have you that my servant has a part in this or any other wrongdoing?"

Holmes gave no answer, but leaned close to Jones, narrowing the space between them to half a foot, and said in a low, sly tone:

"*I have found your map!*"

While Jones' expression lost none of its refined mask, I saw his eyes sharply go out to the right, a mere involuntary flicker.

"A-ha!" Holmes cried.

Quick as a flash of light, Holmes leapt in the direction where Jones' betraying eye had gone, and he called:

"Somewhere here, is it?"

"Sir, I know noth---" the butler began, but Holmes shouted over him.

"Along this wall is that where you concealed it?"

"A map?" Mr. Drew cried out in confusion. "What is this? A map to what, Mr. Holmes?"

"Jones has," I said, seizing onto the facts and leaping with guesswork into the narrative, "made a map leading to a location within this house that he believes conceals a treasure."

"A treasure? In this house?" Drew said. "Madness! The

previous owners were so impoverished they sold out to the developer from London at a fraction of the value."

"And yet," I told him, "this disgraceful man believes in its presence enough to sacrifice a young girl's life on the altar of his greed."

And so, even as Holmes set about pillaging the wall of books toward which Jones had looked, Drew moved toward the butler, violence in his eyes. "Tell me this is wrong!" he fumed. "Say something, Jones!"

"I can only say what I have said, sir," the butler maintained, "which is that I have committed no wrongdoing."

Holmes called out in explanation:

"I asked that the library be the place of this meeting, as concealing proof of his guilt in his small room below-stairs should have left it too vulnerable. There are a thousand hiding places in so massive a house, yet it was the library I found the most logical."

Yet here he paused in his labour.

"I could," he said, "spend the afternoon searching these books, but having eliminated just now the largest and most obvious and found nothing, I will waste no more precious time, not when the girl's life may be draining by the instant."

He strode toward Jones so rapidly that I thought he intended violence against the man, and wondered if Holmes meant to physically shake the truth from him, but instead my friend paused inches from the still-composed butler, and stared deeply into his eyes.

This continued for a minute, in complete silence, and I saw a single bead of perspiration form on Jones' previously frigid brow and drift almost lazily toward his cheek. There was a great silent contest of wills underway, Holmes' deeply-penetrating eyes cutting unblinkingly into his, a most weighty burden under which to find oneself, and I could feel the air grow tense, as if before a storm broke, and finally it came, Jones' eyes jerked away from Holmes, and as if beyond his control fastened onto an object.

Oh, I thought, it's there! For even I could see now the thing toward which he gazed.

Holmes sprang from the man, who in his own right suddenly took off running, shattering his calm stance as he fled out the library door.

"After him!" Drew called, springing from the chair.

"No!" Holmes roared. "Let him go! He is of no further importance and there is not a moment to be lost. I will have him in my net soon enough in any case."

He reached onto the wall and took down a painted Medieval shield that had hung decoratively there, the object Jones, under pressure in his guilt, had betrayed himself by looking toward. He flipped the shield over and pasted to its back was a single sheet of paper, which Holmes snatched.

"He sketched this," he explained to Drew and myself, "because the house can be much different in the light than in the dark, and he, with his evil plot, wanted to be sure he could find the concealed room when he returned to it at some point in the weeks ahead, after the single living witness to its presence was dead, and the energy currently possessing this house had faded away. Come! Let this map lead us!"

And so we rushed behind Holmes as he ran down several long hallways, and finally nearly skidded to a halt at the head of a spiral staircase, where against the darkness he fired a match and lit a small candle he pulled from his pocket. By this flickering light he led us to a floor which lay well below ground level, and to a blank-looking and otherwise unrevealing space of gray stone foundational wall.

"It is here where Miss Liza entered in a spirit of misadventure!" he cried.

"She is somehow within the wall?" Drew all but shrieked. He began to call out for the girl, but only his own voice echoed off the cold stones, and no other was raised, however weakly, in reply.

Holmes threw the map onto the ground and declared:

"I had hoped Jones noted how the aperture was opened,

but he did not, and may not have known, having had to observe from an inconvenient distance, and in nearly total darkness."

Against Drew's frantic cries and pounding upon the walls, Holmes burst out:

"Quiet!"

Startled, Drew ceased his shouting.

"If you please, I require a moment of quiet to think!" Holmes told him,

The candle in his hand continued to burn, flickering with his every movement as he studied the wall before him.

"If a young girl comprehended this challenge....I feel certain I can as well," he said, echoing my own sentiments of but a short while before.

Without turning or removing his eyes from the stonework he thrust the candle to me and knelt.

"As she had no chair to stand on, I might surmise the mechanism was low, or she should not have reached it..."

From running his hands across the stones of waist-high and lower, he stooped and peered at the floor, and with a great jubilant cry, he yelled:

"There!"

I watched as he inserted his left index finger into a slightly wider space between two of the flagstones underfoot, and jerked up a sort of iron lever, creating a discernible popping sound, and a space in the wall, revealed to be merely an inch thick in its falseness rather than the deep width of the stones around it, moved slightly.

Pushing past us, Drew forced the opening wider with his hands, and crying out his daughter's name wedged himself within.

I put the candle into the space and saw it was scarcely wider than a wardrobe but went back more than ten feet into the darkness, where on the stones lay the form of a girl, crumpled and unmoving, her limbs limp, her skin pale. I saw a wasted quality about her face, where the skin looked drawn with dehydration. Oh merciful Heavens, I thought, are we too late? If so I prayed the dastardly butler would himself never see daylight again for his cruelty here.

Yet there was a tiny sound from the girl, barely a sighing cry, almost inaudible, not a word, merely a noise, but it was enough to show life yet remained in her, and I felt a great rising of joy within me. Realizing only then why Holmes had asked that I go for a flask of water, I pulled this from my pocket and rushed forward to kneel before the girl, who was hanging limply, supported in her father's arms, as Drew mumbled declarations of hope and gratitude in an almost sobbing tone.

"Oh, my Liza, my girl," he was speaking in rapid bursts.

"Hold up her head," I commanded, as I fit the flask to the girl's lips and gently poured a little water into her mouth, which, in an excellent sign, she gulped reflexively and greedily even amid her unconscious state. When all the water was drunk, I fitted my fingers to her throat and felt her pulse was weak, but it did not pause. Her eyelids fluttered and her gaze traveled unsteadily about before fixing on her father.

"Papa?" she said, her voice barely a whisper. "Is this a dream? I am so thirsty, so cold, so hungry. It has been so dark… This can only be some nightmare."

She fell into a faint, and her father lifted her into his arms, embracing her, a large, sturdy man un-swayed by the burden, and he said:

"I will bear her upstairs. Let's leave this abominable death-trap."

And so we did, I leading with the light held high above my head, Drew carrying the girl next, and Holmes to the rear.

A thought came to me as we emerged onto the ground floor, the indirect late-afternoon sunlight seeming like the burst of high-noon after the dimness below, and I reflected on the fact the damp, unwholesome room, whatever its original purpose had been, was empty of all save stale, cold air, for despite Jones's wicked expectations, it had held no treasure save the one now being embraced by a grateful father.

"She has endured much," I offered, as I poured a glass of

water from a pitcher for her to half-consciously sip, and then got a clearer look at her in the light of the library as she was set in a reclining pose on a sofa there. "I fear she had not much left in her to expend, being down to a very few hours, I would judge, but I feel indications are good that she will fully recover."

"Then that is the grandest news I have ever received," Drew said, almost choking with emotion.

Within another few minutes the mother, Mrs. Drew, was summoned, and came rushing in amid outcries of overwhelming joy, as she fell onto the sofa next to her daughter and pulled the now slowly recovering Liza to her and set a number of kisses against her cheeks.

"Oh, my child, my child, it was as I said, I sensed you lived but were in some dark place, frightened and trapped. You see?" she cried. "A mother knows! I told you so!"

"And so you did," said Holmes, from a little distance off, smoking his pipe and otherwise staying rather silent as he observed the heart-felt reunion, alongside my efforts to further revive the girl. He added softly, "The power of a mother's bond with her child is not a thing to be discounted, and I have rarely gone wrong when heeding a woman's testimony in such regards."

"What of the vile Jones?" I quietly asked, after I had rejoined Holmes across the room.

"He will face due reckoning in short order," Holmes said with flinty confidence. "I shall see to it."

I asked nothing else, for under the iron-clad bond of such assurance, there was nothing more I needed to know.

And so the mystery of Wyvern Hall was brought to an end after but a single afternoon's investment of time, and despite Drew's offer of rooms til the morning---and his absolute gushing torrents of thanks to Holmes, along with the generous cheque he pressed upon him---it was onto the last train of the evening that we found ourselves, just as the low autumn sun was setting over the wooded hills of Kent. And so with a farewell til the next time, Holmes returned to Baker Street, and I went back to the house I shared with Mary, my wife.

As I sat in the parlour with her while the clock fast approached midnight, and ate a little supper she re-heated for me, I told her all of what had occurred, of the family's relocation from the north to the ancient estate, and of the girl's curiosity in seeking out old records of the place, and taking too much to heart the stories some of those antique books contained.

"Were there really two young people caught up in their romance, hidden away in the same concealed room?" Mary asked me.

"Who can say?" I admitted. "Perhaps so, though I pity them if they were shut off down in so bleak and dark a place, away from the brightness of the world. It seems the mechanism that had been made to open the space from the inside had become broken over the years, so young Miss Liza found it easier to enter the room she had discovered by her long efforts, than to escape again."

"And this butler, Jones, he really believed there was some treasure?"

"He had read some lurid and far-fetched tale in the book concerning hidden Yorkish gold, concealed there in a hidden chamber by King Richard III, just before his own death in battle, and could not conceive of Liza pursuing the room for reasons other than personal enrichment, Jones being the sort who cared nothing for romance, but who had a deep interest in becoming wealthier than the families he served, with what I must certainly admit, seemed devoted excellence."

"One of my teachers told us history has not been kind to Richard III," Mary said.

"So you think he was not the monster of Shakespeare, who killed his young nephews in the Tower?" I inquired.

"We should one day ask Holmes what his view on that mystery happens to be," she said.

"Indeed we should," I agreed, though I can say from hindsight that neither of us ever did.

"Such a sad and horrid situation for that poor girl," Mary

said after a moment, "though you well described the joy of the parents at their daughter's safe return."

"Yes," I quite agreed, "it is something I can but imagine, the joy that surely filled the parental heart when Holmes fulfilled their most ardent hope. The love of a parent for a child surely eclipses all emotions."

Mary was silent for a moment and finally said:

"Someday, John, you will know."

"Know?" I asked.

"What it is to feel a fatherly joy in one's offspring. You will know this, in fact, one day soon."

"Oh, yes, certainly, one day," I said, tired and distracted by memory, and so missing the news she so subtly gave me.

"John," she said patiently, "you will in fact know this sooner than you might imagine. Sometime in the coming year, in fact."

Oh! I was jolted by the magnitude of what she was telling me, and sat straight up from the couch, jarred fully awake, my mouth slightly agape, as I cried:

"My darling, do you mean to say...?"

"I visited Dr. Mullins today while you were away. Our child, dearest John," she confirmed, "will arrive this summer."

"Mary, I...!"

Words failed me as I embraced her, but sheer joy bright as a sunrise lit up inside me, where it would remain for the months which lay ahead, for up til the cruel day when this much-loved child came into the world, she and I would each live amid a greater happiness than either of us had ever known.

ALSO BY C. THORNE

C. Thorne now presents many exciting, never-before revealed adventures of the greatest detective of all time, Mr. Sherlock Holmes. There are many more to come.
Please peruse them all!

Go to:

The Continuing Chronicles of Sherlock Holmes

Made in United States
Orlando, FL
29 June 2025

ABOUT THE AUTHOR

C. Thorne

C. Thorne is a writer who lives in the United States, and a lifelong fan of Sir Arthur Conan Doyle's stories of the world's most famous fictional detective. He is the author of more than a thousand short stories, and nearly three-dozen books of prose and poetry, with even more tomes beneath his belt through the years as ghostwriter, and contributor to a number of college-level textbooks. The Continuing  Chronicles of Sherlock Holmes is his most recent series, and a labor of love. He hopes you enjoy these stories as much as he and illustrator L. Thorne have enjoyed producing them.